ALSO BY NADIFA MOHAMED

Black Mamba Boy

The Orchard of Lost Souls

The Orchard of Lost Souls

NADIFA MOHAMED

Farrar, Straus and Giroux

New York

Mohamed

Farrar, Straus and Giroux
18 West 18th Street, New York 10011

Printed in the United States of America
Originally published in 2013 by Simon & Schuster UK Ltd., Great Britain
Published in the United States by Farrar, Straus and Giroux
First American edition, 2014

Library of Congress Cataloging-in-Publication Data
Mohamed, Nadifa, 1981–
    The orchard of lost souls : a novel / Nadifa Mohamed. — First American
Edition.
        pages   cm.
    ISBN 978-0-374-20914-8 (hardback) — ISBN 978-0-374-70992-1 (ebook)
    1. Women, Somali—Fiction.   2. Triangles (Interpersonal relations)—Fiction.
I. Title.

PR6113.O364 O723 2014
823'.92—dc23
                                                                            2013034411

Farrar, Straus and Giroux books may be purchased for educational, business,
or promotional use. For information on bulk purchases, please contact the
Macmillan Corporate and Premium Sales Department at 1-800-221-7945,
extension 5442, or write to specialmarkets@macmillan.com.

www.fsgbooks.com
www.twitter.com/fsgbooks • www.facebook.com/fsgbooks

1   3   5   7   9   10   8   6   4   2

To Hooyo, Aabbo and Abtiyo Kildhi

If the first woman God ever made was strong enough to turn the world upside down all alone, these women together ought to be able to turn it back, and get it right side up again!

—SOJOURNER TRUTH, "Ain't I a Woman?"

PART ONE

Five a.m. Too early to eat. There is hardly any light, perhaps just enough to distinguish a dark thread from white, but Kawsar washes her face in the basin inside her bathroom, runs a *caday* over her teeth and slips into the day's costume without wasting any paraffin. She feels her way into her underskirt and red shift dress, squeezes thick amber bangles over each elbow and smoothes a heavy silver necklace over her sagging chest, then arranges the sheets neatly over her single bed. She finishes the glass of water on her bedside table and shakes out her leather sandals in case spiders or scorpions have sought shelter in them overnight, before finally locking the door leading from the bedroom to the kitchen. She knows that the day will be long and that she should force a little breakfast inside her, but her stomach is a closed fist. With the sandals on her feet and a long shawl over her shoulders, Kawsar opens the exterior door to

3

find her neighbours, Maryam English, Fadumo, Zahra and Dahabo, mingling in her courtyard.

'What took you so long, *saamaleyl*?' Dahabo swishes the flask in her hand at Kawsar.

'I was oiling my knees,' Kawsar replies with a smile, linking arms with her childhood friend.

The men and women of the *Guddi*, the neighbourhood watch of the regime, have spent the night shouting orders through megaphones of what to wear and where to meet. The women have all dressed in the same traditional outfit and Zahra has torn down branches from a *miri-miri* tree, which she hands out to the women to wave at the stadium – another instruction from the megaphones. The narrow, sandy street ahead is filled with women in similar dress, and behind them even more follow languidly. They pass Umar Farey's eighteen-room hotel, each window blind and shuttered as if the building itself is sleeping; no Hindi songs or Kung-fu sounds come from Zahra's video hall; and Raage's corner shop is just a corrugated tin shack rather than its usual Aladdin's cave.

'See how early they drag us out of bed. Nothing is too much for them, the swines.' Maryam English tightens the strap holding her baby to her back; she has had to leave the two older children locked in at home.

Kawsar rubs the sleeping baby's back and wishes it was Hodan's instead, her child returned as an infant with the chance of a second life ahead of her.

'Look at us, we are the same woman over the ages,' laughs Fadumo, her cane weaving in front of her.

It is true: they are identical except that Maryam English is in her late twenties, Zahra in her forties, Dahabo and Kawsar circling their late fifties and poor Fadumo a hunched-over seventy-something. They look like illustrations in a school textbook, everybody equal in the same garments and just a few lines on the face or a stooped back delineating age. That is the way the government seems to want them – simple, smiling cartoons with no demands or needs of their own. Now those cartoons have come to life – not tilling, weaving or working in a factory like on the shilling notes, but trudging to a celebration that they are forced to attend.

They walk through the backstreets, the sky above slowly getting paler and paler, until they reach the sports stadium. The *Guddi* activists in armbands are asking what neighbourhood they belong to and counting them as they enter the gate.

'There's Oodweyne watching over us,' yells Dahabo, pointing up.

'Shush!' whispers Maryam. 'They'll hear you.'

Kawsar turns back to the *Guddi* to check, but they are preoccupied by the throngs of people pushing through the gate. The mothers of the revolution have been called from their kitchens, from their chores, to show foreign dignitaries how loved the regime is, how grateful they are for the milk and peace it has brought them. It needs women to make it seem human.

Beyond Dahabo's pointed finger is a mammoth painting of the dictator, hanging over the stadium like a new sun, rays emerging from around his head. The painters have tried to soften that merciless, hangdog face but have succeeded only in throwing it off balance – the chin too long, the nose too bulbous, the eyes asymmetrical. The only accurate part is the short, clipped moustache modelled on that German leader.

Workmen hurriedly hang other paintings, slightly smaller, of his acolytes, the interchangeable ministers of defence, finance and internal security, their positions so insecure that by the end of the day new paintings might be commissioned. Fadumo leads the way to the stands and the rest follow, knowing that they will not be comfortable anywhere; there will be no shade, no rest, no sustenance for the next seven hours. Eighty-seven has been a year of drought and the morning sky settles yet again into an unrelenting, cloudless blue.

Filsan hasn't slept for the last three days. She has had charge of three *Guddi* units and they have created problem after problem for her; she could not have imagined a more cantankerous, ineffectual, gossipy group in her nightmares. In the end she sent one of the units back to Saba'ad refugee camp to train a group of children in traditional dance, but she doubts that they can even do that right. One unit is now stationed at the stadium's north gate while the other rounds up stragglers and clears rough-sleepers and debris from the route of the parade. The VIPs are not expected for another hour but the stadium still looks bare, disorganised; most of the participants are yet to arrive and when they do, God knows if they will be in shape.

This is Filsan's first October Twenty-first in Hargeisa and it seems ramshackle compared to what she knew in Mogadishu. It is now eighteen years exactly since the President's rise to power after a military coup, and the celebrations in Mogadishu show the system at its best, everyone working together to create something beautiful. The Military-Governor of the north-western region, General Haaruun, will be the President's avatar in Hargeisa and has arranged the military parade with a flyover to start and finish the day. The civilian part of the ceremony has been patched together by the *Guddi*, who are using it as an excuse to exhibit their amateur singing, dancing and oratory.

Filsan strums the teeth of the plastic comb in her trouser pocket and chews her lip; she looks at the empty dais where General Haaruun will sit with the dignitaries and imagines herself placed in the centre, not as his companion but as his successor, waving down to her subjects. Her boots are polished beautifully, her khaki uniform clean and sharply pressed, and the black beret on her head brushed and angled just so. She has lined her eyes discreetly with kohl and pressed colour onto her lips with her fingers. She looks herself but a little better, a touch more feminine; she has resisted playing these games until now, but if the other female soldiers get noticed this way, maybe she can too.

She shoves the comb deep into her pocket and

straightens her tunic over her rear. As she rushes past the south gate, two civilian policemen salute her, looking to each other with smiles in their eyes. Filsan's face pinches with annoyance, knowing that they will stare at her behind as soon as they can. Beyond the south gate the military convoys are queuing up: tanks, jeeps, armoured vehicles, trucks carrying every type of rocket and missile, soldiers in metal green helmets waiting patiently inside and beside the vehicles. Filsan feels proud looking at them. She is part of the third largest army in Africa, a force that would have conquered all of Ethiopia, not just the Ogaden, in 1978 if the Russians and Cubans hadn't switched sides.

Filsan walks down the convoy, and here the soldiers don't stare at her or smile like the barely trained police; they show her the respect due another soldier. Her life has always revolved around these men, from her father down to her political science teachers at Halane College; it is their judgement that carries weight with her and she still feels small in their estimation. Filsan has volunteered to come north, hoping to show that although a woman, she has more commitment to the revolution than any of her male peers. This is the coalface of internal security, where real work can be done defeating National Freedom Movement bandits who persist in nipping at the government's tail. As she looks around her, she realises it is not inconceivable that members of the banned group are here now, filtering anonymously through the gates between the mothers in robes and uniformed schoolchildren. It is impossible to tell enemy from friend.

It was a hard way to earn a new pair of shoes but for Deqo it was worth it. A month of dance lessons has taught her the *Hilgo, Belwo, Dudi* and the overly complicated *Halawalaq*. She isn't a bad dancer but is better at improvisation than following the steps, and even now she turns left instead of right or jumps forward instead of back. They still haven't seen the shoes but that's all Toothless Milgo has talked about during the lessons. They have earned those shoes with sweat and tears and Deqo intends to wear them like a soldier wears his medals.

'Think of the shoes. Don't you want the shoes? Do you want to be barefoot forever? Concentrate then!' A sharp swipe over their feet with an acacia twig.

They have learnt to dance to the beat of Milgo's rough palm against the bottom of a plastic basin, but at the parade there will be real drums, trumpets, guitars, everything. They will be dancing in front of thousands, even the governor of the whole region will be watching, so they have to *practise, practise, practise.*

Now the day of the parade has finally arrived. Before dawn the troupe of five girls and five boys, all from the orphanage, are herded into the yard behind the camp's clinic and scrubbed half to death. Deqo's eyes are tinged red from the strong-smelling soap and she keeps rubbing them to ease the itch. A truck waits by the dispensary tent and they are dressed in traditional *macaweis* and *guntiino* and then loaded into the back. The truck starts up, a plume of brown smoke bursting from its exhaust, and Deqo grabs hold of the side as they pick up speed. It is her first time in a vehicle and she is surprised to feel such a strong breeze on her face, the edges of her hair whipped about as if on a stormy day. When the truck slows, the breeze disappears again and Deqo squints against the rising grit and clamps her lips together.

While the other children practise the songs they will sing at the parade, Deqo's attention is drawn back towards the refugee camp, the semicircular wooden *aqals* suddenly nothing more than speckles on the surface of the earth. The grain warehouse and various clinics constantly surrounded by milling refugees are invisible from here; the arguments, the bitterness, the sadness far away. The road snakes down towards Hargeisa, the land-scape bare apart from the occasional aloe bush, animal bone and plastic shoe, the only difference from the camp being the freshness of the air. The horizon is all blue sky with just a streak of yellow leading them forward, and it is difficult to imagine anything of substance ahead. Deqo half-expects the truck to reach that yellow streak and then tumble over the edge of the earth, but instead it carries on the badly tarred road until it reaches the first military checkpoint outside the city.

Kawsar and her neighbours squeeze into the second stand; the stadium was made for three thousand specta-tors but today it is crammed with more than ten thousand.

Corpulent women push along the narrow walkway, busy with their own conversations, stepping on Kawsar's toes and using her arm for support without so much as a glance in her direction. The temperature is still cool but will rise steadily until they feel like hides drying in the sun. Her knees are swollen and already she begins to shift her weight from one foot to the other every few minutes.

The October Twenty-first festivals are poor imitations of the Independence Day celebrations, Kawsar thinks – like a bad husband reminding his unhappy wife of the good times they once shared while knowing that they would never return. When the British had left on 26 June 1960, everyone had poured out of their homes in their Eid clothes and gathered at the municipal *khayriyo* between the national bank and prison. It was as if they were drunk, wild; girls got pregnant that night and when asked who the father of their child was, they would reply: 'Ask the flag.' That night, crushed within a mixed crowd as the Somali flag was raised for the first time, Kawsar had lost a long, gold earring that was part of her dowry, but Farah hadn't cared – he'd said it was a gift to the new nation. The party had moved to Freedom Park and lasted into the next morning, the sleepy town transformed into a playground, the youth of the country believing that they had achieved what their elders hadn't. People always half-joked afterwards that that day changed the women of Hargeisa; that they never returned to the modest, quiet lives they had known after that bacchanalian display, that the taste of one kind of freedom led to an insatiable desire for every kind.

A flutter in her womb distracts Kawsar from the marching band tuning up near her. It is a sensation that comes
regularly now, like fingernails brushing the inside of her
skin, a heartbeat pulsing deep in the sea of her. Maryam's
daughter is fussing already, her chubby hands pulling at
her mother's hair as she attempts to wriggle out of the
sling. Maryam slaps the child's thigh to make her settle
but it just infuriates her more. What an easy stage that
was: when a child's only want was to walk around a little
before collapsing back into your arms. Hodan had slept
nestled against Kawsar's shoulder on days like this, when
the people had still been gullible enough to celebrate the
regime with real emotion, when the shine of independence had made everything magical – our first Somali
textbooks, our first airline, everything a wonder. It was
the star that caused all the grief: that five-pointed star on
the flag, with each point signifying a part of the Somali
motherland, had led the country into war with Kenya
and then Ethiopia, had fed a ruinous desire to reclaim
territory that was long gone. The last defeat changed
everything. After seventy-nine the guns that were turned
outward reversed position and became trained on
Somalis instead, the fury of humiliated men blowing
back over the Haud desert.

Filsan hates the squatness of Hargeisa. In Mogadishu
the buildings soar and blind the eye with their white-
ness; here everything clings to the earth, cowering and
subservient, the cheap mud brick bungalows often left

unpainted as if the town is inhabited by giant termites that cobble their dwellings together with dirt and spit. In Mogadishu the oldest residences are made of coral and have delicate wooden latticework and vaulted ceilings that give people a sense of wonder. In the centre of the city where the alleys narrow at points to the width of a man's shoulder blades, you can walk as if in a dream, never certain of what might appear after the next bend: a bare-chested man with a silver swordfish slung over his thin black back, a shoal of children reciting Qu'ran from their wooden slates, a girl milking a white, lyre-horned cow. The place has enchantment, mystery, it moves backward and forward in time with every turn of the feet; it is fitting that it lies beside an ocean over which its soul can breathe, rather than being hemmed in by mountains like a *jinn* in a bottle.

The *Guddi* marching band in indigo tunics and white caps stand beside her, old men tuning their old instruments. What they lack in ability they make up for in their willingness to please; they will squawk and stomp until they are told to stop. The musicians in Hargeisa are amateurs; those who couldn't make it in Mogadishu ply their trade here, in the solitary theatre or in the daytime weddings that take place in bungalows. It needs a real city to pound new rhythms out of life – the tick of the town hall clock, the scrape of a shovel, the whistle of a traffic policeman – it needs all of this for new, pulse-quickening styles to germinate and flower.

The foreign dignitaries step out from their motorcade

on schedule, and Filsan recognises a couple from photographs printed in the *October Star*, the national paper. The US economic attaché leads the group, followed by the Egyptian ambassador and a man in flowing white robes and *keffiyah*. Maybe a dozen other officials line up along the blue and white dais to await the General.

The honk of car horns announces his arrival. A soldier clumsily spreads a threadbare red carpet from the gate to the dais, and then General Haaruun steps out of a black Mercedes. It is as if an electric current passes through the stands as he walks to his seat surrounded by bodyguards, the atmosphere tense, every sound magnified by the sudden, jagged stillness. Filsan turns quickly to monitor the situation behind her: the locals do not shout or throw missiles but their eyes are fixed on the tall, gaunt man in military dress. They crane forward in their seats and appear like an avalanche of bodies ready to fall onto her and bury the stadium beneath them.

At the sight of General Haaruun, Kawsar's heart pounds in her chest. He is like a hyena – sparse, menacing, his very presence seeming to herald death. She blames him not just for Hodan's passing but for her arrest, her disappearance and her decline into a huddled, diminished figure. Despite the crowd, Kawsar feels a wall of black grief descending on her, leaving her blind and deaf and voiceless as if she is at the bottom of a well, only ever able to climb halfway up before losing her grip yet again.

'Stay with us.' Dahabo pats Kawsar's hand and through her numb skin she feels her warmth.

'When is this accursed thing going to start?' Kawsar pretends to return to events around her but her mind is still in that well.

'Now! Look!'

Three MIG aircraft in arrow formation buzz overhead, as grey and long-necked as vultures, swooping over as if racing to a corpse somewhere, the six streaks of smoke behind them fattening out and then tearing apart. The dignitaries stand to attention; they are vultures of a different level, more like marabous in their finery, roosting with full stomachs for the moment, the eyes behind the dark glasses are always alert and watchful.

It is only Dahabo who touches Kawsar now. Every month or so they meet in Kawsar's house for tea and lamentation, and Dahabo makes a point of resting a hand on Kawsar's thigh as she speaks, as if she knows how chilling it is to live alone without any human sound or touch. Dahabo squeezes, kneads, pats according to the topic of conversation, but her hand is never far away; it is a hard, calloused hand with nails bitten down low, but it comforts, transfuses more than just heat. That is another thing about getting old, the constant need for heat. Kawsar's bones ache for sunlight, and she has taken to sitting out for an hour most days just after the worst of the midday sun and basking in her orchard like a lizard. But her sense of distance and loneliness is not shifting today, despite the warmth of the sun scaling up the sky and the proximity of so many bodies all around her.

The large speakers garble announcements, but it's not necessary because the sequence of the parade is well established already. Soldiers come first, their legs snicking like scissors, then the heavy, older policemen and women in their blue uniforms, then civilians in their work clothes – teachers, civil servants, students. The only enjoyable thing for Kawsar is spotting her neighbours and their children amongst the marchers, their blind eyes and lunatic grins as they strain to search out family members from the identical figures in the stands. The *Guddi* come last, waving branches and carrying images of Lenin, Kim Il Sung and Mao, the communists who once provided inspiration to the dictatorship but whose pictures have faded, carted out just once a year like church relics. The regime now seeks out friends of any description, be they Arab, American or Albanian.

On the way into the stadium Deqo has seen tatty-looking girls her own age gathered in the market, sweeping with short brooms made from dried grasses. Even as poor as they are, each has a pair of plastic jelly sandals on her feet.

Now she watches from behind Milgo's legs as the soldiers begin their parade. They march as one, a tribe of insects with green shells on their heads, their thousand feet scuttling across the dirt, their thousand eyes pointing in the same direction. She has never seen so many men in one place; the camp is mostly women and children, all squabbling and fighting with each other. The soldiers are young, powerful and unified. They seem to belong to each other while she belongs to no one. Milgo ululates as the men pass beside them and Deqo tries to emulate her, swinging her tongue in her mouth and yodelling. She decides, as she looks at the soldiers, at the crowd, at the aeroplanes above, that this is the best day of her life, the day when everything in the world is laid out for her to see and enjoy. No more of the camp and its dust and flies. She feels her stomach fluttering with excitement; soon she will be out there to take her place at the centre of the earth.

In the stand opposite Kawsar there is a sudden shifting, an exhalation from thousands of lungs as the spectators bend down and arise with placards in their hands. At the instruction of *Guddi* activists in traditional dress these placards are turned over and held up. Within a few seconds the stand has disappeared and a shimmering portrait of Oodweyne faces Kawsar. A few rebels refuse to hold up their placards, making tiny little holes in his face, but the message is clear: the President is a giant, a god who watches over them, who can dissolve into pieces and hear and see all that they do. The young nomadic boy who knew how to hobble a camel and ease a tick out of a sheep's flesh has become a deity. A blasphemer, thinks Kawsar as his face floats up at her, both he and his servant Haaruun. Before she remembers where she is, she spits violently at the sight, drawing a gasp from the spectators around her.

'What are you doing?' Dahabo exclaims, squeezing Kawsar's upper arm tightly.

Kawsar doesn't know, she isn't really there; she just saw a face that disgusted her and reacted. The expressions in the aisle below reflect shock and fear that she has drawn attention to them, but Kawsar cannot comprehend that fear anymore, it seems so paltry and pointless in comparison to what she has lived through. What more can they hold to ransom when they have taken away her only child? It is fear that makes the soldiers brave, that emboldens the policemen to loot, that gives life to that old man in Mogadishu. She does not care enough about her life or possessions to keep abasing herself.

'Now! Let's go, let's go!' shouts Milgo.

The children stream out onto the ground, Deqo third in line. Sound explodes from every corner: drums, shouts, roars. Deqo can't hear her own voice as she sings. Already, the whole routine has left her mind. She follows Safiya's movements but her limbs are heavy, her mind swimming. She knew these dances, was better at them than Safiya, but now she is lost. She is suffocated by the dust beaten up by the shield-and-spear dancers which still hangs in the air, and the discordant band music unsettles her even further. This wasn't how it was meant to be.

Milgo comes running towards her, her hand held up ready to smack.

Deqo continues to dance, but her eyes are fixed on Milgo's enraged face. Other women come behind her, just as angry. A thin, dark stream of urine trickles onto her feet.

Grabbing Deqo's arm, Milgo drags her away so fast that when she opens her eyes she is in the dark recess between two stands.

The blows come as soon as she is out of sight of the crowd, hands and feet attacking from all sides and words stinging her ears. Milgo shouts one insult after the other, the music still blaring loudly behind them.

At the heart of the swirling mass of dancers Kawsar notices a still point, an emptiness that seems to reflect how she feels. Within the circle is a forlorn girl in red staring at her feet, unconscious of where she is. The sight touches Kawsar, a moment of truth within this fiction. The serene calm lasts a second before the *Guddi* descend on her and Kawsar watches as the little girl is pulled away by the arm, four or five women crowding around her; she can tell by their expressions what they are going to do and rises before they take her away. Kawsar feels something has broken loose inside her, something that has been dammed up – love, rage, a sense of justice even; she doesn't know what, but it heats her blood.

'Where are you going?' demands Dahabo.

'I'll be back, stay here.'

'Kawsar, wait!'

But she is gone, pushing past the women in the aisle, stepping on their toes and clambering over them when they don't move quickly enough. A couple of steps down and she is free of the crush.

'Whore . . . imbecile . . . bitch,' shout the *Guddi* beside the stand, and there she is – an anguished face pleading for mercy.

'Give her to me,' Kawsar says with more calm than she feels.

'Go back to your own business,' replies a young turbaned woman dismissively.

'This *is* my business. I said give her to me.' Kawsar charges forward and reaches for the girl.

The young woman holds Kawsar back. 'You want us to call security, you old fool? You want to be thrown in jail?' she shouts.

'Do what you like, you can't hurt me. I am from this town, I was born here, I won't be told what to do by you.' Her voice is shrill as she lunges yet again for the girl.

The *Guddi* block her and form a semicircle around the child. 'Milgo, go and call security, this mad woman wants trouble,' the young woman says, and a gaunt older woman runs back to the entrance.

The little girl breaks free from her captors and runs away at full pelt.

'*Naayaa! Naayaa!* Don't worry, I will catch her.' The youngest girl in the group follows in pursuit.

Their attention returns to Kawsar. 'You want a night in jail to show you how things are? Old women have hard heads and learn too late sometimes.' The group's leader presses her finger into Kawsar's forehead for emphasis.

Kawsar brushes her hand away. They stand inches apart as if in a duel.

A petite female soldier wearing a beret approaches with two male soldiers on her heels. She looks disgusted by the whole scene and gestures impatiently for Kawsar to follow her. The *Guddi* make space and Kawsar departs with her head held high.

'Kawsar! Where are they taking you?' Dahabo asks, leaning over the edge of the stand, Maryam beside her.

'Jail,' replies the soldier, 'and we'll take you too if you don't return to your seat.'

'Go back, I will see you later.' Kawsar is strangely jubilant; she is the one making things happen now.

Deqo carries on blindly into the strange city. Looking behind, she sees her pursuer still running clumsily after her. She accelerates, taking wide, elegant strides. In Saba'ad she had never been able to run freely between the crowded *buuls*, the women's legs outstretched in the small spaces between them; it was an environment that enforced slowness, wariness rather than childish abandon. She imagines now that there had been hands grabbing at her skirt and pulling her back, down into the earth that sucked people in every day. Here there is space, endless space, wide roads and boundless buildings.

She pumps her legs and arms, her lungs heaving, her heart pounding, testing her body to the edge of its capacity. She feels faster than the cars on the road, the crows in the sky, the bullets in the soldier's rifles. She races against herself until the stadium is far behind her; the thud of her feet hitting the dust matches the beating of her heart. She is a slick machine in complete possession of itself. She reaches a bridge and crosses the vibrating concrete. Past the two-storeyed Oriental Hotel with Land Rovers pulled up near its entrance and the glass-fronted pharmacy, the mechanic's shop with black tyres piled up outside, the scrap metal merchant's corrugated tin shack. The streets are empty of people, little piles of dust and leaves gathered in corners every few metres as if sweepers have just been there; a single bus passes her as she speeds towards the market.

The old woman is quiet in the back of the van, her nose in the air as if she's in a taxi; haughtiness is all she has to hide behind now but it won't work. She will have to spend a night on the floor like all the other miscreants, use a bucket to relieve herself and wait until she is told she can leave. This isn't the oldest troublemaker Filsan has had to deal with – the market woman who pelted General Haaruun's motorcade had to have been over eighty – but this one looks wealthier, well-bred.

They pull up beside the central police station. Filsan

hasn't bothered to handcuff her – what's the point? She can hardly outrun anyone. The old woman pulls her headscarf around her cheeks but Filsan yanks it back to reveal her face. It is only then that their eyes meet, the old woman's full of reproach and contempt. Filsan grabs her arm and leads her into the police station; she will report her behaviour in the stadium to police officers and then leave them to take care of her.

'The cells are full,' the policewoman at the desk barks, not even looking up from the paper in her hand.

'She has caused a public nuisance during the celebration.'

The policewoman raises her head and looks at the suspect. 'What did she do?'

'Harassed and threatened women from the *Guddi*.'

The policewoman laughs and bends over the tiny public nuisance. 'Are you not too old for this? Are you not ashamed of yourself?' She is maybe twenty years old with streaks of bleached blonde hair peeking out from under her cap. 'Where do you live?'

'Guryo Samo.'

'Name?'

'Kawsar Ilmi Bootaan.'

She jots her details into a form and then shoves the pen behind her ear. 'She won't take up too much space, I guess.' The policewoman sighs. 'Hand her over.'

Filsan watches as Kawsar is escorted to a group cell. She walks slowly but shows no emotion; she moves like a tourist on a tour of the place, looking left and right as if to say, 'Yes, yes, everything is as it should be.' The barred doors click behind her and then she is gone, swallowed up in the guts of the police station to be digested and excreted out another day.

Saylada dadka, thinks Kawsar. This is where her journey ends, in the 'people market'. From here the fortunate ones will be ransomed out while others end up in the hospital morgue or disappear into prisons all over the country. This was the place that had broken her child. She looks around, imagining where Hodan might have sat that first night after she was arrested with her class- mates. The cell is large with walls that had once been painted white but are now gangrened and blackened with mould. It is little more than a dungeon with around thirty women and girls spread across its concrete floor.

'Take a seat, *eddo*,' an inmate breast-feeding a child calls out.

Kawsar hesitates. It is clear from the woman's jaun- diced eyes and gaudy dress that she is a prostitute. The woman shifts over on her mat and pats the floor.

'What's a lady like you doing in a place like this?'

'I couldn't take any more of them, I realised.' Kawsar crouches down slowly onto the woven straw mat.

'What did you do?' she prods, teasing her nipple back into the baby's mouth.

Kawsar shrugs. 'What can I do? I just told the *Guddi* to stop beating a child.'

'Those bastards. You were lucky they didn't beat you.

Look here,' she points to the infant's temple, 'see that dent? It's where a policeman's stick caught him during a raid. No apology, no nothing.'

Kawsar strokes the fine, smooth skin of the boy's forehead. Before he has even reached his first birthday he has been marked by the violent world surrounding him; perhaps he will be unable to see or hear or walk in the future and that won't matter to anyone but this drunk, sloppy mother feeding him her poison through her milk. 'He's beautiful,' she says.

'He should be, his father was very handsome, a real Ilmi Boodari.'

Kawsar smiles. 'You look too young to know anything about Ilmi Boodari.'

'He died the year I was born.'

'Of love . . .'

'Of course, of love! He was the most romantic Somali man to ever live or write poetry, but no one knows his songs better than me. I have each and every one on tape.'

An addict of love as well as drink, thinks Kawsar. That makes sense, from one high to another.

'What is your name?'

'People call me China.'

A laugh escapes from Kawsar. 'Why? Are you a coolie? Do you build roads in your spare time?'

'No, but I help the men who do.' China meets her gaze and raises an eyebrow flirtatiously.

Kawsar imagines the baby in a drawer under the bed while coolies with dirty hands climb into bed with his mother.

'Don't look so pious. When it's not the coolies it's prob-ably your husband or son.'

Kawsar rises from the mat feeling small and vulnerable.

'Go! Go to hell! It was my mistake to show you any kindness. Go and sit over there on the cold floor,' China bellows, pushing her away.

Kawsar walks to the opposite wall where the smell of the waste bucket has cleared a circular space. Her breath is shallow and pained. She knows women like China always carry a weapon.

'Please, Dahabo, come quickly, get me out of here,' she prays. Whatever rush she had got from standing up to the *Guddi* has now evaporated. She wants nothing more than a cup of strong tea and to be back in her clean, safe home.

Deqo skids to a stop. Ahead of her is the woman who had come to her rescue in the stadium, climbing down from one of the jeeps that had overtaken her. She had looked so tall and brave when she confronted Milgo, but now the soldiers tower over her. She follows behind a female soldier, up the concrete steps, her knees seeming to buckle on the fourth step before she regains her balance and enters the building. Deqo crosses the road and stares up from the bottom of the stairs. The fragrant incense on the woman's clothes is powerful and sweet and Deqo inhales deeply, imagining the home this smell comes from – it will have pots bubbling on the stove, clothes drying on a line in the sun and a bed piled high with pillows and soft blankets. A full stomach and a good night's sleep were necessary to make people kind, Milgo said, when she went too far with the hidings.

Deqo decides to wait in the shade across the road until the gentle lady returns to thank her; it had been rude just to run away like that and leave her in trouble. Maybe she hasn't got children and would let her live with her, she has seen that happen before – women arrived at the hospital, browsed the cots and took a baby home. Deqo could cook, clean, run errands; she was better for an old woman than a whining baby.

A few people emerge from the wide, dark entrance of the jail but not whom Deqo wants. They come out shielding their eyes from the light, their clothes crumpled and stained, but Deqo feels certain that her woman is unsulliable; she will smell as good on her release as she did when she went in.

A reverberation emanates from the direction of the bridge she has just crossed. Deqo takes a few steps towards it and watches a group of women, all dressed like her saviour, come slowly into view, a wave of red, white and brown crashing over the road, singing out in praise of the President and Somalia as they wave branches in the air. They march in rows of ten, some in the road, some clambering onto the pavement, an army of housewives invading the silence. Deqo ducks into an alleyway in case Milgo appears alongside them.

A Somali film crew run past. With their lumbering cameras, bags and microphones, they remind her of the foreign photographers who descended on Saba'ad during the cholera outbreak, stepping on people's fingers and shoving cameras into their faces as they died silently on the ground. They had seemed friendly until they began to work, dominating the clinic as they littered it with cables, generators and so many different machines. They had filmed Old Sulaiman crying over his dead family, all four children and his wife wrapped in thin sheets ready for burial, his tears coursing down into his beard, their cameras less than a step away. He had survived but left the camp, not even a bundle on his back, abandoning his possessions for his neighbours to pick over. Some people said he went back to the Ogaden, others into the city, but he was never seen again.

The marchers wave their placards and shake their branches until the flow peters out, leaves and twigs are stomped into the tarmac in their wake. They take the life in the street with them and leave her with images of corpses lined up for burial outside of the clinic walls, the smell of them clinging to her skin like oil.

The stadium events are finally over and the dignitaries rise as the national anthem is played over the speakers. Filsan stands in a phalanx of soldiers just beneath General Haaruun. With the *Guddi* units safely despatched she has eased her way to the dais. There are two other female officers nearby but she is the closest, and she casts a competitive glance at them, hoping that the General will notice the sharpness of her uniform, the straightness of her back, the smartness of her salute. She has not eaten all day and her eyes are turning scenes into dreamscapes: spectral figures waving to her from the edge of her vision, the stands undulating with hands at their tips like surf, fires burning wherever the sun hits metal. A tap on her shoulder makes her jolt as the final strains of the anthem float away.

'His Excellency wants you to be introduced to him.' A sergeant with a star on each epaulette speaks in her ear.

'Huh?' She has waited for this moment for so long and that is all Filsan can say.

'Quick, he is waiting.' The sergeant turns his back and clicks his fingers for her to follow.

She rushes around the barrier and up the steps. Large electric fans stir the blue and white silken sheets covering the dais, and she feels like she is standing on a cloud as the wind pushes it across the sky.

Filsan dabs the sweat discreetly from her hairline and salutes General Haaruun.

'At ease, soldier.' His voice is smooth, soft, so comfortable in his power that he doesn't need to bark it. 'I always like to meet female comrades, encourage them in their career. What is your name?'

'Adan Ali, Filsan, sir.' She can't look at him.

'Which agency are you in?'

'Internal Security, sir.'

'Look up, comrade.'

Filsan raises her face and meets his gaze.

'Are you from a military family?'

'Yes, sir, my father is Irroleh.'

'I trained with him in East Berlin. A wonderful soldier.'

It has worked. Her father's name is like a key clicking in a lock; she can almost hear the door swinging open to her.

'How is he?'

'He is very well, sir, he is based in the ministry of defence,' Filsan lies. Her father has been suspended and is currently at home while under investigation.

'I will have to look him up next time I'm in Mogadishu. And you, how long have you been here?'

'Just three weeks, sir.'

He smiles. 'It's a village, isn't it?'

She smiles in return. He is like the men who carried her on their shoulders as a child, friendly giants with big hands and big laughs.

He turns to one of the foreign men and pushes his chair out, still addressing her. 'Why don't you accompany us to the Oriental Hotel, we can talk further there.'

Filsan grins and reveals her small, overlapping teeth. 'Yes, sir!' A knot of guards surround the General and she joins the outer shell protecting him.

He steps into his black Mercedes and drives away in a convoy. The sergeant who had called her now ushers her into his jeep. Let the *Guddi* clear up and deal with the stragglers and argumentative old women. She has studied and trained to take her place at the heart of things. The jeep speeds to the Oriental Hotel near the bridge, the grandest and oldest hotel in town.

General Haaruun enters ahead of them, his hand lightly touching the back of an Asian ambassador's wife; he bows and lets her enter before him.

Filsan jumps out of the jeep and follows the dignitaries into the main hall. She has an urge to rush to the toilet and check her make-up and hair in the mirror, but the professional side of her rejects the idea. She has never set foot in this place but was practically raised in the hotels of Mogadishu, eating her meals in them while her father drank coffee and networked all day long. After her mother left and before they had found their house-keeper Intisaar, they had barely lived in their villa, only returning at night to sleep. She is deeply intimate with hotels – their structure and schedules, the smell of the blue soaps found in every hotel bathroom – but standing here surrounded by these worldly people she feels like a big-booted Bedu staring at the mirrors and gilt-effect chandeliers. She wants to wrap herself in the long window drapes and hide like she did as a child when there were too many strangers in the house.

General Haaruun has a tumbler of drink in his hand, the same colour as the whisky her father enjoys; he swills it around the ice cubes as he speaks. He doesn't look at Filsan at all but she waits awkwardly close, busying herself with the details of the room: the red bow ties of the waiters, the matching velveteen of the sofas and curtains, the lacquered finish to the dining table in the centre of the room. She isn't sure what to do with her body, what role she is meant to be playing – protector, supplicant, daughter. Her back stiffens, slackens and stiffens again. Turning for a moment she grabs a glass from a passing tray and throws the drink down her dry throat. Cheap white wine sloshes over her taste buds and hits her stomach; pulling a face, she returns the glass to the tray and swivels back into position. She will wait until Haaruun is ready for her.

He is deep in mirthful conversation with the American attaché. English sentences from her school days come back to her and make her smile: 'Could you please tell me how to get to Buckingham Palace?'; 'I am waiting for the ten thirty to York'; 'I have an urgent need to see a physician.' She imagines Haaruun and the attaché speaking these sentences to each other, their whole conversation full of random declarations and questions.

None of the other guests approach her. Maybe if she weren't in uniform they would think she was worth speaking to, but now they just crane their necks to look around her. There are soldiers outside that she can talk to but then General Haaruun might forget about her, jump into his car and drive away into the half-light of the late afternoon. She needs the patience of a *bawab*; those bare-chested black men in turbans standing in the background of harems, as immobile as stone, simultaneously absent and present, their eyes as bright as a cobra's in the dark. She has nowhere better to be – just her tiny, bare room in the barracks with its slimy toilet and lumpy mattress.

'Comrade! Come join us.' It is Haaruun.

Filsan's knees click as she walks to his side.

The American has his hand on Haaruun's shoulder, his grey shirt wet under the arms.

'You speak English, right?'

'I do, sir.' Filsan is self-conscious about her strong accent but has studied well.

'I was just telling our American friend how strong Somali women are, that we don't have any of that purdah here. Women work, they fight in our military, serve as engineers, spies, doctors. Isn't it so?'

'Absolutely, we are not like other women.' She nods fervently.

'I bet you this girl could strip a Kalashnikov in a minute,' the General boasts, placing his gold-rimmed sunglasses on top of his bald head.

'Yes, and she could annihilate an Ethiopian battalion while unicycling. I don't doubt it,' the American laughs.

'Look, buddy . . .' General Haaruun grabs Filsan's hand and raises it before twirling her around. 'You're going to tell me that American women can be trained killers and still look this good?'

Filsan fixes her gaze to the floor; she can feel others looking her up and down, eyes flicking over her like tongues.

'Not bad, not bad. I wouldn't want to meet her down a dark alley. Or maybe I would if it was the right kind of alley.'

General Haaruun clasps the attaché's shoulder and hoots his approval before recovering himself. 'Keep your capitalist hands to yourself.' He mock-wags his finger in his face.

Filsan's face burns hot, bringing tears to her eyes. She rushes away before they roll down, back to her corner as the lamps and chandeliers are lit across the room. She straightens her back and stands tall. Even in her uniform they see nothing more than breasts and a hole. He knows who her father is but still parades her like a prostitute. A waiter stops to glance at her; chest puffed out, barely a breath escaping her lips, she must look ready to burst.

'Go to hell!' she hisses.

He purses his lips to blow a kiss and grabs an empty glass from a nearby table.

One tear escapes down her left cheek and she scrapes it quickly away. The sky is black outside now, her reflection in the window shortened and stumpy-looking; she looks like an abandoned child on the verge of breaking down.

'Comrade. Why don't you let me drive you back to barracks?' General Haaruun approaches and gestures to the door.

She hesitates but wants to salvage some of the hopes she had for the meeting, he might still offer her his patronage. Rearranging her features into an expression of gratitude, she nods acquiescence.

The Mercedes is parked two metres away from the hotel entrance. A young soldier bends to open the door but he waves him away. 'Stay in the jeep,' he orders.

General Haaruun holds the door open for Filsan and she slides in, holding her boots away from the upholstery. The windows are tinted black, and once the door has slammed shut they are in complete darkness with only the dials on the dashboard casting a fine red light over them.

Hargeisa is eerie at night. The electricity supply has been cut to make life difficult for the rebels, but the darkness feels portentous, and apparitions pass across the black windows as they race along, the glow of an occasional paraffin lamp radiating from a street-side shack. They are submariners passing through the deep sea, perhaps able to make it to dry land, perhaps not, strange creatures glubbing along on the other side of the glass.

'Take your hat off.' The General's voice is more sober now.

Filsan unpins the hat from her head. Her hair is bundled up on top.

'Let it out. Let me see it down.'

Filsan responds quickly to orders, she always has done, her father made sure of that. 'Do it quickly and do it well,' he instilled in her.

It takes a while to find and remove all of the metal pins; she gathers them in her lap and teases her hair down to her shoulders. It feels good to release the tension in her skull; her scalp tingles now, her fingertips making circles over it.

General Haaruun moves closer to her, the back seat squeaking beneath his weight. Filsan stares out of the windscreen, sees stray dogs and civilians diving into the headlights.

His hand is on her cheek, stroking it, his skin softer

than she had expected, the smell of lotion faint on his fingers.

He moves closer again.

The driver's eyes are framed in the rear-view mirror, looking back at her.

'*Ina* Irroleh, daughter of Irroleh, look at me.'

The mention of her father is like a thunderbolt striking her ears. He is watching her now, she knows it; he can see her sitting in the back of this car and the veins in his temple are rising and tightening.

General Haaruun holds her chin and turns her face to him. 'I can make your life so easy, whatever you want is yours.'

'My father wouldn't like this.'

He moves his hand down, brushing her thighs and then squeezing her knee. 'You think your father doesn't do this to girls he meets?' He pushes his hand up her thigh and against her crotch. 'You're a virgin, aren't you? A clean girl,' he whispers in her ear.

Filsan is deep underwater now, unable to breathe or even swallow; she will never make it to dry land.

'Please stop, my father . . .' she hears herself mutter.

'Who cares about him? He is an old drunk. Think about what is good for you.' Both his arms wrap around her, one hand padding around for her belt and zip.

The driver's eyes are still on them.

Filsan grabs General Haaruun's hand and throws it away. 'No! No! No!' She hits his chest with both palms at each word. 'Don't touch me.'

'Stop the car!' he shouts.

They screech to a stop and the jeeps behind fan out around the car.

Reaching around to the door handle, he opens the passenger door and pushes Filsan out of the car. '*Abu kintiro*, you cunt, make your own way home.'

Filsan lands on her knees in plain view of maybe twenty soldiers, the jeep headlights making the scene as bright as day.

The door thuds behind her and the Mercedes skids and then drives off. Darkness huddles around her as the convoy pulls away. She rises to her feet, her head whirring, and walks to the nearest light source.

The jail is where people's stories end, thinks Kawsar. Whoever you are, whatever ambitions you nurse, however many twists and turns it has taken to arrive there, it is like the heart of a spider's web that you eventually wind your way to. More women and girls have entered the cell and there are about fifty prisoners now. No one has used the bucket but the prostitute's son has made a mess that still stinks an hour later. The lack of space means the youngest inmates are forced to stand; some of them are street-looking girls who seem unruffled by the whole experience, while others tremble in school uniforms. They crowd around her for comfort and she wishes she could extend her arms around all of them.

'Kawsar? Where is Kawsar?' The policewoman raps on the bars.

'Here!' It takes three attempts to rise to her feet, her knees making a loud crack as she finally succeeds.

'This has been delivered for you.' She holds up a bundle wrapped in a towel.

'Is she still here?' Kawsar asks plaintively.

'No, I sent them home.' She unlocks the door and hands it over. 'Be careful, it's hot.'

It smells good even through the cotton: coriander, pepper, cloves, garlic.

She is the first to be given food, but she can't eat while the others go hungry. She approaches the young girls and gestures that they should eat with her.

She unwraps the towel and inside is a lidded saucepan with a stack of round *roodhis* folded to the side of it. Steam escapes as she lifts the lid. A lamb and potato stew fills the pot, more than she would ever be able to eat alone. Gingerly, like cats, the girls gather around the food.

Kawsar passes the bread around and there are still four or five in her hand; she turns to China, 'Come and eat, you need milk for your son.'

China scrunches up her nose and shakes her head. 'I have my own *asho* to wait for.'

Kawsar dips a piece of bread into the stew, twisting it around a cube of potato. The bread is Maryam English's and the stew Dahabo's – she knows their cooking well enough. They must have paid *laluush* to ensure that it didn't become the guards' dinner; she makes a mental note to repay them.

The girls have overcome their shyness, reaching deep into the stew. Their fingers are dirty, so are her own, there is no way of cleaning them, but it still makes Kawsar queasy to look at the thick line of dirt under one girl's fingernails. Her stomach is tiny these days, one small meal a day is sufficient; she finishes one *roodhi* then leaves the remainder to them.

'Kawsar! Come out, you're wanted,' the policewoman bellows through the bars.

'What is this? The Kawsar hotel? What about us? I have been sat here all day with my infant,' China shouts.

'Hush, *dhilloyeh*! Whore! Keep your mouth closed if you don't want us to shut it for you.'

Kawsar is embarrassed. She wonders if Dahabo has told them that her husband had once been chief of police in Hargeisa.

'This way.' Amber light fills the corridor; they turn the opposite way to the exit, even deeper into the building, and then down narrow concrete steps into the basement.

'Are my neighbours back? Have they paid?' she asks the policewoman.

'You're not free that easily.' She knocks on a yellow door and then pushes the handle and looks inside the room. 'Here she is.'

'Let her in,' a voice says.

'Watch what you say,' the policewoman whispers and then opens the door wide.

It is the female officer who brought her to the police

station. She is less polished now, with her hair stuffed clumsily under her beret and her make-up smudged under the eyes. A bare light bulb of low wattage illuminates just the table and her pale face and hands. The windowless room still smells of the prisoners who have passed through – their exhaled breath, their sweat and the tang of their blood.

The officer points to a metal chair opposite her. It screeches as Kawsar pulls it along the concrete floor. The chair is tall and her toes can just about reach the floor when she sits down; a small murmur of pleasure comes from her as she relaxes into the padded plastic seat.

'I am Officer Adan Ali.' The woman clears her throat before continuing. 'I am investigating the disturbance today at the October Twenty-first parade in Hargeisa stadium. What is your name?' She produces a notebook and pen from her lap and jots down Kawsar's name, neighbourhood, age, marital status, clan details. She has the same concentrated intensity to her face as Hodan once had.

There is a pause before either of them speak again. Kawsar takes in the solitary decoration in the room – a poster taped askew to the back wall showing Ogadeen refugees huddled under an acacia tree in one half and the same refugees smiling broadly in a fishing boat after they have been resettled by the government in the other segment; her eyes keep meeting those of a teenage boy in the picture instead of her interrogator's.

Officer Adan Ali tugs at her collar and brushes a strand

of hair behind her ear. 'It was reported that you tried to assault members of the *Guddi*. What do you have to say in reply to this accusation?'

'I neither raised my hand to anyone nor threatened to,' Kawsar explains.

'Are you saying the *Guddi* are lying?'

Kawsar hesitates and takes a deep breath. 'Yes.'

Violent writing into the notebook. 'You understand that defamation of public workers is an offence?'

'An offence to God? To you? To me?'

'To the country.'

Kawsar shrugs her contempt.

Officer Adan Ali slams the pen onto the table and throws her back against her chair; another petulant little girl in authority.

Filsan feels her leg jiggling underneath the table; it is a nervous habit that appears when she is about to lose her temper. This is her first ever interrogation; she had walked into the police station and demanded to see the old woman. The night shift guards were already red-eyed and bleary and let her in without much discussion. She had wanted to clear her head, focus on work rather than what had just happened in Haaruun's car. Deep down she is terrified of returning alone to her little room. This old woman, Kawsar, has not only cleared her mind but is kindling a fire of anger in it; she thinks she is a gangster or something, refusing to look at Filsan and shrugging nonchalantly at questions.

Filsan has forgotten a standard question and she asks it now. 'Do you have any children?'

'Not anymore.'

Filsan's suspicion grows; if the mother is this disrespectful, maybe she has sons amongst the rebels in Ethiopia or in the Gulf, sending them money. 'When did they leave the country?'

Kawsar sighs. 'About five years ago.'

'Where did they go?'

'Heaven.'

Another pause.

'Do you think this is a game? If I want to I can make you disappear into Mandera or prisons that you have never heard of, where no one will find you.'

Filsan wants to take a hammer to her face. For some reason people feel they don't need to respect her. 'I am going to give you one last chance: tell me what happened between you and the *Guddi*.'

Kawsar spreads her hands on the table, her wrists just bone and bulging veins; the fingers curve as if the knuckles need oiling, the henna on her nails half grown out leaving small harvest moons at the tips.

'I went to the stadium as instructed. I sat quietly with my neighbours watching the parade. I am old, I am tired, I have no energy for these all day events but I obeyed. I saw a scrap of a girl dancing in the stadium until she was dragged away by the *Guddi*.'

'That is when you intervened?' Filsan's heart rate slows down.

'Yes. They were thrashing her, four or five of them against a child. I didn't want to just watch.'

'So what did you do?'

'I approached and told them to stop. I didn't touch anyone but I was pushed more than once.'

'What happened to the girl after you flew to her rescue?'

'She ran away.'

'Is this your first conflict with public officials?'

'I was once fined.'

'Why?'

'I was wrongly accused.'

'What of?' snaps Filsan.

'Listening to NFM radio,' murmurs Kawsar.

'Are any of your family mixed up with the rebels?'

'I don't have family. I am alone.'

'So why is a woman of your age tuning into childish propaganda?'

'I wasn't, but even if I did, aren't these my own ears? Given by God to do with as I please?' Kawsar's hand flicks her right ear lobe.

The blows come one after the other. The first to her ear as loud as a wave hitting a rock, then to her temple, cheek, neck. For a moment they stop as Kawsar clutches Officer Adan Ali's hands in hers but after a few heartbeats they resume. A swirl of sound and sight engulfs her until a punch to the chest knocks her from the chair onto the cement floor. Landing on her hip, Kawsar hears a crack beneath her and then feels a river of pain swelling up from her stomach to her throat, obstructing her breath. Resting her weight on one hand, she lifts an open palm to the soldier. 'Please stop!' she cries.

The girl shakes her head, tears in her own eyes, and rushes out of the room. The thud of her boots as she runs down the corridor gets quieter and disappears.

Every millimetre of movement electrifies Kawsar's nerves. She can neither pick herself up nor lie flat on the ground but is fixed in an awkward, lopsided pose. Her head sways with the enormity of the pain pulsing through her body, bile at the back of her tongue. Even if someone did arrive to help, how could she let them move her? It would be better to take a bullet to the back of the head. Her palms are clammy and she loses her grip, slipping closer to the ground, where drops of blood stain the white concrete. Kawsar licks her upper lip and tastes more blood. She rubs a hand under her nose; it comes away red.

The door is flung open and the policewoman with the blonde highlights and a man gather around her.

'What the hell did you say?' the policewoman asks, leaning over Kawsar's face.

'Don't touch me! Don't touch me! I beg you,' Kawsar sobs.

The policewoman hooks her under the arms while the policeman grabs her ankles.

'My hip is broken. In the name of God, put me down, I beg you, put me down . . .' Her words become screams as they lift her into the air.

They shuffle out of the interrogation room and a curtain of black descends over Kawsar's eyes, all feeling and hearing fading away.

Hidden in a narrow alleyway, Deqo peeps out at the crowd that has gathered outside the police station. Around ten women in red robes shout at a policeman, more policemen arrive and the women retreat but continue to shout. 'Give her to us,' she hears one say.

A civilian car drives past and one woman jumps out in front of it, banging on the windscreen until it stops and the driver steps out to speak with her. Behind them the shouting ceases as a prostrate figure emerges on a stretcher between two young policemen.

Deqo tiptoes out into the street, the area suddenly bright as cars slow to observe the commotion, their head-lights revealing the face of the woman on the stretcher.

It is her.

Deqo rushes across the road. Nobody seems to see her; this is a trick she has, the power to become invisible. She wipes the blood away from her saviour's face and pats her cheek. The women are shouting over her head, one older woman threatening the police with a cane; two of them take hold of the stretcher and push it into the open doors of the waiting car.

The car doors slam before Deqo can slip inside with them. A squeak, a crunch and the car starts, throwing up a plume of dust into her face. She chases its lights through the darkness, a pair of eyes looking back at her through the rear window. Deqo looks down at her garments glowing ghostly white and her limbs paled to the same colour. She realises how far away Saba'ad is, how exciting her life has become in the few hours she has been in Hargeisa, and she knows she cannot go back. The car begins to pull away from her and she quickens her pace, her legs eating up the road; the car turns and she follows, her feet now numb. Another acceleration and Deqo strains to keep up, her heart banging against her ribs. Her eyes focussed on the lights ahead, she misses the large pothole right ahead of her and falls in, scraping her knee and collapsing into it. The car slows to turn another corner and then disappears. Deqo is alone once more.

PART TWO

DEQO

Deqo steps barefoot across the festering mulch that slides beneath her feet. Her red plastic thong sandals hang delicately from her fingers, and beads of water drip from the trees as if the branches are shaking their fingers dry, splashing her face and neck in mischief. She hides behind the wide trunk of a willow near two crouched figures, her face framed in a scorched cleft where lightning has flung itself in a careless fit. She whispers her name to give herself courage. The men's talk is distorted by the music of raindrops falling over thousands of trees in the ditch, their leaves held out like waxy green tongues. The drought that had tormented her in Saba'ad is over, but she is in no mood to enjoy the downpour.

On either side of the trees are the stray dogs, thieves and promenading ghosts of Hargeisa. The swish of cars crossing the bridge and the susurrations of secret policemen come to her through the darkness. The barrel in which she sleeps is cold, too cold. The scraps of cut-off fabric that usually line the bottom are floating in kerosene-rippled water, the emeralds and sapphires of a peacock's tail flashing on its moonlit surface. She shivered with goose-pimpled skin for as long as she could bear it and then sought out the drunks and their fire in a moment of reckless desperation; she wonders what they will do for her, to her. She wants to know if hyenas can only be hyenas when confronted with a lamb. The heat of the men's fire blows over her, its crackling and its colours warming her. They have built a bombastic blaze, full of their alcohol; it lurches at the dark, quivering trees before stumbling and falling back into the barrel. She breathes in the smell of damp smoke, the taste of fresh ash.

'*Waryaa, hus!* Can you hear something, Rabbit?' one of the drunks slurs to his companion.

'Oh Brother Faruur, only the complaints of my poor stomach,' the other replies.

Faruur doesn't reply, his ear cocked to the side, his face concentrated and stern. He reminds Deqo of a dog, his body taut, his ear attuned to the hiss of faint breath, his twitching nose-hairs trapping and tasting the sour-sweet odour of blood.

'There is someone over there in the bushes,' Faruur says triumphantly.

Deqo steps out with a thudding heart, preferring to reveal herself than be caught; she marches straight to the burning barrel and puts her palms out to drink in the heat. Her brazenness works; Faruur and the other man look down in confused silence, both of them anxious that their hallucinations have returned.

The fire holds her hands and beckons her closer. It is like bathing but without the sting of water in her eyes or the awkward exposure of her naked body while unseen eyes watch.

Faruur's eyes are sick soups of yellow and pink, glossy like an infant's, the bottom lids slack. He looks Deqo up and down.

'Get away from here, from our fire!' He picks up a piece of wood with a nail spiking out and grasps it aloft as if to strike her. Beside his unlaced shoes leans a bottle of surgical spirit, half drunk.

Deqo meets his gaze. He thinks he can chase her away, they all think that. 'Man, be a Muslim. Let me get warm and then I'll leave you in peace.'

Faruur keeps his arm up and Deqo remains calmly by the fire, her hands like two explosions. Slowly his arm relaxes and falls to his side, the weapon still in his hand.

The other drunk reaches out to grab at her thigh; she jumps quickly beyond his reach. '*Oof*! Go grab your father, you disgusting old lizard,' she shouts.

The two look to each other and laugh, the hacking, husky, wheezy laughter of men with tuberculosis.

'Now, look here, Rabbit, we go to the effort of building a fire, collecting wood, buying matches, sacrificing our precious alcohol to get it started on this wet, godforsaken evening, and then this . . . this *kintir* . . . this

overgrown cunt comes along to steal our heat.' A moth
flits around Faruur's head as he speaks. 'What has the
world come to?'

Rabbit raises his hands in mock prayer and gazes up at
the dark-veiled heavens. 'Let the end be soon, there are
only so many injustices a man can stand before he
despairs.'

Deqo readies herself to run in case they both come at
her; her skin is hot, her muscles limber, she can disappear
into the night as if winged.

Faruur throws his stick to the ground and waves his
hand dismissively at Deqo. 'Do what you like. I am too
old, drunk and cold to chase after anyone.' He bends
down and picks up his bottle.

Deqo hopes they will fall asleep soon so she can spend
the night beside the fire, warm and well, rather than
wide-eyed in her barrel, her knees pressed up against her
chin, her back against the cold metal, trapped like a
breech birth in a hard, dead womb.

Rabbit and Faruur are pulling at their bottles, eyes
sealed, as peaceful and distant as infants drugged with
breast milk and soft, scented lullabies.

She has seen these two in town, laid out along the steps
of the warehouses near the hospital, sleeping through the
hot, shuttered hours between noon and afternoon prayers;
the hours which she spends collecting guavas, pomegranates, mangoes, bananas and papayas from the farms along
the ditch. She gathers them in a cloth sheet which she
spreads in the *faqir* market, guarding her patch until the

sun relents and the maids and cooks appear with their straw baskets to purchase cheap food for their own families. She makes up to fifty shillings a day like this – enough to buy a baguette filled with fried lamb, onions and potatoes. Girls are not allowed into the tea shops so she has to eyeball the schoolboys until she finds one honest-looking enough to go in for her. She has only been fooled once, taunted through the glass door as the khaki-uniformed boy stuffed her baguette into his grinning mouth, his hips swinging side to side as he scoffed it. She kicked him hard in the stomach when he finally ambled out of the teahouse, her daily bread tight and swollen under his skin.

She hates schoolboys. There are, in fact, only a few people whom she likes: Bashir, who sells well water from the back of his donkey but fills her tin cup for free; Qamar, the tall, plump, fragrant divorcee who wraps her up in fat arms and pets and kisses her in the market; and the blind *ma'alim*, Eid, who teaches the market boys and girls *Kitab* under a willow tree near the museum.

Rabbit's sarong has gathered up around his knees, his snores quietly audible beneath the fire's burning. Her legs are tired, her eyelids eager to drop, but she can't sleep here with them. She sits down heavily on the mulch and crosses her legs. She will wait until the sunrise and then tip out the water from her barrel and sleep for a couple of hours.

A dawn loud with birdsong erupts around her, black wings flapping in the diffuse sunlight between the trees.

Deqo quickly turns to where the drunks were sleeping and is relieved to find them still slumbering in a heap by the burnt-out fire. She gets to her feet and heads for the pathway to Hargeisa Bridge. It is early enough for her to reach the central mosque before the free bread and tea they give out in the morning is exhausted. Already the heat has dried the night's rainfall; only a faint dampness remains in the undergrowth, causing her plastic thongs to squeak. She had found them blown beneath a *whodead* stall one evening, too battered for the stall holder to bother picking up before he rushed home for the curfew. They don't match, one being larger than the other, but they stay on her feet. She has grabbed all of her clothing from the wind: a white shirt caught on a thorn tree, a red dress tumbling abandoned by the roadside, cotton trousers thrown over a power line. She dresses in these items that ghosts have left behind and becomes an even greater ghost herself, unseen by passers-by, tripped over, stepped on.

Clutching onto the scrub she pulls herself up the steep embankment, avoiding the thorns pressing into her skin and the excrement piled up in the dirt. There are only two bridges across the ditch, this concrete one and another made of rope near the Sha'ab quarter that swings precariously as you cross it. The bushes beneath the concrete bridge are crammed full of rubbish from the pedestrians above. In the six or so weeks Deqo has been in Hargeisa she has met many people she knows or dimly recognises from the camp along this bridge. The men stand out in sarongs of navy and maroon check, probably sold all over Ogaden by one trader from Dire Dawa. These men look uniformly old and familiar: sunken cheeked, bow-legged, hunchbacked and wild-haired. Some meet her gaze with a sharp, sidelong glance that pierces the clouds of her memory, and then she remembers them from Saba'ad: he rented out a wheelbarrow, he volunteered at the clinic, he sold goat milk.

There are only a few people crossing the bridge today, and she can run her hands along the peeling white iron railings without moving aside for anyone. Toyotas and trucks slow down beside her to navigate the gutted tarmac of the bridge. As she crosses from north to south Hargeisa she hears chanting. A flotilla of small clenched fists appears in the distance, approaching her as if pulled in by the tide. Local schoolboys and girls in pastel-coloured uniforms pump the air shouting, 'No more arrests, no more killing, no more dictatorship!' Their faces are frank and happy, the outlines of their individual bodies obscured by the flow of their movement. They block the road ahead so Deqo waits on the bridge to get a closer look at them. The bridge vibrates underneath, one hundred or two hundred feet drumming on the fragile structure. Deqo can see a few children without uniforms and some young men, too old for school, within the group. They sing a song she has never heard before: 'Hargeisa *ha noolaato*, long live Hargeisa.' The children closest to her look her up and down and scrunch up their noses.

Deqo wraps her arms around the iron railings behind her back and stares as the children make a spectacle of themselves. She has spent her whole life observing; hers are the eyes that always peer from behind walls or rocks, infuriating everyone with their watchfulness. But since she lost her friend Anab there is no one to lie down with at night, no one to divulge her secrets to; instead they put down roots in her mind and grow in the mulch of her confused life.

The schoolchildren are tightly packed onto the bridge, a shifting mass of blue, pink and khaki. She looks towards the north side of the bridge and sees red beret soldiers lined up across the road. Deqo finds them attractive: she likes the dark bottle-green of their uniforms, the gold on their epaulettes, the jaunty angle of their famous hats; she even likes the silver pistols that hang like jewellery from their hips.

The schoolchildren are silent, nervous, and when a whistle blows they scream and run back in the direction they came. The lean, tall soldiers pull out batons and chase the children. Deqo is caught in the melee and joins the stampede to avoid getting trampled. She feels like a sheep being herded into an enclosure. Hands grab her and push past, some almost dragging her down, but there is nowhere to escape to, the south side of the bridge blocked by another line of soldiers. The schoolchildren fall over each other trying to avoid the rigid, stinging batons. Their fists are now open in surrender, held aloft as if in promise of good behaviour.

Deqo trips over a boy and falls at the feet of a soldier; he grasps her dress in one hand and the boy's arm in the other and drags them over to a massive lorry waiting beside the road. The bed of the truck is so high the soldier has to let the boy go to throw Deqo into it with both hands; the boy follows and then other captive students. Reaching for the soldier's hand, Deqo tries to plead with him to let her go but he slaps her in the mouth. The taste of blood on her tongue, she looks around in shock at the flying skirts and limbs, as more and more children are forced into the vehicle. Black netting covers the side but that is the only difference between it and livestock trucks. An older boy with long ringlets down his neck tears a hole in the netting and clambers out the side, and other brave ones follow him. Deqo peers down at the distant ground, too afraid to try.

The vehicle is soon full of clamouring schoolchildren pressing against her on all sides. A girl sits next to her, crying open-mouthed, choking on her sobs. Deqo can feel the girl's bones and flesh grinding against her own as the truck's engine starts and they roar across the uneven road. Even in this teeming truck the girl smells fresh, her skin and uniform so scrubbed with soap that her perspiration has the heady, detergent scent that wafts out of the *dhobi*-houses.

'Don't cry,' says Deqo, placing a hand on the girl's arm.

'Don't touch me!' she shouts, pushing Deqo away.

An older pink-shirted girl throws her arm proprietorially over the crying girl's shoulders and kisses her head. '*Shush, shush*, Waris, I'm with you.'

Deqo turns her head away and purses her lips. I don't owe you anything, she thinks. In fact I should be angry with you for causing trouble, stupid girl. She doesn't understand why the schoolchildren and soldiers keep fighting. They all have food, all have homes and parents, what is there to squabble over? They should go to the refugee camp and see what life is like there. She covers her feet with her hands, ashamed by her dusty, long-nailed toes, the calloused, scaly skin, her red cotton smock fraying at every hem. Pulling her knees together she draws away from the boys sitting nearby. They do not hold their bodies as far away from her as they do the schoolgirls, she notices; there is barely an inch between her and any of the boys' limbs. They always nudge her in the street too, making her feel small and grubby. There isn't any *dhobi*-smell about them, only musk as sharp as vinegar that rubs onto her skin as they fall against her with the truck's tortuous drive.

The truck dips into one last pothole and then stops, the engine still trembling under the hood. To her right is the central police station, the first place she saw in Hargeisa after the stadium. A red beret pulls down the lip of the truck bed and ushers out the children. Ordinary policemen in white shirts lead them to the station, holding two in each hand by their shirt collars.

Finally it is Deqo's turn and she recoils as the red beret reaches for her; he is like a figure in a bad dream, silent, cruel and persistent. She squeals in pain as his vicelike hands grasp her ankle, another hand moves to her thigh and he yanks her out. Her body is not her own, she thinks; it is a shell they are trying to break open. A policeman with his trousers belted over his fat gut and his flies half done up swears at the prisoners, slapping the back of Deqo's legs with a flat, hard palm and wrangling her arms behind her back. Holding her wrists and those of the fragrant girl's in one hand he marches them through the haze of dust that the struggling protestors have kicked up and ascends the tall, rain-stained concrete steps into the police station.

In the dingy, dark corridor a young guard sits on a metal chair to the right. He looks at the passing school-children with big, melancholic eyes. 'Help me,' she mouths as she skids over the green-tiled floor, but he doesn't shift, just cradles his gun with long, large-knuckled fingers, veins twisting under his smooth skin. Deqo feels as if she is treading water, pulled into a current she can't escape.

The schoolchildren are led through to the cells, the girls put into one communal cell and the boys pushed deeper into the station. Deqo's wrists burn where the big-bellied policeman has been squeezing them and she shakes them in the air to cool. A few steps into the cell she is overcome by the stench of excrement. Older prisoners have to sit up and move to make room for the protestors and complain loudly at the intrusion. Four young women with their hair in thick plaits huddle together along the back wall. One of the large women kicks at them and shouts, '*Roohi*, move it'; they obey and she spreads out her rush mat in the small space they had shared.

Some of the schoolgirls start snivelling again as they look around the cell. Deqo rolls her eyes at them; she feels superior to these naive, sheltered girls who protest while knowing nothing of what the real world is like. They cannot appreciate the roof above that will keep them dry, the bodies that will keep them warm, the dripping tap in the corner that will quench their thirst. The women and girls shift constantly, trying to stand as far from the waste bucket as possible. Every breath Deqo takes is shallow and cautious; this smell sends her back to the refugee camp and the cholera outbreak that ended Anab's life and nearly her own, both of them falling asleep but only one of them waking up. In the ditch she has at least become accustomed to space and the fresh scent of trees.

Some of the prisoners look comfortably at home. One young woman is breastfeeding her baby and chatting, her legs stretched out. Her friend is dressed gorgeously in pink and silver, with black hair dyed gold at the tips. They seem untouched by the situation around them. In contrast, the girls with the plaits appear to have been in the cell for weeks. One of them is barefoot, her trousers blood-stained near the crotch, another has small, circular scorches all over her bare arms. All of them are emaciated, their hips like metal frames under loose trousers, their necks long and drawn, their dark-lashed eyes sunken into black holes. Policewomen in navy uniforms pass by the cell bars, their trousers tight across their back-sides. Deqo wonders what the girls have done to be treated so badly and if she will be kept inside with them. Looking between them and the pretty women, she ma-noeuvres closer to the pretty ones to see if their good luck will spread to her.

'. . . that he is free, that the last child wasn't even his own,' the one with gold-dipped hair is saying.

'You believe him?' replies the mother.

'No, but what can I do? I have been bitten by love.'

'Well, bite it back,' she laughs.

Deqo laughs too and they look up suspiciously.

'Didn't anyone tell you it's rude to eavesdrop?'

Deqo smiles apologetically.

'Let her be, she's not doing any harm. What are you doing here? You stole?'

Deqo shakes her head violently. 'I don't know, ask these people,' she gesticulates dismissively towards the stu-dents, 'they put me in trouble.'

'Is that so?' she smiles. 'What is your name?'

'Deqo. What's yours?'

'Nasra, and this is China and her son Nuh.'

'Why are you in here?'

The women look to each other and chuckle.

'It is part of our job,' Nasra answers coyly.

The policewoman has a neat beret perched to the side of her pinned-up hair and possesses a strange combination of femininity and menace.

'Which one of you is Waris Abdiweli Geedi?' she calls in a harsh voice.

The fragrant girl pushes past the others and presents herself before the policewoman, who beckons her out of the cell with a henna-painted finger before locking the door again. The prisoners ease into the small space the girl has left behind. To Deqo's amusement, fragrant girl does not so much as look back at those she has left behind; the girl who had thrown her arm over her in the truck is left to stand there, head hanging. Deqo is pleased: when arrogant people like that are are forced to see how little they really matter she feels a small charge of satisfaction.

One by one the schoolgirls are called, bailed out and hustled home by their fathers, mothers, uncles and elder brothers. They are released before the boys to protect them from shame; the shame that grows and widens with their breasts and hips and follows them like an unwanted friend. Deqo has long been aware of how the soft flesh of her body is a liability; the first word she remembers learning is 'shame'. The only education she received from the women in the camp concerned how to keep this shame at bay: don't sit with your legs open, don't touch your privates, don't play with boys. The avoidance of shame seems to be at the heart of everything in a girl's life. There is at least a chance in this women-only cell to put shame aside for a while and flop down without wondering who might see her legs or who might grab her while she sleeps. She finds a space near an elderly destitute woman on a rush mat.

'Get me a cup of water,' the woman croaks.

Deqo looks at the reclining figure, so old and self-important. 'Get it yourself.'

The woman sighs. Deqo notices that she is missing all of her front teeth. The woman nudges her with her foot. 'Go on, my sweet, just get me some water, I have an axe slicing through my head.' She makes kissing noises to cajole her.

Deqo tuts and rises to her feet; she will ask for water for herself too, fill up her stomach a bit. She waits by the bars; she can hear the policewoman talking at the end of the corridor.

'*Jaalle, Jaalle*! Comrade, Comrade!' Deqo cries out.

No answer.

'Comrade Policewoman with the hennaed fingers and black *koofiyaad*, we need cups here.'

The policewoman approaches and pushes a tin cup through the bars. 'Don't try and be funny here, little girl.'

'I wasn't trying to be funny, I just wanted water.'

'Aren't you too young to be selling yourself? Or have you been stealing?'

'No! I haven't done anything, honestly. They mistook me for a protestor.'

'Where are you from?'

'From Saba'ad.'

'So what are you doing here?'

'I work in the market. I never steal, never!'

The policewoman's face softens a little; she tilts her head to the side and looks over to her colleague.

'Luul, this refugee girl is here by mistake; she was pulled in with all those protestors this morning.'

The other policewoman comes to join her. She is tall and flat-chested, unable to fill out her uniform like her friend.

She pulls a face. 'Let her out, we're not going to get anything for her.'

'True, she's a waste of bread,' laughs the policewoman with the henna on her fingers.

The door chimes open once again and Deqo runs to the old woman on the mat to hand over the cup before stepping out into the corridor of freedom.

'See you another time, Deqo,' Nasra calls out.

Deqo waves back.

The policewomen walk on each side of her in silence.

'Jaalle, when will that woman be released?' asks Deqo, before being led out of the station.

'Never you mind, you should stay away from women like that, they will drag you down into their nasty ways. Stay away, you hear?' She adjusts the beret on her head.

'Is she a . . .' Deqo hesitates at that powerful word that has plagued her throughout her short life.

'A whore? Absolutely, and much else besides.'

Deqo marches back to the ditch with her eyes to the ground, deep in thought. She still has time to collect fruit from the farms and reach the market before it closes for lunch. Her legs propel her forward robotically but her mind is whirring with memories from Saba'ad, stirred up by her encounter with Nasra and China in the cell. 'Whore's child, whore's child, whore's child!' That's what the other children in the camp had yelled at her for as long as she could recall, but she hadn't known what a whore was; it sounded bad, like a cannibal or a witch or a type of *jinn*, but no adult would describe what made a whore a whore and the children didn't seem to know much more than she did. She was born of sin, they said, the bastard of a loose woman. From the children's story her nativity went like this: a young woman arrived in the camp alone and by foot, heavily pregnant and with feet torn to shreds by thorns. The nurses at the clinic bandaged her feet and let her wait for the child to be delivered. She refused to give her name or her husband's, and when Deqo was born she abandoned her own child without naming her either. Deqo had been named a year later by the nurses when she climbed out of the metal cot the orphans were kept in and began disappearing; Deqowareego was her full name, 'wandering Deqo', and she had learnt that the one thing she could do that the other camp children couldn't was drift as far as she liked. She belonged to the wind and the tracks in the dirt rather than to any other person; no watchful mother would come after her shouting her name in every direction.

At first she had believed her mother was a *jinn* who had changed into a human for only a short while and then had to change back, but she was always too cold to have had a mother made of fire. Then she thought her mother may have been blown away by a typhoon, but too many older orphans said they had seen her walk away on her own two feet. Finally she decided that her mother, this 'whore' they talked about, was not like other women who lived and died beside their children, but another kind altogether, who knew that her child would be clothed and fed, just not by herself, like a bird who lays her egg in another's nest.

So Deqo had grown up thinking herself a cuckoo amongst the other camp children, whose parents were all refugees from the fighting and famine that had swept across eastern Ethiopia from the seventies into the eighties; some were Somali, some were Oromo, but they all had their families or even just their family names and clans to help them. Deqo deeply wishes she had a second and third name; she won't be greedy and ask God for a whole *abtiris* of seventeen names or anything, just two more would allow her to puff out her chest and announce her existence to people. When she was too young to know better she had taken the name Deqo Red Cross because that was the name of the clinic she lived in, but the frowns on the white-uniformed nurses' faces let her know it wouldn't do as a replacement name. She lived as just Deqo, or sometimes Deqo-wareego when the nurses shouted at her, and waited for her prayers to be answered.

When Anab Hirsi Mattan came into the orphanage at around six years old, head shaved for lice and wild with grief, Deqo was charged with looking after her. When she ran away to the burial ground Deqo was in close pursuit, nervously waiting and watching while the little bat-eared girl beat her hands on the mound of earth covering her mother. The older graves were marked with rocks, planks of wood, or thorny acacia branches, but the newer ones were unadorned, rolling up the hill in a wave. The cemetery resembled the vegetable plot between the dispensary and orphanage, pregnant with plantings that would never grow, watered with nothing but tears. Anab shovelled her hands into the dirt as if she was trying to dig up her mother or bury herself; eventually she tired, defeated, and laid her face down on top of the grave. Deqo had then approached and stretched out her hand; Anab took it, her fingers bleeding, and sloped back with her to the orphanage.

Deqo took ownership of Anab from that day, sleeping and eating beside her in the large tent that housed fifty-two orphans and strays. Every day she and Anab ate *canjeero* for breakfast, played beside the standpipe where the earth was damp and malleable, followed funeral processions to the cemetery, had an afternoon nap and then played *shaax* with mud counters before the unchanging supper of rice and beans and lights out. Lying in the dark, whispering and tittering, Anab called her Deqo-wareego Hirsi Mattan; they were newfound sisters, thrown together like leaves in a storm.

The myriad buildings that Deqo is slowly learning the names and purposes of appear in the edges of her vision as she steps into the pitted road. The library for keeping books to learn from, the museum for interesting objects from the past, the schools in which children are corralled and tamed, the hotels for wayfarers with money in their pockets – the existence of all these places brings pleasure, despite her belief that as a refugee she is not welcome inside.

In the weeks since her arrival in Hargeisa she has learnt something every day just from observing the life around her. In the first few days she slept in the market, led there by electric lights and children's voices. She huddled rigidly under the stalls with a few girls and many, many boys fighting and sniffing all night from little bags that gave them leaky noses. She left there and found a concrete area in front of a warehouse that was swept clean and raised above the dust of the street. She found a little sleep there until one night a pack of stray, short-haired dogs found her, growling and barking as she hid her face in her hands. They drew the attention of the watchman who frightened them away and then banished her too. She had then stayed a week outside the police station, hoping for their protection against boys and strays, but instead there was the constant disruption of police cars, of foot patrols and military vehicles sweeping up and down the road. Eventually, she had gravitated closer and closer to the ditch, lured by its quiet thicket and isolation, to the point where she is now perfectly comfortable sleeping within its deep darkness, unafraid and undisturbed, unless it rains and a deep chill enters her bones.

Deqo reaches the ditch and turns off at the red-berried shrubs that mark the path towards her barrel, speeding down the slope and only staggering to a stop when it comes into view. It is a mysterious sanctuary that swallows her up at night; she doesn't know who brought it here and only found it herself by accident one moon-bright night. She scoops up the rainwater that had so tormented her the night before and quenches her thirst, the taste of kerosene faint at the back of her throat. Then she pours the rest over her head and torso, squeezing the excess from her thin smock. It will dry in the time it takes her to collect all the fruit she needs from the farms.

She hurries over to Murayo's plot which lies near the right bank of the dry waterbed, far from the noise of the road, where a flock of birds roosts and chats, their nests like bad imitations of wicker baskets. They fly up and hoot at her approach as if to warn Murayo. It depends on how Murayo is feeling each day as to whether she will allow her to glean the fruit, but since Deqo alerted her to the burglar crouching on the roof of her mud-built home she has been generous. Deqo scans the ground for the squishy, over-ripe mangoes she can eat herself before bothering with the hard, green fruit still ripening on the branches. Today there is only one lying splattered in the weeds, its orange flesh trembling with black ants.

Up in the trees she checks the foliage for snakes. She once grabbed a sleeping green snake as she climbed, its mouth suddenly yawning, rigid and white in her face, making her fall clear out of the tree. She spits into her palms and hugs the slimmest trunk, above which are a clutch of mangoes that have a nice red blush to them ready for picking; her hands hold her up while her toes slip against the smooth bark. Before she loses her grip she grasps the branch that holds the mangoes and plucks them off one by one, throwing them gently to the ground, then edges back towards the trunk and slides down, enjoying the sensation of the trunk against her skin. She collects the mangoes in her damp skirt and rushes away before Murayo comes to water her crops. The next plot is larger, dominated by dense banana trees, some so laden that the bananas hang near her head; she takes six, all that she can carry in her skirt, and turns back to town.

At the *faqir* market Deqo retrieves her piece of cardboard with the slice of advertising still visible on it from the pile on the ground and lays out her merchandise in two rows of six, alternating banana and mango. She has tried other jobs: collecting scraps of *qat* to sell to the dealers, pulling grass to sell as goat feed to housewives, sweeping the main market when there aren't enough girls in the evening, but this is her favourite. Her workday is over early and she has no boss to tell her what to do, and on the days that there are no customers she can eat the pilfered fruit herself.

Most of the other sellers are middle-aged women, with hefty arms and feet overflowing the edges of their sandals. The only one of them who is always kind to her, Qamar, is not there today so Deqo sits on her haunches and waits for customers. They come slowly, browsing the other stalls before deciding they can get the cheapest price out of her. She watches how the other sellers haggle and imitates their impatient gestures and harsh words. 'Take your shadow off of me if you're not interested,' she shouts. 'You are blocking people with more than lint in their pockets.' She says this with a straight face despite her tiny ramshackle body and the twigs in her hair.

The bananas go first to a woman carrying a toddler on her back, and then the mangoes disappear in ones and twos. She holds the money in her hand with satisfaction; there are no dramas today, no thieves encroach and no arguments take place. She hates those days when honking, clumsy women stampede through her patch in pursuit of someone or other.

She rises and shakes the dust off the cardboard.

'*Yaari*, little one, come over here a minute,' calls a woman with a blue and gold threaded turban on her head.

Deqo walks to her and stands stony-faced with her hands on her hips.

'I'll give you a few shillings if you deliver something for me.'

'How much?'

'Twenty?'

'Forty.'

'Thirty.'

'Fine,' Deqo smiles in triumph. 'What do you want me to take?'

The woman reaches behind her back and pulls out a package wrapped in the light-blue-inked official newspaper *October Star*.

Deqo takes it in both hands and feels the shape of a glass bottle inside.

'Don't drop it and don't you dare open it. The person waiting at the other end is called China – you hand it to her and no one else. If any police approach you just throw it away, you listening?'

Deqo nods, intrigued.

'Hold it like that!' The woman's upper arm wobbles as she arranges the package in an upright position under Deqo's arm. 'Tight, tight, squeeze it.' The whole exchange has raised sweat beads on the market woman's forehead. 'Go, keep your head down and look for the blue painted house on the street leading left off the end of this road.'

The area the woman points to is a part of town Deqo has been frightened to venture into before. The market women refer to the place as a kind of hell in which dead souls live; people who have left behind any semblance of goodness congregate in its shacks – drunks, thieves, lechers and dirty women.

The road tapers into a narrow alley, the market disappearing more with every yard until there are just fragments of it: a cloth, a squashed tomato, a torn shilling note that Deqo picks up to add to her stash. The sun is high above and the smell of goat and donkey droppings grows stronger in her nostrils. She passes fewer stone-built bungalows and more mud brick and traditional *aqals* modernised with tarpaulin and metal sheets in place of wood and animal skins. It will be easy to pick out a blue bungalow from these neighbours. She sees children everywhere, bare-bottomed and tuft-haired, five-year-olds carrying two-year-olds on their hips or staring out from entrances with solemn, hostile expressions. '*Dhillo*! Whore!' one little boy in a red shirt that stretches to his knees shouts at her.

She picks up a small rock and lobs it at him, missing him by a short distance; he ducks back into his shack with a squeal.

Her sandals are full of grit; she stops to shake them out and notices a gully of dirty water running to the side of the track, small jagged bones lodged in the mire as well as pieces of plastic and twisted wire. This side of town seems abandoned by the rest, left to sink and slump and rot; she wonders why anyone would stay here if they had the whole of Hargeisa to choose from.

She finally spots a small, blue breezeblock bungalow and knocks on a metal door painted in diamonds of orange and green. The tin roof buckles loudly in the sun and flies buzz in the wire mesh covering the windows. Beside the blue bungalow is a jacaranda tree with a goat happily lost in its high branches, nibbling at fresh shoots.

Deqo waits a long time before knocking again; she checks around the sides of the house for any movement.

'Who is it?' someone shouts from inside.

'I have a delivery,' Deqo answers nervously.

NADIFA MOHAMED

Three locks click open and then a figure takes shape within the gloom of the hallway.

Deqo recognises her hair first, the broad band of yellow at the tip of her waves.

'Give it to me,' Nasra says yawningly.

'I can't. I need to give it to China.' Deqo looks down as she speaks.

Nasra throws her head back and groans; she doesn't seem to recognise her.

'Take it to her.' She pulls Deqo into the bungalow and locks all three latches again.

Nasra leads her into the courtyard and her pale pink *diric* lights up in the sunlight, engulfing her body like a flower bud. The bungalow smells incredibly sweet despite the rashes of black damp growing up the interior walls, and Deqo inhales deeply.

Nasra knocks on the bare wooden door on the opposite side of the whitewashed yard. *'Isbiirtoole,* drunkard, your nectar is here,' she calls.

China opens the door and the courtyard fills with music in a foreign tongue. 'Give here.' She snatches the package before Deqo can hand it over. 'I know you . . . It's our little jailbird. I didn't know you were in the trade.'

'What trade?'

'The booze trade, of course.'

'I'm not. I have a stall in the market.'

'There is no need for pretence here; one thing about Fucking Street is you can be yourself.'

'Where do your family live?' Nasra asks.

'I have no family.'

'No grandmother, no aunt, no cousins?'

Deqo shakes her head. 'No grandfathers, no step-siblings, no half-uncles. I look after myself.' Each time she says this it feels more true.

'So where do you sleep?'

'Over in the ditch.'

Both of the women tut.

'Ooh, you have a stronger heart than me sleeping in that haunted wasteland,' China says, unwrapping the newspaper and unscrewing the lid of the bottle.

The ethanol clears every other smell from Deqo's nose.

'It's not haunted, I'm not bothered there.'

'Until someone comes to slit your throat while you're asleep,' Nasra says.

'That won't happen, no one can find me where I sleep.' Deqo feels a shiver along her spine despite her words.

The women look her in the eye. They see her in a way that most other people don't; she doesn't constantly lose their attention.

Nasra rubs a hand over Deqo's hair. 'What is it like being all alone in the world at your age?'

The question hits Deqo like a falling branch. She shuffles her feet a little and tries to pick through the words lodged on her lips: frightening, tiring, free, confusing, exciting, lonely. She mumbles incoherently and then stops. 'I can still have a good life.'

Nasra looks down at her with tears in her eyes.

'With enough luck you can. You lucky?' China asks, her voice suddenly louder with the drink.

Deqo cocks her head and smiles. 'Sometimes. I just found this torn shilling outside, that's quite lucky.'

'You are going to need more luck than that, child.' China throws her head back and lets out a laugh that echoes off the walls and tin roof. Her baby wakes and begins to cry inside the room. 'Oh, shut up!' she yells before slamming the door shut.

'Give this money to the woman who sent you.' China counts out one hundred and fifty shillings from a huge roll and then squeezes back into the narrow room. 'Good luck, little girl,' she says as she waves Deqo off.

Nasra leads Deqo back to the front door and pushes another ten shillings into her palm.

Just as she is about to walk away, Deqo stops and turns back to Nasra.

'Can I ask you something?' she says in a faint whisper.

'Huh? I can't hear you.'

Deqo bends in closer. 'Can I ask you something?'

Nasra nods cautiously.

Deqo licks her lips nervously. 'Are you a whore?'

Nasra tenses with anger but Deqo doesn't run or laugh, she is waiting, eyes wide, for an answer.

A few moments pass and then a twinkle enters Nasra's eyes and her smile answers the question.

Deqo crouches down by the roadside an hour later, chewing on a lamb baguette; the bread is stale, the lamb cold, but she doesn't care. In her mind she goes over and over her exchange with Nasra. If she is a whore then China must be too, so why had she kept her child? If it wasn't necessary to abandon him then why had her own mother abandoned her? Deqo swallows with difficulty as the notion that her mother might have kept her enters her mind. Did she see something wrong with her? Was she running away from a child whose bad luck was written across its face? As if to punctuate this thought a car drives past and sprays dirty water from a puddle over her legs. She rises and brushes the drops and breadcrumbs away, kicking a stone in frustration at the back of the car. Sour-faced and melancholic she walks back in the direction of Nasra's house.

The heavens break open and she trots forward, skipping and sliding. The rain smells fresh, heady and green; it cleans the town and makes the paintwork on the buildings shine again. On a wall beside the market is a portrait of the old man with protruding teeth, the President. She has noticed it many times, but the raindrops now falling over his face look like tears and she stops, suddenly arrested by the sad expression on his face; despite the military khaki and gold braids he looks out to her with infinite loneliness. The dark clouds and the empty street drag down her already low spirits; in this kind of weather you should be at home with a family, dozing, playing and sitting snug by a fire. She feels cheated, cheated and spurned by the world. She wipes the tears off the portrait and continues up past the main market and antenna-eared radio station, along the perimeter wall of a large school loud with loved children and through her *faqir* market.

She reaches Nasra's street shivering and with rivulets of water running down her nose and the inside of her dress. The street has changed entirely; it is full of wild children dancing half-naked in the rain and lifting wide-open maws to the sky. Chickens flap between their feet and goats are forced to dance on hind legs in their arms. A cacophony of music blasts from each dwelling: songs from the radio, others warped by over-played cassettes and a few trilling from the women inside the homes. The previously thick waste in the gully is now flowing away in a small stream and the plastic bags caught in the tree branches shine like balloons. A girl of about eight with hair plastered to her face runs up to Deqo and drags her into the melee; holding her tight to her chest she spins like a whirling dervish, cackling. Deqo laughs too, enjoying the delirium; her sadness floats above her, hanging there for the moment, then the girl slips and they both crash to the mud, limbs intertwined.

'What's your name?' Deqo pants.

'Samira, you?'

'Deqo.'

'I haven't seen you before.' The girl smiles and reveals small brown teeth.

'I am from far away.' Deqo knows the way smiles fade when she tells people she is from the refugee camp.

A woman with bare feet leaps towards them; she is

thin and angry. 'Samira! Samira! Get up off the dirt, you little pig!'

'I have to go.' Samira rushes to her feet before the woman can slap her bottom. She runs into the shack and the woman follows, her feet like a wading bird's as she navigates the mud.

'Deqo, is that you?'

Deqo lifts her head from the mud to find Nasra squinting at her. She slides up and wipes the stripes of dirt off her face.

'Come inside, you'll get sick,' Nasra orders.

An incense burner heats up the room as Nasra rubs a towel over Deqo's hair and body. 'There isn't any water at the moment, you'll just have to stay a little dirty for now,' she says.

Deqo looks around the room as the warmth returns to her skin: at the pink walls decorated with film posters, the fur rug on the blue lino floor, and the white furniture crowding around her. This is the finest room she has ever seen. Totting up how much all of the furniture, clothing, ornaments, knick-knacks and cosmetics must have cost in the market, she takes a sharp inhalation of breath. *Whores live well*, she thinks.

'Let me put some milk on the stove.' Nasra drops the towel on her bed and leaves the room.

Deqo tiptoes to the framed photos on a table; all the pictures are of Nasra, but in only one of them is she smiling. Her eyes move aside and she picks up nail varnish bottles one by one: pale pink, bright pink, dark red, electric blue – she would like to paint a fingernail in each colour. Everything in the room is gorgeous, made for pleasure; the soft rug is bliss against her tired feet, sequins twinkle on the gauzy purple curtains, the bed has pillow upon pillow. She struggles to see what shame there is in being a whore if it brings such luxury to a life. Nasra seems incapable of any work apart from beautifying herself; she is too delicate and too pretty to labour in the dust of the market or to wash someone's floors on her knees.

Nasra returns with two mugs of milk. 'I was thinking about you earlier.'

Deqo smiles and quickly hides her mouth behind her hand.

'It is wrong for any child, but especially a girl, to be sleeping anywhere near that ditch, with the wild dogs and even wilder men. If you wanted to, you could stay here; there is space for bedding in the kitchen and you'll be warm at night. We need help around the house, cleaning, preparing food; you could look after China's baby too. You would like that, wouldn't you?'

Deqo looks her square in the eye. 'Why do you want to help me?'

Nasra puts her mug on the floor and sits back on the bed. 'Because I was once not too different from you: lonely, hungry, uncared for. I hitched a ride to Hargeisa and arrived with nothing more than a toothstick and a change of underwear. I know how it is to be a girl on the streets.'

'I can really stay here? You won't send me away?'

Nasra smiles. 'Not unless you do something terrible.'

'That is China's room as you know, over there is Karl Marx, and in the corner the new girl, Stalin.' Nasra points to three closed doors made of rough planks on each side of the courtyard. 'You have to clean their rooms but if the doors are closed you leave them alone.'

'Are they foreign? Their names don't sound Somali.'

'No, those are their nicknames; every girl has a nickname on this street.'

Deqo skips beside her. 'What is yours?'

'Every girl but me. I liked my own name well enough and didn't care about anyone finding me.' She opens the kitchen door to reveal pots, pans and long knives dumped in a large plastic basket in one corner, and a mat, blanket and cushion in another.

'It's not the Oriental but it's better than the ditch, no?'

Deqo nods. Falling asleep in a warm kitchen with the smell of proper food in her nostrils is good enough for her.

'We all like to cook for ourselves but you might be asked to help chop or watch over dishes. When you're not cleaning stay within earshot in case we need you to run an errand.'

That night, as Deqo huddles in the kitchen, imagining her barrel in the ditch empty and miserable without her, she hears men's voices. She jumps up to peer out of the doorframe. All of the doors to the women's rooms are thrown open and light spills onto the courtyard.

'Stay away from me!' a young girl shouts from the hallway. 'Oof! I don't want you anywhere near me, you cannibal.'

Deqo guesses that it is Stalin.

An older man appears, carrying a leather bag into Karl Marx's room. He looks back, smirking, as Stalin continues to pour curses onto his head. He enters the room without knocking and then the glowing strip of light underneath Karl Marx's door is extinguished.

All through the night Deqo is woken by slamming doors, raised voices and other more mysterious sounds. She feels more anxiety here than in the ditch, but also insatiable curiosity. She suspects the origins of her own story lie in a place like this, that it is time to uncover the facts of her birth. Her eyes remain wide in the dark, her ears attuned to every little squeak, her dreams evaporating like mist. It had been far easier to sleep in the ditch, where it was too dark to see and so quiet at times that she could hear the blood rushing through her veins.

The morning comes, bright and demanding, just as Deqo is falling asleep. She resists its call for as long as possible before realising just how late it is. She eats the *canjeero* that someone has placed beside her on a tin plate and washes her face and arms under the weak flow of the courtyard tap, unsure if she is allowed in the bathroom.

Shaking her arms dry, she peeps into Stalin's open door

and, finding it empty, grabs a cloth from the kitchen to start work. To her it is just an excuse to touch interesting things; she has no idea how to clean the various jars, instruments and trinkets scattered around the room, but she enjoys handling them, turning them around in the light and imagining their use. Eventually her attention turns to the mattress on the floor with its sheets entwined into floral ropes; she shakes them out, smoothes them back over the bed just as she has seen the nurses do in the hospital, and then lifts the striped pillow. She does a double take at the sight of the butcher's knife hidden beneath it. She doesn't touch but leans over to take a closer look: the blade is a long, wide slice of silver, the black handle has grooves moulded into it so that it can easily fit into a hand, and around the point where metal meets plastic is a dark stain that might be rust or old blood.

'Get out of here, thief!' a girl shouts before pushing past Deqo and grabbing the knife, pointing it at her face. 'Who told you that you could enter my room?'

Deqo raises her hands in terror and points to the court-yard. 'Nasra,' she stutters.

'Nasra! Did you bring this street kid into the house?' the girl yells.

Nasra joins them in the tiny room and pushes the knife away from Deqo. 'Stalin, what are you thinking? I said she could work here. You can't just stick a knife in every stranger's face.' She sighs. 'Didn't you see her asleep in the kitchen?'

'I went out to buy my breakfast.' Stalin looks Deqo up and down. 'You shown her to anyone yet?'

Nasra glares at Stalin before ushering Deqo out of the room. 'Go to Karl Marx's room, she won't say anything to you.'

Nasra closes the door and stays behind with Stalin.

Deqo looks over her shoulder. Still trembling slightly, she decides to stay out of Stalin's room in future and leave her to clean it on her own. Stalin is the opposite of Nasra: stocky, muscular, stern-faced, her hair pulled back from her face and pomaded – she looks ready to beat someone to a pulp. What did she mean about showing me to someone, wonders Deqo. I am not a wild animal, there is nothing to see.

She crosses the yard to Karl Marx's room and knocks before entering. It takes a few seconds for her eyes to adjust to the gloom, but when they do she sees Karl Marx on her back with her palms on her chest. Deqo stands beside the door, unsure if the shape on the bed is breathing or not.

'Come in, I'm not dead. Not yet anyway,' Karl Marx says without opening her eyes.

'I have come to clean your room.' Deqo holds back the sneeze tickling her nose.

Karl Marx doesn't move a muscle; her profiled face is sharp and pale against the blue wall. 'Clean it then.' Her words seem to come out through her large ears or thin nostrils as her lips do not move.

Deqo takes the cloth and sweeps a layer of dust off

the windowsill, but it is inhibiting having another person in the room. Karl Marx begins to shift, flinging her legs to the side of the bed and yawning loudly. Deqo glances at the woman's skeletal naked body, her protruding collarbones forming a yoke around her neck, bleeding sores crisscrossing the skin on her meagre thighs. Deqo examines her discreetly and sees a woman who should be in hospital. Karl Marx grabs a corner of the bedclothes and dabs at the blood on her legs; she is unperturbed by her appearance and slowly rises, showing the two triangular bones of her buttocks as she retrieves a *diric* from the floor.

Deqo feels a lump in her throat and hums softly to distract herself.

'You one of Nasra's?'

'*Haa,* yes.'

'You selling?'

'Selling what?'

'The thing between your legs.'

Deqo takes a minute to decipher what could be worth selling or even possible to sell between her legs. 'No! I clean and run errands only,' she says hurriedly. She imagines Karl Marx doing what the goats and stray dogs do when they mount each other and is disgusted. That is what makes a whore a whore, she realises, and her eyes widen.

Karl Marx sits down heavily and looks at Deqo with lowered eyes. 'I was your age when I started this.'

Deqo cannot see what anyone would want with Karl

Marx; she looks like she has TB, typhoid and every kind of sickness going. In Saba'ad people would have run from her.

'Look at me,' she says.

Deqo stops and looks her squarely in the face.

'How old do you think I am?'

There are already white hairs on her head, her breasts beneath the sheer *diric* hang down to her navel; she is far into old age in Deqo's estimation.

'Go on, say it.'

'Fifty? Fifty-five?'

Karl Marx laughs, revealing broken khat-stained teeth. 'You little bitch! Take twenty off that and you're close.'

Deqo smiles in return, not believing her words but too polite to challenge them. 'Why are you called Karl Marx?' she asks.

'Because I have shared and shared and shared until there is nothing left to give.' She clutches at her bosom and sighs.

'What about Stalin and China?'

'Stalin is named after *Jaalle* Stalin of the Russians for her brutality, and China is a favourite of the coolies. Nasra doesn't want a name.' Her attention turns to the store of white medicine boxes on the floor, and while Deqo straightens the bed she crunches tablet after tablet in her mouth.

'What will your name be?'

'My name is Deqo, I don't want it to change,' she says firmly. If Nasra didn't need a new name to live here then nor would she.

'Wash those clothes for me, would you?' Karl Marx points to a pile by the door.

Deqo hesitates, unsure if laundry is one of her duties, then decides to ingratiate herself with Karl Marx; it can't hurt to have another ally against Stalin within the house. She picks up the laundry and leaves.

Deqo drops Karl Marx's clothes into a basin in the court-yard and then scrubs them under the tap with a green soap; the trickle of water is so slow that she leaves the basin and attempts to finish the rooms before returning. After knocking three times on China's door and not receiving a reply, Deqo pads across to Nasra's room, where incense burns in a white clay urn. Nasra has just had a shower and her hair is wrapped in a towel away from her long neck. The skin above her knees and elbows is paler than the rest and mottled with small moles that rush over her chest and thighs; she rubs a milk-white cream on her body with a rough motion, kneading the flesh between her fingers and pulling it away from the bone.

'Take some.' Nasra holds out the bottle.

Deqo squirts a tiny amount into her palm and returns the bottle. The scent of the lotion, the razor blade and the myriad jars of perfume on the dresser seem to express the metamorphosis from little girl to woman, the necessary grooming and management demanded by a body grown large and wild. She rubs her hands together and puts them to her nose, the lotion's scent is overwhelmed by soap, charcoal, bread and sweat.

Nasra rips the towels from her head and body and stands in all her splendour before the wardrobe. Deqo averts her eyes, but the difference between Nasra's solid thighs and backside and Karl Marx's makes her want to look again and check how a grown woman is meant to be; to see how many changes her own body will undertake.

'You slept well?' Nasra flicks through the folded piles spilling out of the wardrobe.

'Yes,' Deqo replies enthusiastically, despite the fact she barely closed her eyes.

'Good. Maybe you will stay with us then.' Nasra dresses, choosing her clothes carefully. 'You have to tell me if you need anything. I want you fat and happy, understood? I want you to be my little girl.'

'Yes, Nasra,' Deqo smiles broadly.

'Have you ever seen the sea?'

'Never.'

'I will take you to Berbera one day, to see my family.'

'What's it like there?'

'The same as Hargeisa but with the sea next to it, and fishermen selling their catch on the beach and Yemenis touting *qudar*, a kind of date drink, and my mother with her scissors cutting my hair every month.' Nasra smiles.

She turns on the stereo and then changes the cassette, searching through tape after tape, declaring the provenance of each as if she is a radio presenter: Indian, Arabic, Congolese and American. Deqo cannot tell them apart but likes them all; the room suddenly feels crowded and animated by invisible musicians, singers and dancers. Nasra finds a Somali song and then settles back on the unmade bed, a photo album in her hands. She flicks through it; the photographs have the texture of distant, half-forgotten memories behind the opaque paper and Nasra's smile fades.

Deqo looks over her shoulder at the images: barefooted young girls playing in the surf, a hard-faced matriarch glowering in front of a savannah studio backdrop, a thin, wild-haired man standing proudly in front of a white boat.

'Who is that?' Deqo jabs a finger at the photo.

Nasra wipes away the greasy mark left on the film before answering, 'My father.'

'Is he a fisherman?'

'He was.' She turns the page quickly and skims through the other photographs without really seeming to see them.

'I don't know who or what my father was,' Deqo says with a nervous giggle. She tries to place an arm on Nasra's shoulder and then thinks better of it.

'You're from the camps, aren't you?'

'Yes, Saba'ad.'

'Well, he was probably a poor nomad then, and your mother a long-haired sultan's daughter from a village by a river, and they met and ran away together for love and had you. Is that right?' Nasra jumps from the bed and shoves the album in a drawer.

Deqo almost purrs with delight; Nasra's story fills her with light and warmth. 'Yes! Yes! Yes!' she wants to shout, but she just swings her arms instead.

The truth is so brutal in contrast. She has no knowledge at all of where the rest of her family are; there are no stories passed on by cousins, no villages to return to, no genealogy to pass on if she ever has children of her own. She is like a sapling growing out of the bare earth while others are branches on old, established trees. Her teenage mother had a mark on her neck the shape of a crescent moon and dots burnt into her chest like an old woman, Nurse Doreen had said. That was all the description she had. No face, no body, just burnt dots and a crescent moon to remember a mother by.

'Who has flooded this damn place?' shouts Stalin from the courtyard.

'Oh no,' whispers Deqo and rushes back to finish the laundry.

As the courtyard shifts from blue to indigo to black, Deqo picks dirt from under her fingernails and feels the bones of the house cracking as it eases into the night. Soon each corner of the house is lit by paraffin lamps, and she falls into a light sleep that dulls the noise around her but doesn't silence it: footsteps, clicking locks, laughter, faint music, discussion, bed springs, silence. The smell of tobacco wafts over from Nasra's room to the kitchen.

It is late when Deqo hears a rapping on the back door, insistent bursts every ten seconds. She scrambles to her feet and places her ear close to the door. She peeps through the keyhole and sees a waste ground where rubbish is dumped and charcoal made. She is frightened at the thought of letting that darkness in.

'Who is it?' she demands with more courage than she feels.

'Open up! I'm here for Nasra,' a deep, male voice replies.

'I am not allowed to let anyone in.'

He kicks the door. 'Either let me in or I will find my own way.'

'I can't let you in!' Deqo jams her shoulder against the door.

Silence, and then the scrape of feet up the wall and over the corrugated tin roof. Deqo ducks down as if he might fall on top of her. Within moments a huge man in a long overcoat leaps down into the courtyard. Deqo can just pick out his nose and sneering lips under the shadow of a military beret pulled low over his forehead. He straightens his knees and disappears towards Nasra's room and Deqo hears Nasra's door lock just after he enters; she hides in the hallway as first Stalin, then China pop their heads out of their rooms.

She returns to the courtyard and crouches to spy through the window into Nasra's room. Deqo's eyes and ears strain to take in as much of this drama as she can, her face creeping upwards, her nose jabbing the glass. The man towers over Nasra; he hasn't removed either coat or hat but paces around her as she stands erect in just a red satin underskirt pulled up to cover her breasts, a cigarette burning between her fingers. They don't speak or touch. Nasra catches sight of Deqo's eyes in the window and slams her palm against the glass.

Deqo rushes back to the kitchen, ashamed to be caught spying, and throws the blanket over her head; she balls up her hands and digs her nails into her flesh, angry that she has made Nasra angry. She doesn't cry but sits with her back to the wall feeling bereft. Nasra doesn't come and eventually she hears the man leave through the back door. She spends another sleepless night in the kitchen, her sense of safety breached, waiting for more giants to jump over the wall and appear right before her in the middle of the night, with guns, or knives, or with nothing but their strong hands to squeeze the life out of her.

Deqo wakes late to footsteps all around her. The charcoal stove burns a few inches from her feet and Stalin kicks her leg to move her out of the way.

'Deqo, get us some sugar from the shop,' Nasra asks, as she fans the fire and takes a bundle of notes from her brassiere.

Picking up her *caday* from the mat, still bleary-eyed, Deqo stumbles out into the street, brushing her teeth while she walks. She is met by a cacophony of crowing cockerels, braying donkeys resisting their harnesses, young boys play fighting in school uniforms, women shaking buckets of feed at their goats, and the drumbeat of adolescent girls beating carpets with sticks. She stops to watch a cat suckle the kittens mewling around her and then continues on to the corner shop feeling content with her new place in the world.

In the camp it was as if each day brought a new threat – maybe a fire, or flooding, a new outbreak of illness, or someone would die inexplicably; life was just a tightrope to be walked pigeon-toed. Deqo and Anab would imitate the German doctors in the camp by checking each other's pulses, feeling their foreheads for fevers, and knocking sticks against their joints; they made a joke of it but the fear of falling sick was always there. Of the children in the orphanage, five had already died, three from disease and two in a violent clash between different clans. She remembers the tubes of reed matting they had been wrapped in before burial, the rolls so narrow and small they resembled cigarettes.

During the fighting that killed the two boys, the aid workers were sent away for a few days, and it had occurred to Deqo then that they belonged somewhere else, that this camp was just one of many camps they had seen, that their real homes were far away, safe and rich. Nurse Doreen was the only one to stay behind. She was like a mule, tireless and uncomplaining; the harder it was in the camp, the more excited she seemed. She had tried to describe her childhood in Ireland to Anab and Deqo; she had a pony, she said, and cows, and it rained nearly every day she could remember, and it wasn't the kind of rain people looked forward to here but a hard, cold, stinging one that made her grandmother's bones ache. Deqo had enjoyed playing with Nurse Doreen's long, grey-streaked hair as she spoke and imagining it the tail of her own horse; Nurse Doreen had liked Deqo to place her cool fingers on the red, burnt skin of her shoulders where it refused to go brown like the rest of her arms. Nurse Doreen was good, was goodness; she gave that word meaning in a way few people did.

Deqo feels a pang of longing for the woman her life had once orbited around. She wonders how the *Guddi* will explain her disappearance to Nurse Doreen. They will probably just scratch her name off the register and give no explanation; no one dares challenge them, least of all the aid workers who have to do what they are told by the armed policemen who bounce around the camp in jeeps.

Just a few paces from the corrugated-tin store, Deqo's attention turns away from the blue sky criss-crossed with vapour trails to the street, and the blur of flared jeans, afros and tight shirts as dozens of young men and boys pelt past her. They are pursued by soldiers in various vehicles. As the street narrows the soldiers disembark and chase on foot, jumping on their quarry as they scramble up walls and seek shelter in the rambling confusion of yards and alleyways. A young boy inside the store creeps out of the back of the structure and hides inside a derelict goat pen nearby. It is like a huge, furious game of hide and seek that Deqo is excluded from, one reserved just for boys.

A lorry pulls up to block the far end of the street and some of the captives are led to it, heads bowed, arms twisted behind their backs. A woman bars the entrance of her bungalow with her body, but two soldiers throw her out of the way and drag a boy out by his long hair. The woman trots behind, pleading for his release: 'Let him go, he is all I have, he is too young for conscription, let him go, *walaalo.*'

Deqo stands on the outskirts of this scene, enveloped by dust and holding her arms protectively over her chest; she is reminded of the slaughter of animals during *Eid* at the camp, when nomads arrived with sheep and goats and sold them to the wealthier families, the animals separated violently, bellowing. She enters the empty store, takes a packet of sugar from a shelf and leaves the money in its place before fleeing to Nasra's house. The women are at the door when she reaches the bungalow; they peer up the street. Stalin has a smirk on her face but the others look anxious.

'It's the second time this month. What do they want with all these kids?' China shouts.

'Cannibals, they want to eat the fruit of our wombs,' replies Karl Marx.

'Look at them run! Wasn't that the bastard who threw a rock at my window? Not so tough now, is he?'

Nasra chews the corner of her headscarf and doesn't join the conversation; she places a hand gently on Deqo's back and leads her into the house.

Deqo stands in the darkness of the bathroom and shivers as cold water pours out of the bucket above her head.

'Scrub your hair,' demands Nasra.

Thick lather drops into her eyes and sits on her neck; the shampoo smells so good that Deqo keeps stopping to take deep inhalations.

'You'll look beautiful by the time I've finished with you.'

'Where are the soldiers going to take those boys?' Deqo asks with her eyes closed.

'To the south, to train for the military.' Nasra fills another bucket from the tap and throws it over Deqo.

'Don't they want to become soldiers?'

'No! Why should they? This government isn't on their side.'

'But the President cares about us, he is our father.'

Nasra laughs. 'Well, that is what the songs say, but I don't think that is the truth. You learn that in Saba'ad?'

Deqo nods and shows off the dance that Milgo taught her, her feet squeaking against the wet floor.

'Steady yourself, that dance won't win you any friends here.'

Nasra slides her hand up and down Deqo's bare back, washing away the last trail of lather.

Stalin appears and leans against the doorframe. 'You have your work cut out with this Bedu. Look at her chicken legs – and she's not even circumcised!'

Deqo cups her hands around her privates; it had felt natural being bathed by Nasra, as if she was an older sister or mother, but the way Stalin looks at her makes her shrink. The woman's eyes pick her apart and seem to say, 'Look at you, no one loved you enough to even circumcise you; you're wild and dirty.'

'You don't have anywhere better to be, Stalin?' Nasra says dismissively.

'Not now, no. I've got a knife if you want me to cut it off, hey Deqo?'

Deqo edges away from her, her legs pressed tightly together.

'You think you looked any better when you arrived? You were followed by fleas wherever you went. Get out of here!' Nasra scatters water at her.

'If you're not careful, I will sell her from under your nose,' Stalin retorts before retreating.

'What did she mean by that?' Deqo asks, her eyes to the ground.

'Nothing, she's just a fool and jealous that you're better looking than her.' She cups Deqo's face and squeezes her cheeks playfully. 'Don't let her bother you. I am your protector now and no one gets the better of me.'

Just as the curfew is about to bite, Deqo is stirring a lamb stew that Nasra has put on the stove when someone bangs at the main door.

'Open it!' shouts Nasra from her room.

Deqo finds Rabbit, the old drunk from the ditch, swaying on their doorstep. He pushes into the house and without looking at her makes a clumsy beeline for China's room. 'My darling, *habibti*, it is your friend here,' he croons, beating his yellowed palm on the splintered wood.

'Who told you to come here?' China bellows, pushing the door open and shoving his shoulder.

'My love, you have two things I want, let me have just one and I'll be on my way.'

China reaches into the pockets of his grey trousers and pulls out the empty white lining. 'Do I look like the Red Cross to you? I don't service beggars or accept them in my house.'

'Just give me a swig of whisky, then.' He holds out his hands and cocks his head to the side. 'I was a good customer when I had money, you know I was. I might even be that dear boy's father.'

'In your dreams.' China grabs Rabbit's padded shoulders and lifts him off his toes. 'As if you have anything in you apart from disease and alcohol. You have nothing to do with my child!'

Nasra enters the courtyard with a smile on her face and then Stalin and Karl Marx join the audience.

'Beat the fool!' shouts Stalin.

'You still owe me a hundred shillings.' Karl Marx bends down and takes the battered shoes off the man's feet. 'I'm keeping these till I get my money.'

They are like cats with a mouse, Deqo thinks, batting him around for pleasure.

'Ladies, I am a poor man, I give when I can. You should have mercy on me.'

'This isn't a place for mercy, you know that, Rabbit,' Nasra says, winking conspiratorially at Deqo. 'The world hasn't done us any favours, why should we help you?'

'I'm not like the others, I have never hurt you. Don't humiliate a helpless old man!' He sounds pitiful, on the verge of tears.

Deqo giggles guiltily; it's true he hadn't hurt her, but it's exciting to see him dangling in the air, being taught a lesson in respect by these women.

Stalin kicks him in the backside and then they all pounce on him.

'Throw out the trash,' they shout together.

While Deqo holds the door open, they each take a limb and carry him out, swinging his body a few times before slinging him into the street.

'A curse on all your heads,' he shouts as he hits the dirt with a thud. Deqo closes the door on him.

The women slap each other's backs and seem more joyful than Deqo has seen them so far; it feels as if it is not just Rabbit that has been expelled, but some tension or cloud has been lifted too. They laugh and laugh until they are bent over and weak.

'Poor man!' wheezes Karl Marx.

Deqo leans against Nasra and wraps her arms tentatively around her waist, beaming too.

Just as Deqo has become accustomed to the heavy drum of rain on the corrugated tin lullabying her to sleep, the rainy season comes to an abrupt end. A whistling draught replaces the leak of water from the rusted roof as *jiilaal* winds try their best to sneak into the bungalow. Nasra stuffs the holes with cloth when Deqo complains of the cold and leaves the stove burning a little later into the evening. The shrieking wind reminds Deqo of the hardships the *jiilaal* would bring to Saba'ad: red, infected eyes from the grit, old people perishing from the night chill, fights between the refugees over water. It was a time of forbearance and endless waiting. The only good thing it brought was deep, cloudless skies. She remembers clambering up the barred window onto the flat roof of the orphanage with Anab and watching the camp settle into sleep. If there was enough moonlight they could see pale mountains in the distance and beneath them a swathe of the camp. Everything crisp and clean, the sky blue-black and the stars like a thousand kind eyes watching over the forgotten people, smoke from cooking fires spiralling up like prayers. She feels a pang for that view, for that moment in life when Anab was beside her and the world they knew was calm and peaceful; there is no way to reclaim it even if she returns to Saba'ad.

The routines of the house have become familiar to Deqo and she knows which customer is for which woman: the younger, smartly dressed men go to Nasra, the middle-aged husbands hiding their faces behind sunglasses to Stalin, the drunks and gangster types to China, and the humble workers to Karl Marx. Nasra complains that there are only one or two customers willing to brave the curfew most nights and they are China's type rather than hers. Once upon a time they had journalists, and businessmen with dollars in their pockets, she said, rather than hawkers, drunkards and criminals.

The last night of the year arrives and the only male voices to be heard in the house are from the radios; it is too cold, dark and blustery for even the drunks. The evening passes glumly with Deqo sitting on Nasra's bed, watching her rearrange the room; she moves the furniture from one place to another and throws out many of her possessions because she claims to be bored with them. She leaves the pile in the hallway for Deqo to pick over and then throws herself face down on the bed.

'What I wouldn't do to leave this place!' she says, squeezing a pink cushion into her eyes.

Deqo lightly strokes the back of her hair.

'Who would have said my life would come to this? I'm clever, you know. I'm not a drunk like China or illiterate like Karl Marx. I could have been someone. Once you do this it's like you can never get out, never be anything else. I go outside and people look at me as if I'm a ghost walking around in the daytime.'

'Is that why you don't leave the bungalow much?'

'That and I feel as if I have nothing left out there. Why am I even telling you this?' She drops her head onto the quilt and then brings it up again. 'I don't feel like a real person. I have no family, no friends, no husband, no children. Every day I open my eyes and wonder why I should bother getting up, or eating, or earning another shilling. No one would miss me, in fact my mother would be happy to hear that I have died, she would clap her hands and say that her shame has been lifted.'

Nasra hides her face and sobs, and with wide, anxious eyes Deqo sits up. 'I would miss you, Nasra,' she says hurriedly, patting her back.

Nasra doesn't reply and Deqo understands that she is not enough for Nasra, not by a long way.

The first day of 1988 is bright and blue-skied, the street outside littered with leaves and broken twigs blown about the previous night. Deqo holds a hundred shillings tightly in her right hand, a gift from Nasra to celebrate the arrival of the new year and to maybe apologise for her tears. The little girl who danced with her in the rain is sitting with her mother on a large cement step, resting her face on her knuckles; Deqo waves in greeting but when the girl raises her hand her mother yanks it down. The wiry woman narrows her eyes at her. 'Keep walking,' she shouts. Deqo holds up her head and marches on, but her stomach does a small flip as Nasra's words return to her; she doesn't want to become another daytime ghost.

Looking down at her freshly painted red toenails and the clean, lotioned skin of her feet, Deqo sees no reason for anyone to look down on her. She looks good in her mind, better than she ever has before. Her cheeks have filled out and the constant headache she used to have from hunger has gone, but she also feels heavier, slower and less sharp-witted now that she doesn't have to graft for every little morsel. She feels as though she is in disguise: dressed in Nasra's hand-me-down green skirt and white shirt, she wonders if anyone will recognise her at the market or if she will pass for one of the plump and carefree local girls.

Deqo veers off to the left to explore an open area she hasn't noticed before; there are scrubby bushes in a sand-pit and boys kicking a rag ball. Deqo and Anab had sometimes joined the footballers near the wide, empty riverbed beside Saba'ad; for no obvious reason some matches would just grow until maybe a hundred players gathered, creating a gravelly pitch that stretched for a mile in each direction. More makeshift balls would have to be made from rags tied up with shoestring when the others crumbled under the stampede of toddlers and teenagers, girls and boys – the girls often just picking up a ball in their hands and running to the goal because they couldn't understand why they shouldn't. On those after-noons, when the girls abandoned their *buuls* and chores and the camp was veiled by the dust they kicked up, Deqo had run and run and leapt for the golden sun, a bright medal just beyond her reach.

After watching the boys kick the scrappy ball around listlessly for a few minutes, Deqo skirts the sandpit and strolls up to a crossroad with four tracks leading away from it. She chooses one randomly and passes the giant power station, the Pepsi factory with rows of trucks parked outside, and then after another patch of scrub-land there is the ditch, full of trash and spirit bottles, and a rope bridge to the other side of town. Looking down on the ditch from the swaying bridge, it is hard to believe that she once spent her nights there; it is a wild, dark jungle, a no-man's-land full of threat and danger, her barrel probably full of snakes or scorpions by now. It is the kind of place where human skeletons might sink into the soil undisturbed and unmourned. She is a different girl now to the one who had sought shelter in that wasteland; she must have outgrown and abandoned some kind of shell or cocoon there.

The market has been her salvation, its noise and smells and rough interactions have kept her human, and she reaches it with relief, clasping the treasure in her hand more tightly. She has never had a hundred shillings before and has to fight the desire to hide it from herself for a rainy day, but Nasra made her promise to buy something frivolous with it. The spot where she had sold stolen fruit is hidden behind the large backs of several middle-aged market women. Children swarm around her newly long legs – pallid glue sniffers, shoeshines, pickpockets, religious students in long white robes and prayer caps, street sweepers – there are enough of them to populate a small town of their own, with hierarchies, feuds and alliances to match anything the adults can muster.

No one recognises her, her transformation complete; who would believe it is the same Deqo who used to sleep in a rusty barrel? She catches her reflection in a mirror hanging up in a clothes stall and sees a girl with neatly pinned up hair holding her nose imperiously high.

Nothing grabs her attention enough to part her from the hundred shillings until she reaches a corner stall with animals. The trader, sitting on a stool with a white lamb cradled in his arms, has dark, pitted skin and oily straight hair and smiles a generous smile as she approaches. A tortoise crawls lethargically around his feet, tied by a leg to the stool, various birds squawk and flap inside cramped cages, and in the depths of the stall she can see a small brown-mottled fawn sat on its haunches. Deqo quietly kneels beside it and the fawn looks at her with terrified, wet eyes.

'How much?' Deqo asks the trader.

He scratches his jaw before answering, 'Give me five hundred.'

She runs a hand over the animal's back; it trembles with each rapid heartbeat. It should be with its mother. 'I only have a hundred.'

'Oh, forget it, then.' He turns back to the street and spits.

'What do you feed it?'

'Cow's milk. Why don't you ask your mother for more money if you like it so much?'

'I don't have a mother.' She scratches the fawn under its chin and its ears flick in response.

'Or your father then. Or . . .' He drags a straw basket over to his stool and tips it so she can see inside; a flurry of yellow chicks fall over each other and chirp in alarm. 'You can have one of those for a hundred. Pick one.'

Deqo pats the fawn on its head and then examines the chicken orphanage. She pities their fragility; it would be easy to crush one in her palm. She sticks her hand in and strokes the downy chest of one flailing on its back. The first two years of her own life had been spent in the overcrowded cots that contained the camp's youngest orphans, where they were left to clamber over each other and poke curious fingers into unguarded eyes. Somehow she had emerged from that cage and learnt to walk and talk and feed herself.

'I'll take her. And when I have enough money I'll come back for the deer,' she says resolutely.

He mock salutes her and takes the money. 'I'll be waiting for you!'

Deqo walks back to the house slowly, tickling her face with the chick's fuzz; she hopes that it will one day grow into a proud, bright-plumed hen, the matriarch of her own ever-expanding brood.

China steps over Deqo to set the kettle on the charcoal burner; she harrumphs and makes indistinct complaints aimed either at Deqo or the baby tied to her back. The boy's face is squashed hard against China's back; it looks uncomfortable but he doesn't whimper. Deqo is half grateful, half envious that she has never been carried like that. The chick is on her lap, walking up and down the length of her thighs.

'I thought you were meant to work in this house, not just sit there with that thing and eat our food?'

'I have finished the cleaning, China. Is there anything else you would like me to do?' she replies calmly.

'Well, take this weight off my back for a start.' She unwraps the boy and dumps him into Deqo's arms.

Nuh's arms flop to the side of his body; he smells as strongly of alcohol as his mother and seems drunk too, his eyes half closed and motionless. She looks up sourly at China. Why did you get to keep your child when you can't even care for him? she thinks.

'Deqo!' Nasra exclaims. A tall man with a wooden cane stands behind her in the courtyard. 'You're back. Is that what you bought?' She points to the new chick. 'Have you named it?'

Deqo shakes her head. 'I'm still deciding.'

'Does that child belong to her?' the man asks. He lifts his sunglasses up to look at her more closely, muttering something into Nasra's ear.

'Of course not, that is China's son.'

The man steps further into the kitchen and bends down over Deqo; he smiles and reveals two gold canines. 'Pretty girl,' he says, catching her nose between his tobacco-stained fingers.

'You're in good health, aren't you, Deqo?' Nasra gently pulls him away from her.

Deqo nods shyly.

'Let's talk in my room,' Nasra says, leading the visitor out of the kitchen.

'Oh, you're set for the chopping board, little one,' chuckles China.

'What do you mean?'

'You'll soon find out.' China takes Nuh from her and walks back to her room with a flask of tea.

Deqo shoves the chick into her skirt pocket and stands

beside Nasra's door, but she cannot hear the conversation no matter how hard she presses her ear to the wall. Deqo goes back to the kitchen, telling herself to not be so suspicious; Nasra wouldn't let anyone hurt her.

The new year brings new customers – soldiers and plenty of them; the man who jumped into the courtyard returns nearly every night and brings his comrades with him. The house of women has become the house of men, and even Stalin seems humbled. Unhindered by the curfew, they arrive at midnight and leave before dawn, but by that time the bungalow is in chaos, with displaced cups and glasses everywhere, broken plates thrown into the kitchen, cigarette butts and empty bottles littering the courtyard, washing pulled from the line and trampled, urine all over the toilet floor.

The women sleep all day, exhausted, while Deqo cleans. The old customers do not come, afraid of the soldiers, and she misses their neatness. It is hard to sleep when there is music all night and footsteps a few inches from her head, but it is their voices that really bother her: Why do men speak so loudly? They shout rather than talk and laugh like the world needs to know they are laughing. She covers her ears while they boast about how the city is theirs, how they can do what they like and no one says anything, and as if to prove that, one of the young conscripts likes to run into the kitchen, pull up her skirt and then escape while the others guffaw. They declare each week that planes and artillery and bulldozers are on their way to Hargeisa, but Deqo never sees them. The chick, now named Malab after her honey-coloured new feathers, has also come under threat from a strange young soldier with a shaven head, who tries to stamp on her if she leaves the safety of the kitchen.

The presence of the soldiers has made the neighbours even more hostile than before and the front door is streaked with goat shit. Deqo begins to cover her head and a little of her face when she heads for the market after Stalin is caught by local women and beaten with brooms. They are angry that their husbands and sons have been taken away, and some had come to the house earlier to plead with Nasra to find out from the soldiers where their loved ones had gone. She had refused. It was Nasra they were after, Stalin said when she staggered in, bruised and limping, but the neighbours would send a message through any of them.

After the dry season ends, Karl Marx packs a suitcase and leaves one night without bidding farewell to any of them. Nasra, China and Stalin remain behind but are subdued; they take what they want from Karl Marx's room and continue to play act with the soldiers, laughing dryly at their jokes and dancing strangely with them in the dark courtyard.

Nasra is glassy-eyed and drinks from China's bottles; she looks through Deqo when she tries to talk to her, her words slurred and incoherent. She has lost weight despite the money she is drawing from the soldiers. Deqo asks why she doesn't send some of them away if they are upsetting her, but Nasra pushes her away and tells her to leave her alone.

The air warms up as the months pass but little rain falls; the one tree in the courtyard is desiccated, and even the plastic vine Nasra decorated it with is bleached and brittle. Only Malab thrives in the bungalow, growing fat on the corn Deqo feeds her; everyone else is tired and fragile. None of the women cook anymore; there is just bread, fruit and biscuits to eat and Deqo can feel her wrist bones again.

On her way to the *suuq* she often passes children tied by the feet to a barrel or stake outside their home. They stand for hours as punishment for some misdemeanour, staring at her with absent eyes, rubbing the places where they have been whipped or beaten. Everyone is angry – even the sky is grey and motionless; there doesn't seem to be space for anything but silence and obedience. A new checkpoint is set up at the top of the road and she recognises some of the soldiers from the night visits; they let her through easily while others are stopped and searched. The market is bare and each item is sold at a new, higher price every time she goes there. Many of the traders have disappeared altogether and there are large dark spaces where their stalls used to be. The animal seller has departed along with his tortoise and deer.

Deqo feels herself retreating into the past. Memories of Anab alive are eaten up by images of her dead, the quiet penetrated by her cries, the heat and then the cold of her skin as the cholera emptied her, now washing over Deqo in waves. What had made the life seep out of her body but not Deqo's? Had she just wanted to return to her mother enough to leave her little doll body behind and vanish from the earth?

Carrying a string bag of papayas and oranges, Deqo opens the door and sees a wide pink suitcase in the hall-way. The door to Nasra's room is ajar and she peeks in. The floor is covered with clothes and shoes and Nasra picks through them in a panic and stuffs them into a shoulder bag.

Deqo continues to the kitchen before Nasra can shout at her. Malab scuttles excitedly beneath her feet, pecking at her bare toes; she is almost fully grown and her sharp beak stings. Deqo pushes the hen away and begins to peel an orange when Nasra calls her name.

The old man with the sunglasses is smoking behind the door while Nasra stands in the middle of the room, dressed in black and wearing a headscarf. She holds her arms out and gestures for Deqo to come closer.

'Little one, I have to leave for a while. I need to go to Ethiopia to find a new job, but you won't be alone, Mustafa is here to look after you. You have to do what he says, OK? He will keep you safe.'

'Can't I come with you?' She reaches out.

Nasra pushes her hands away. 'No, that would be too much trouble for me. You stay, you can take my room, you can have all of my things while I am gone.' Her eyes don't meet Deqo's but flit around from one corner to another, and her hands tremble slightly as she throws garments from the bed towards her wardrobe. 'You'll be fine, Deqo. Mustafa is a good man,' she says, but her voice cracks unconvincingly.

She watches mutely as Nasra wanders the room, stuffing documents and random belongings into her handbag: red nail varnish, tweezers, comb.

A car horn sounds outside the bungalow.

'But Nasra . . .'

'But nothing! I have to go, stop nagging me.' She yanks her shawl over her head and rushes to the hall, dragging the heavy suitcase with both hands she reaches the front door and slams it shut behind her.

Deqo's attention turns to Mustafa. He raises an eyebrow at her. 'Let her go, what do you need her for?'

'When will she come back?' Deqo says, holding back her tears.

'Come sit down with me.' He stubs out his cigarette on a dirty dish, puts an arm around her shoulder and leads her to the bed. 'You've grown since the last time I saw you. That's the thing about little girls, you change every day.'

Deqo shrugs his arm away but he grabs the back of her dress and drags her to sit. 'Come on now, don't be like that. We can start off in a good way or you can thrash around and make it worse than it needs to be.'

'I don't want you! Get off me!' she cries, twisting away from him.

'Deqo!'

She bristles at the sound of her name in his mouth.

'Watch her leave if you want.' He points to the window with one hand while still holding her dress in the other.

Deqo clambers over the bed and catches a flash of Nasra darting from the boot of the white vehicle to the passenger door. She disappears behind the tinted glass, the engine revs and with a blast of saxophones and drums from the stereo she is gone.

Mustafa lets go of her and leans back on his arms. 'I will take better care of you than she ever did.'

Deqo cups her face in her hands and tears flow onto her palms. She feels her strength seeping out of her and into the soft, rumpled bed. Mustafa's presence encompasses her; his breath, his sprawling flesh, his silent menace.

She takes her hands away from her eyes and checks the distance to the door. Her legs are folded under her while his dangle over the side of the bed.

'How much did Nasra tell you about what she does?' he asks, scratching his stubble.

Deqo shakes her head but doesn't reply.

'Don't look like your world's caved in, good girls like you are usually the most popular, you'll make a fine living.'

Deqo bolts for the door before he has finished speaking but he grabs her ankle and wrestles her to the floor.

As she screams he covers her mouth with his hand; his fingers taste of tobacco and ghee. Deqo bites down on them until she tastes blood, but he rips his hand away and punches her mouth.

'China! Stalin!' she cries.

'They won't help you!' he sneers.

He pulls her skirt up; she is not wearing knickers because she had washed the two pairs that she owns in the morning.

She sees a black stiletto on the floor and reaches for it while he is trying to prise open her legs. He doesn't see it coming as she forces the heel into his eye. He is thrown back in pain. She pitches the shoe to the side then escapes from the room.

She runs blindly into the street, her pulse pounding in her temples. She heads instinctively for the market, past the first checkpoint and into a deep throng of shoppers. She navigates around the dawdling figures, clawing her way through until a flat-bed truck parked horizontally across the entrance to the market stops her flight.

The crowd is transfixed by the sight of three dead bodies on the bed of the truck: three old men in red-checked sarongs, brown bloodstains like bibs on their white shirts, camel leather sandals on their feet, a nomad's *hangol* staff beside one of them. Around each of their necks is a board with 'NFM' written on it in red ink. The soldiers seated around the bodies look like hunters posing with the wild animals they have caught, an element of embarrassment on their faces at the wizened, toothless specimens they have found. One of them adjusts the position of the head nearest to him with his dusty boot.

No one says a word, neither soldiers nor spectators, it

is a silent lesson; a blizzard of flies hovering over the truck makes the only sound. Already the corpses are beginning to turn in the heat; their faces have ceased to have any kind of spirit in them, just slack skin over bones.

KAWSAR

Inside the green, wailing walls of the hospital there are too many annoyances: the clumsy cleaner clanking her heavy metal bucket against the cement floor, the feuding nurses who never come when they are called and the self-pitying amputee who never stops calling them. Kawsar can tell there is a *miri-miri* tree outside the window by the constant chirruping of tiny *yaryaro* birds; the din of their '*jiiq, jiiq, jiiq*' call and rustling feathers is so dizzying – as if there are mice scurrying through her head – that she hopes they will take flight with the tree and eat its seeds someplace else. In her aluminium bed, its rank mattress so thin she feels the bars of the base against her back, Kawsar pulls the nylon sheet over her head and hides from the visitors tramping through the ward. She concentrates on facing the pain that girdles her. It is a complex agony: a pulsing, electric high-note over something messier and deeper – similar to the post-childbirth sensation that her bones and flesh had been ground down to mush. She is not able to sit up, stretch, turn over or even shift without a crackle of pain rushing through her nerves. She is taut, her jaw clenched tight, the breath held in her lungs, the tendons in her neck rigid, trying to antici-pate this pain before it engulfs her in its swell.

'Broken hip. Broken pelvis,' the doctor declares, but she doesn't trust him; he has spent no more than three minutes examining her, his eyes misted over with other thoughts. He seems to feel that her time is rightfully up, that her leaf is about to fall.

'Can you not operate?'

There is annoyance in the doctor's voice, 'You're too old, your bones would not stand up to it. Osteoporosis. The hospital is short of equipment for surgery anyway. I think all we can do is make sure the pain is under control.'

'But will I walk again?'

Kawsar's eyes have been fixed on the ceiling through-out the whole exchange.

There is no reply from him and a few seconds later he walks out of the ward with a nurse a few steps behind.

When she wakes later in the afternoon, she sees Dahabo glaring down at her. She lightly touches Kawsar's bruised face. 'Look at you.'

'How the mighty have fallen. She beat me like a diso-bedient donkey.' Kawsar smiles wanly, one of her eyes swollen and the left side of her vision blurred. 'I'm surprised she didn't kill me.'

'*Joow*, you are made of leather and bitterness, nothing can kill you. But if I could get my hands on her, I would skin her alive and make a handbag out of her hide.' Dahabo squeezes the pillow in demonstration of her anger.

'She is a child of her time.'

'No, it is the other way around: Those with sick hearts have made the time what it is, and what did you think you were doing anyway? Rushing away from us at the stadium like that? Did you lose your mind?'

'Maybe. Hodan must have got it from somewhere.'

'Kawsar. You have got to stop blaming yourself. No one can derail a person from their fate. She was loved more than any child I know, including my own.'

Dahabo's voice never drops from the volume it takes to yell across a street.

'Shush, Dahabo, can you not speak in a normal voice?' Kawsar hisses. She doesn't want the ancient woman in the bed beside her to overhear.

'To hell with them, Kawsar, listen to me. You could not have done more for her. You bought the pills you were meant to, had the imam read her the Qu'ran, you kept her out of that place.' She gestures through the window to the hospital madhouse. 'What else? What else could you have done? Or I? Or anyone?'

'I know. I know. Let's not go over this again,' Kawsar says quietly.

Dahabo clutches her shoulder. 'You are old now and fragile, you have to be kinder to yourself.'

'I want it to all end, Dahabo. Is that wrong?'

'No, but your time will come, as will mine. Wait. You can't throw yourself in danger, breaking a hip here, an arm there. Leaving me with another mouth to feed.' She reaches down to pick up a basket. 'I've put a few meals in here. I want the plates cleared, do you understand me?'

'I can't . . .' Kawsar feels guilty eating into Dahabo's hard-earned income while hidden under her own mattress at home there are hundreds and thousands of shillings.

'You will. Maryam and Raage will come to collect you tomorrow. Don't fight anyone in that time if you can help it.'

Maryam and Raage arrive early in the morning to collect her, before the rush at his store. 'Don't forget the basket, it's Dahabo's,' points Kawsar from the trolley, 'check under the bed too, I might have dropped something.'

'Yes, *eddo*,' Maryam bends down to check, 'nothing.'

'Good, let's *roohi* then.'

Raage takes the lower end of the trolley and pulls it out of the ward.

They roll along the uneven, grey-tiled corridor, past queues waiting outside the TB clinic and paediatric wards. The strangers stare at her, grateful for a momentary diversion from the endless waiting. They stare most at Maryam; she was born and raised in Hargeisa, but the long nose she has inherited from her English mother points her back to Europe. With her wisps of yellow hair and light brown skin she has always made Kawsar think of a plastic doll that has been left out too long in the sun.

Kawsar has not visited the hospital since Hodan's death and does not remember being brought in from the jail. She is in the main, low building left over from the British; the maternity and other small wards are scattered around it, and hidden beyond a high barbed-wire wall is the psycho-social unit. The morgue is a more recent extension, built to cope with the victims of Ethiopian bombing sorties over the city. The hospital is falling into ruin, the inside walls are cracked, the plaster peeling, creepers snaking their way through the windows.

An orderly in a khaki jumpsuit stops them at the main entrance. 'You cannot take the trolley beyond this point,' he says, grabbing hold of the rail above Kawsar's head.

'We are just taking her to the car. She can't walk,' Maryam argues, trying to pull the trolley with her.

'Leave it here, don't you have ears?'

'You put a donkey in uniform and see what happens,' Maryam shouts back.

'What? Should I call the police? You can tell them what you think about donkeys and uniforms.'

'To hell with you.'

'Let's go, Maryam, quickly please,' Kawsar begs.

'*Ko, labah, sadeh,* one, two, three . . .' Maryam and Raage pick up the thick woollen blanket underneath her and lift Kawsar into the air. Neither is strong and they struggle to walk without losing grip of the blanket, but they persevere until she is safely manoeuvred into the long, grimy boot of the red Toyota.

Raage starts the engine and drives out of the hospital grounds. 'Go as slowly as you can,' orders Maryam.

Kawsar does not hear if Raage replies; there is a sudden numbness to her senses from the painkillers, a cushioned distance between her and the rest of the world. She looks through the dust-haloed back window, streaked with the scum of dead flies, at the passing trees bowing down to her and fluttering their green fans.

Kawsar seems to float a few precious inches as the car dips into potholes and weaves around ditches. 'Where are we?' she asks, disorientated.

'Going past the old women's college, our college,' smiles Maryam, squeezing her hand.

'Near where I met Farah . . .'

'What did you say?' Maryam bends down to hear.

'Nothing,' she replies, closing her eyes.

She had first seen Farah while dawdling home from the Women's Technical School with Dahabo. It was a languid, dry season day, her shadow huge and black behind her, and they were teasing each other as they held hands. A lunatic was on the run from the mental hospital, weaving his sticky web of insanity over the town. Kawsar always imagined him as a man-spider who had clambered out of the English asylum they'd trapped him in and sailed back to Somaliland on driftwood. The girls passed telegraph poles in which his teeth marks were visible, his hundred white incisors imprinted onto the fresh black paint. Kawsar had heard at college that devil voices pursued the madman through the telegraph wires, his mind burnt up by the fire in their words. At every junction policemen lay in wait for him before he killed again. A tall, young policeman was standing with a red-haired Englishman at the crossroads ahead. There was no main road in south Hargeisa then, just a track tramped down by camel caravans, and the girls crossed to the other side so the men would not come too close. Dust hung in the air between them, lit gold and orange by the weary sun, and she accidentally caught the eye of the Somali policeman as she watched it glitter.

'We're here, *eddo*. I'll get help from the hotel.' Maryam crawls out of the car. She returns moments later with a crowd of men, their silhouettes black against the sun, their voices and hands indistinguishable, innumerable.

Each holds a scrap of the blanket and Kawsar believes for a moment that this is her funeral, that they will wrap her in this blanket and grasp handfuls of sand to throw over her, burying her wide-eyed and pliant.

'This way, this way,' Maryam leads them to Kawsar's bungalow.

A break in the men's bodies reveals a slice of October Road: children in their scruffy playclothes watch the hullabaloo with quizzical expressions.

'Just here.' Maryam bangs the metal gate with her fist.

Kawsar expects to see Dahabo but the door is opened by a stranger, a young girl in men's clothing.

'Let us through,' orders Maryam.

Kawsar and the girl's eyes meet as they pass, suspicion reflected in both.

Kawsar is propelled through the hallway and into the bedroom, which smells peculiar – a sharp cocktail of sweets and cheap perfume – and falls onto the bed with a soft thud.

The bedroom is dark, gauzy blue. At the end of a shaft of moonlight is the girl, asleep under a thin sheet on the floor. Her ribcage rises softly under the covers, a small, beautiful quiver of animated air. Nobody else has slept overnight under this roof since Hodan died. Kawsar's pulse quickens. She is excited to have someone to watch, to hear in the background; she will share this space that she has roamed alone for so long.

The next morning the girl wakes Kawsar by wiping a wet cloth over her face and neck as she lies in bed.

'What are you doing?' stutters Kawsar.

'I was told to bathe you.'

'Are you an undertaker preparing me for burial? Can't you wait until I am awake?'

'I thought I would save time.'

'That is not the way to save time.' Kawsar snatches the cloth from her hand. 'What is your name, who are you?'

'Nurto, I am a cousin of Maryam's. I am here to look after you.'

She is a tall girl, all legs and arms, with a sharp, belligerent face atop a thin neck.

'You will only stay with me if I'm happy with your work.'

'So what do you want me to do now?'

'Go to the market, there is no food in the house.'

Nurto leaves for the *suuq* and does not return for hours.

It is strange to think that Nurto will be the one to find her lifeless one day. What will she do – scream, say a prayer, or quickly throw a sheet over the stiff, wide-eyed corpse? For some reason this imagined scene makes Kawsar laugh – the perfect revenge of the old on the thought-lessly young.

A loud bang heralds Nurto's return and Kawsar listens as the girl goes straight past the bedroom to the kitchen and unloads the basket into crates on the floor. Later, she pushes open the bedroom door with her foot, her skinny legs in black corduroy trousers, and enters carrying a tray.

She has bought the things she desires with the shop-ping money: pastries, *halwa*, biscuits, and now makes a show of presenting them to Kawsar on a tray, as if she could want these things.

There is a knock at the door and Nurto rushes to open it. Maryam pops her head into the room. She kisses Kawsar's cheek and feels her forehead.

'How is Nurto behaving?'

'She's fine,' Kawsar says curtly. 'Take a seat.'

'I can't stay right now. I just wanted to give you these.'

She pulls a packet from her alligator-skin handbag. Her English mother had left behind powerful painkillers and Maryam reads the instructions aloud, carefully and slowly, struggling to translate terms such as 'hypertension' and 'water retention'. But as soon as Maryam follows Nurto into the kitchen, Kawsar takes six of the pills and waits expectantly for the girdle of pain to release a fraction.

In the afternoon light her room looks institutional, with just a single iron bed, a metal chair, a bare light bulb and two large wardrobes full of clothes she never wears and never will again. Above the bed hangs her art: the fine, abstract textiles she has hand-loomed herself, woven straw hangings she bought in Juba, her wedding photo in a frame she painted in the blue and white of the Somali flag with crescent moons and irregular exploding stars. The only ostentatious thing she dares exhibit is a silver necklace covered in coins and amber beads that her jeweller grandfather made for her wedding day. She hopes that it is too old-fashioned for the policemen who shop for their wives and daughters in the homes they raid. It dangles over the handle of the larger wardrobe, its gentle tinkling reminding her daily of the magic in her grandfather's fingers.

She closes her eyes and imagines the street beyond her walls: the sandy lanes the colour of threshed wheat, everything else splashed with blue – the indigo gates to the bungalows, their turquoise compound walls, their navy water barrels rusting in the yards – the drought has made her neighbours paint themselves underwater, succour against despair. The desirable modern stone bungalows built by teachers, civil servants and engineers are now dependent on donkey carts for their water supply. She feels as though she has made this street, has claimed it single-handedly from the colony of baboons that had lived in the juniper forest that stood near here, her bungalow once a besieged fort in hostile territory, her washing torn and orchard raided.

When she had arrived with Farah in sixty-eight it had been at the outer edges of Hargeisa, the air fresh, the land cheap, distant enough from her mother's house in Dhumbuluq for her to feel free but close enough to visit each day. They had bought a large plot of land, expecting to raise a brood of children, but it didn't happen. Instead her neighbours gathered around her slowly, incrementally, like coral around a shipwreck, creating a new suburb. They used her well before building their own, gathered on her doorstep in the evenings and called for her help when delivering their babies. These clanspeople and the strangers they had married were her family.

She remembers standing inside Raage's *dukaan*; it is like a doll's house, sunlight glinting off tin cans as bright as mirrors. In there Kawsar always felt she had regressed to childhood, holding her mother's money in her palm, the sweets and chocolates on the counter filling her eyes. The simple square structure of corrugated tin is packed to the last inch with everything a housewife

NADIFA MOHAMED

might need: soap powder in cellophane twists, fresh bread rolls, matches, toy guns and sweets for well-behaved children, plastic hoses to beat misbehaving ones. Raage planted behind the wooden counter – tall, gruff, with weary, drooping shoulders. He arrived in seventy-two at the age of fifteen or sixteen, selling milk for his divorced mother, and slowly built a shop from his earnings. He works robotically now, exchanging the same short pleasantries with each customer, the little radio beside him constantly tuned to the BBC World Service. He performs his dawn prayers in the shop and is still there late at night, fussing over details like a bird over its nest. The only variance is on Fridays when he wears a skullcap over his prematurely smooth head and closes for half an hour to pray at the mosque. A scrappy beard, long at the chin but threadbare along his jaw, has appeared on his face making him look mystical and wise.

'Everything well, Raage?' Kawsar would say.

'*Manshallah*, praise God.'

'Business good?'

'As good as it needs to be.'

'*Nabadgelyo.*'

'*Nabaddiino.*'

Words simple as birdsong passed between them.

Kawsar could have done most of her shopping with Raage, but had still preferred to trek into town every day, to feel the buzz of town life against her skin.

Still with her eyes closed, she turns back from the shop

and stands in front of Umar Farey's hotel, the windows are tinted green and always shut, and shadows flit behind the decorative masonry on its roof. He built the hotel using his police pension in seventy-six, the same year he lost four of his fingers to a stray dog. It had been frequented by Somalis returning from jobs overseas, sailors and oil workers mostly, and Farah would spend his evenings over there talking politics. Between seventy-eight and eighty-one the hotel made the neighbourhood lively with weddings and the reappearance of long-lost men. But then in eighty-one the tone of the place changed; there was no joy, just congregations with furrowed brows gathered to lament the ever worsening situation. First the doctors in Hargeisa hospital were arrested for trying to improve conditions for their patients, then the student demonstrations broke out following their death sentences, and finally the National Freedom Movement, formed by Somalis living in London, began military action to remove the dictatorship. Since then the hotel has cast an ominous pall over the street. Unsubtle spies pace its perimeter by day and return at night to drag guests away at gunpoint; it has become a secretive place from which you can almost hear the ticking of a bomb.

Soon after Maryam leaves, Dahabo comes bustling into the house, another covered basket thrust in front of her. She dumps the basket on the metal chair near the bed, the frayed rattan seat flimsy under the weight.

'Can you pass me the glass of water?'

'Forget water, you need milk to build you up.' Dahabo whips the cloth off the basket. The first item she reaches for is a plastic yellow can, made to carry petrol but now used by nomads to sell camel's milk in town. 'Start with this. I have cow's, sheep's and goat's in here too.' She pours the thin milk into her black thermos cup and hands it to Kawsar.

Kawsar sniffs it before putting her mouth to the cup. She is incredibly thirsty but hates camel's milk; it is so acidic, frothy, it rises back up her throat as she drinks.

'*Ka laac*! Drink it all up!'

'I'm trying to.' Kawsar sips at the last few terrible drops before holding the cup upside down in front of her friend.

'You infant, come here.' Dahabo wipes away the milk's froth from Kawsar's upper lip with the back of her hand.

'Ah, your poor children, you have a hard hand.' Kawsar's skin stings from the touch. She has yet to see her reflection but the bruises are still tender.

'It's soft when it needs to be.'

'That doctor from Russia, Hassan Luugweyne's son, said I have a broken hip and pelvis.'

'May Allah break his pelvis, hips and legs. What does he know? I will take you to Musa, he will mould your bones back together again. Remember when my Waris fell from that hill and all those fools said she would die? Who but Musa Bonesetter would have known how to bring her back?'

'We'll see, but this pain is killing me.'

Dahabo returns to her basket, piled up with apples, bananas, dates and anonymous bottles and flasks, 'In here is something that will help with the pain but it is very strong. Don't eat too much of it, understand?'

'What is it?'

'It's special, don't ask too many questions, it will work, trust me.'

'Give it here.'

A harmless-looking bark in a plastic bag falls into Kawsar's hand.

'Just chew a couple of pieces at a time.'

Kawsar complies. The bark is soft in her mouth; it has been smoked and tastes faintly of cinnamon. She can imagine the dirt on it as it dissolves on her tongue.

'Rest now. I'll be back tomorrow . . .'

'*Bismillah*, don't make a fuss. Go and attend to your family.'

'Keep an eye on that basket, there are thieves everywhere, and remember to eat.' Dahabo tilts her head to the kitchen where Nurto is clattering the dishes as she washes them. 'See you tomorrow. I'll want to hear what kind of dream you have.' She bends down, the tassel of her prayer beads tickling Kawsar's neck, and kisses her three times, her lips dry and rough against her cheeks.

Kawsar is barefoot, alone in a cemetery with boulders marking the graves. Her arms are numb and immobile. She knows not to turn around; there is something monstrous behind her, its bristling shadow cast over the ground. Her breath won't come, her legs are too heavy to move, the thing is licking the back of her neck. The shadow is a sharp black now, eight legs that spread from one corner to the other, with a bisected head looming over. Two legs embrace her, squeezing her breasts down and lifting her gently into the air. She sways with the creature's movement; its grip is tender, paternal almost, except for the constant movement of one leg over her body. It is taking her away into the anonymous shrub outside town. She is carried over thorn bushes, acacia trees laced with armo creepers and termite mounds to a desert she knows only from ghost stories.

'Gaallo-laaye!' shouts Dahabo triumphantly, slapping her palms onto her thighs.

'Who?'

'I should have known his spirit would never rest quietly, a hard life followed by a hard death.'

'Gaallo-*laaye*?'

'How can you forget him? He brought you and your beloved together, didn't he? It all makes sense that he would come back to you, but may Allah keep him in his grave.' Dahabo reaches into the basket and brings out two apples, peeling them into a bowl on her lap.

'I don't know who you are talking about . . .'

'You are a fool to forget.' Dahabo jabs her hand into Kawsar's face. 'He was that man who had all of Hargeisa scared when we were little girls. He thought he was a spider.'

'You mean Mohamed Ismail?'

'*Na'am*! That was his real name but everyone called him Gaallo-laaye, the whiteman-slayer, because he shot five Englishmen dead in a drinking den while living there. They put him in a madhouse then sent him back here. One day he goes crazy again and starts shooting everyone up.' Dahabo pretends to shoot Kawsar with her finger.

'I remember, I remember.'

'What kind of spider did he think carries pistols? We shouldn't talk about the afflicted, but remember when he was finally cornered in the cemetery and everyone came out to see his battle with the police? He was throwing rocks, firing his gun, running from boulder to boulder. I swear it looked like he had grown extra arms and legs, and he was such a beautiful man to look at, so long-limbed and open-faced. I find madmen the most handsome, *wallahi*.'

Dahabo offers the bowl of apple slices and Kawsar fills her palm with a few slivers.

'You have a *jinn* inside you that makes you say these things.'

'Why? There is no shame in it. They are part of God's creation too, aren't they? They are men in every way; it's just that their eyes are open to the things we can't see.'

Kawsar's pain is tamed by Dahabo's presence but is still coiled tightly around her like a sleeping serpent. 'Mohamed Ismail,' she repeats softly.

'What a man! Imagine what he would do to the idiot police now.'

'I was there in the cemetery. I saw his dead body. His hair white with sand, he wore a light yellow shirt and there were three red wounds in his chest. Here, here and here . . .' Kawsar points to imaginary holes in her own chest. 'His eyes were open, looking up at me, and I bent down and closed them.'

'*Maskiin*, poor man.'

'I was angry with myself afterwards. I thought that touching a dead body so close to my wedding would bring bad luck.'

'Nonsense. It surprises me that I have never touched a corpse, even after all these years.'

'I have touched too many. Maybe I should never have approached that first one.'

Dahabo visits her every day at noon, when the streets are at their hottest and the shops close for lunch and midday prayers. When Maryam English and Fadumo can join they eat communally with the radio on in the background and sift through the rumours spreading across Hargeisa – the government is going to shut down the schools, or is going to put chemicals in the water supply to make the population more docile, or is already planning to demolish all the cities and villages in the north-west – Kawsar only believes what the BBC Somali Service broadcasts from London report, they are far enough away to not succumb to the propaganda or hysteria. In the brief time that Farah had been chief of police in seventy-six he had warned that the government was capable of anything; it saw the country as a blank canvas that it could paint in whatever likeness it wanted. The police, army and bureaucrats were just the brushes they used. He lasted a few months before he was told to take early retirement. The police service had purged all of those who challenged the government's edicts and now no outrage was inconceivable. Oodweyne's proclamations were becoming more menacing; his nickname 'Big Voice' was intended to mock his radio interludes but the words he spoke in that deep percussive drawl were increasing in violence and hubris. He wanted all citizens to know that no one would get the better of him; that it would take death to unseat him.

The weeks after Kawsar's return from hospital float by in an opiate-induced torpor. She dozes as much as she can and spends the rest of her time alternately bickering with Nurto and brooding. She can bear the girl's messiness, the rough way she runs a wet cloth over her in the mornings, but she cannot bear watching her leave every day to do the same circuit that she has done for the last forty years. Cocooned within a tight wrapping of petticoat, *diric*, jumper and blankets, her skin pale and clammy, Kawsar feels like an enormous, delicate silkworm cloistered from the sun. If only damp wings could unfurl from her back and bear her away. Instead, there are bedsores. When Nurto returns after the shops have closed at one the never-ending conversation starts again.

'What have you done with the rest of the money?'

Kawsar asks, examining the change the girl has slapped onto the bed.

'That's all of it,' Nurto pants. Her cheeks are flushed and her clothes pungent after chasing her friends around the market.

'You think that my mind is gone rather than my hip?'

Nurto ignores the comment and stomps towards the kitchen.

'I'm talking to you. Come here now or I'll send you back to that tin shack you come from.'

Nurto reappears at the door.

'How much was the kilo of rice?' Kawsar continues, training her eyes on the girl.

'One thousand shillings,' comes the defiant reply.

'And the tomatoes?'

'One hundred and fifty shillings.'

'Since when?'

'Since they got more expensive.'

Kawsar reaches for the leather sandal sitting unused next to her bed and holds it aloft.

'One month ago a bag of tomatoes cost eighty shillings and now you expect me to believe the same dried-up tomatoes are a hundred and fifty?'

'Believe what you like. I was lucky to even buy the rice before it was sold out. People were fighting over the last few bags, punching and kicking each other. God above knows that I am telling the truth.'

'God knows that you're a cheating, ungrateful, untrustworthy liar.'

'What would you know? You're just a . . . a . . . smelly old woman.'

Kawsar throws the sandal but Nurto makes a show of not flinching and contemptuously tidies up the basket of wool and half-finished knitting it tips over.

Nurto's presence in her home has long lost the pleasure of novelty and is instead suffocating. This is her life now, no orchards, no family, no movement. She is just a stomach to be filled and a backside to be wiped, and these daily contests with the maid are one of the few things that remind her that she is still alive. Her mind spins between what is lost and what remains. The bungalow is often filled with sea-silence like a giant shell, her days empty, clear of appointment or duty. Instead of helping Dahabo at her market stall or looking after Zahra's children she watches Nurto like a spectre. She has become one with the bed; from a two-legged creature she has grown four metal feet, the mattress moulded to her flesh, its springs entwined with her ribs. Trapped within a skin within a bed within a house, only her two peeping eyes feel mobile, alive; they flutter about the room, settling hesitantly on her dusty possessions, the mysterious bundles and packages that litter the nests of old women. The urge to preserve, store and shroud her possessions had manifested itself quietly; she cannot remember when she began collecting the flakes at the bottom of the spice tin, the too-short-to-knit-with lengths of wool and the dried-up medals of soap, yet everywhere she looks rests another knot of plastic or cloth hiding the detritus of her existence. All has been condensed into tight bundles, her fifty-something years of town life – the papers, the gold, the money, the photographs, letters and cassettes – can be packed up, carried away on the back of a camel and blown away or destroyed in a rainstorm. Her bungalow with no heir will slump into old age and crumble back into the sand, her life of solidity and bureaucracy and acquisition leaving less of a print than the circles scorched into the desert by long dead nomads.

It is time for the weekly wash. A metal basin of lukewarm, soapy water and a facecloth are the extent of her bath, but Kawsar makes Nurto light an urn of crystallised incense to fragrance the room. It is a good day to feel water on the skin; there has been a thunderstorm, jagged spears of lightning impaling the sky through the window, the thunder as enveloping and threatening as an angry father and the rain as sibilant and soft as a mother's comforting words. The air pregnant with moisture as the drought finally lifts. It is a day to sit in cosy, expensive smoke and be lulled by the music of the sleepy, sodden town just outside the walls. She has taken a few painkillers just to savour this mood that glides her back to her childhood. Her mother used to wash her in the backyard with the fat, warm raindrops of the *Gu* season gathered into a barrel and poured from the tin cup in her mother's hand. Her mother's spare hand held Kawsar's thin upper arm tightly while she splashed and giggled in the tight circle around her feet, her curly hair slick and cloying against her back. This was around the same time she'd had the *gudniin*. Dahabo had had hers first, disappearing for two weeks before reappearing in new clothes and shoes, a purse dangling from her bangled arm. 'How'd you get them?' Kawsar asked, her mouth dropping.

Dahabo put the purse carefully on the step and quickly looked over her shoulder; she grabbed the corners of her skirt and flicked it up at the front, her bangles giving a little flourish as if to say, 'Now you see it, now you don't.'

Kawsar's eyes widened at the half-healed wound where Dahabo's shame had been. 'Does it hurt?' She wanted to ask to see it again but their mothers might appear suddenly.

'When I *kaaji* it stings.'

'When did it happen?'

'My cousins came in from the *miyi* and they did us all together. Today is the first time we have been allowed to walk, we had our legs bound for days and days.'

Kawsar reached to touch the bangles; their glitter came off on her sweaty, jealous fingers.

'You should get done too,' Dahabo chirruped, but there was no need, there was no way Kawsar would allow herself to be left behind, be called dirty names and left out of games. If it was Dahabo's time then it was hers too.

That very night she gathered close to her mother and told her she wanted to be made *halal* like Dahabo.

'But you are a year younger than her and smaller too. You are not ready, Kawsar.'

Younger, smaller maybe, but Kawsar as the only child of a widow was not used to being denied, and by the morning she had forced her will on her mother. Within the fortnight a middle-aged woman appeared at the front door with her circumcision kit.

'Kawsar, Kawsar.' Nurto shakes her leg.

'Yes?' she says with a start.

Nurto squeezes excess water from the small towel and slaps it into Kawsar's hand; this is the signal for her to wash between her legs.

Nurto turns her back to the bed and picks up the basin to refill it in the kitchen.

Kawsar's hand slips down past the sprigs of grey hair that have grown sparse with a lifetime of shaving and runs over the smooth shield of skin that lies over her genitals. She scrubs at the scar tissue and slack flesh, hoping to erase the musty smell she fears clings to her for most of the week. She bears no kindness to this part of her body, it has brought her nothing but pain and disappointment, and if she could scour it away she would feel no regret. It sometimes seems as if that cutter, looking around that finely furnished room, at the thick mattress Kawsar reclined on and at the rips in her own garments, had decided to play a trick on her. Maybe she had stitched the opening completely closed or cut too deeply or even planted thorns in her womb to make it barren. She certainly appeared to have been diminished in some respect that day, while Dahabo and the other girls recovered from their circumcisions stronger than before.

Whichever bitter old sorceress devised this practice back in pagan times must have convinced the others that this was the way to winnow the strong from the weak; that girls who could not survive this were not worth the milk it took to raise them. If a few managed to hobble along, neither dead nor properly alive, well, they could be suffered as long as they didn't get in the way. This philosophy had given generations of women – kept like Russian dolls one within the other – the same hardness, the same ability to not look back to whoever was left behind until eventually it was them who dallied at the rear.

Nurto returns with the basin, the hardness visible in her brow too. Kawsar drops the cloth to the floor and lets the girl scrub her back with a splayed brush. It feels good as the numb skin rushes back to life, but the brush soon approaches the two bedsores standing pink and proud above her buttocks.

'That's enough,' she says, sucking in air through her teeth.

Nurto rubs her dry with a towel stiff with detergent and then helps her into fresh, incense-infused clothes.

It isn't the cleanliness she is used to – patches of her skin have not touched any water at all – but it is enough to make her feel human again; soap, warm water, and the touch of another's hand has that power now.

A heavy rain shower pelts at the windows, distracting Kawsar from her thoughts; the beacon of a police car maintaining the curfew spreads a thin yolk-yellow light into her room. Cold, violent rainstorms have a contradictory effect on Kawsar – they bring warmth, a sense of fullness and well-being, the memory of Farah's palm stretched over the beating heart of her womb. Those shuttered green colony days of their youth have seeped into her flesh: the tin roof clattering above them, the wind whispering through its grooves, and Farah sleeping beside her on the low divan bed, his wandering hand pinned down by her petticoat's waistband. Kawsar remembers tugging his arm closer, moulding his body around hers and watching him through half-closed eyes on those mornings or afternoons that he refused to travel through the yellow sludge to his office. She never loved him more than in those dazes, when they seemed nothing less than twins curled up within the same skin, their limbs so entwined that she could not feel where his flesh ended and hers began or separate her scent from his. Hours passed in sleep so cavernous, so voluptuous that she knew how drunks felt as they slipped into unconsciousness by the roadside, a secret smile on their lips. When Farah finally began to stir, the rain spent to a tepid, half-hearted spray, there would be the separation, the readjustment of limbs, hair, and clothes as he became the husband and she the wife. But now, the only thing to be distilled from those hundreds of mornings and afternoons was the heat of an absent hand on an old, empty womb.

It is Friday, cleaning out the house day. All over the neighbourhood, all over the town, all over the country, rugs and mats are thrashed, windows opened and rooms dusted, floors washed and scrubbed, bed linen stamped on in wide basins, squeezed and hung out on bushes and washing lines, only to be brought in a couple of hours later bone dry, smelling of the sun and thick with pollen. Nurto has Friday afternoons to herself and Kawsar fears another long day watching the door, secretly hoping and fearing that someone will visit, her loneliness bearing knee-sharp on her chest. Her ears follow the footsteps on the street outside, her pulse quickening if they pause nearby. Once Maryam English's nanny goat had butted open the door, frightening Kawsar who thought that the soldiers had returned for her. The huge, horned animal looked around the room in surprise, chewing simple-mindedly on a mulch of grass, her hooves like castanets on the cement. 'Shoo, Shoo!' Kawsar had shouted, flinging her arms, at which the animal had obeyed, turning around and walking calmly away as if she agreed that there was no point wasting her time on an old woman.

Dahabo, Maryam, Fadumo, Raage the greengrocer, Zahra, Umar Farey, these are her occasional visitors. She knows maybe hundreds more though they do not come; people hide behind the excuse of curfews but their hearts have hardened, they cannot bring themselves to care about yet another misfortunate when they are already so overburdened. Women are running their families because the streets have been emptied of men; those not working abroad are in prison or have been grabbed off the street and conscripted into the army. If

Farah were still alive he would be like the others – hiding in his house, meek, prematurely wizened, like a woman in a harem. Nurto reported that the old *askaris* who used to gather around Raage's *dukaan* at five p.m. and wind their West End watches by the dings of the BBC broadcast have been banished, and the BBC banned in all public spaces. The regime doesn't just want to black out the city but to silence it.

Kawsar's heart wavers between recrimination and understanding. Times have changed so deeply; life had been cheap, easy and slow-paced, but now it is cheap in another way, certainly not easy and the hours of darkness have been stolen and made dangerous. People are made to scuttle about in the daytime, trying to live full lives in half their allotted time. The shops are bare as the subsidised rice and flour have disappeared to allow the government to obtain more foreign loans; instead of home-grown maize and sorghum, sacks of USAID donations smuggled in from the refugee camps are on sale in the market at ridiculous prices, Dahabo reports.

Nurto shoves a chipped enamel bowl into Kawsar's hands. Inside is her daily meal: chopped tomatoes, onions, coriander, chillies drenched in lemon juice, all bulked up with the boiled rice that the girl insists on. 'I don't want anyone saying that I'm not feeding you,' she says, raising an eyebrow accusingly.

Kawsar does not want the rice; it dilutes the intense, sharp flavours that feed her memories. Chillies she had first eaten in a restaurant in Mogadishu that Farah had taken her to. She had planted a lemon tree in their new police residence in Salahley and added home-grown coriander to every one of his dishes because he loved it so much. She craves tart flavours that suck emotion out of her; even her tea is over-spiced with ginger, cinnamon, cardamom – just like the concoctions she had made while breastfeeding. She doesn't want food that prolongs her life; she only wants to sustain her soul while it remains in her body.

'I'm going to a wedding now, I'll be back in a few hours,' Nurto says, placing a glass of water on the bedside table.

'A wedding? At this time?'

'Yes, the curfew, remember. We have to be in by seven.'

Kawsar rolls her eyes to the sky. 'Oh, I remember.'

Nurto's face is hidden as she struggles to squeeze into a black sequinned top and emerald trousers that balloon out at the hips and taper in at her bony ankles. They are *whodead*, that she has bought from the *suuq*. The rumour goes that foreign corpses are stripped down and the garments they breathed their last in are sold in the local markets.

'I wouldn't be attracting anyone's eyes to legs like those,' laughs Kawsar. 'A man wants a woman with sturdy ankles, not those scrawny *minjayow*.'

'Do you want anything from outside?'

'No, just don't break your ankles in those ridiculous shoes, there isn't room for another invalid here.' Nurto has slipped into her wooden platforms and is clomping her way to the door, trying not to hold her arms out for balance.

'*Nabadgelyo,*' shouts Nurto before banging the door behind her.

'Silly girl.' Kawsar laughs, but her smile withers when she catches sight of her reflection in the mirror. It looks as if a coconut has been coddled in many blankets, her face a blinking blurry smudge in the dingy room, her once thick black hair now as short and fine as a baby's. It had nearly all fallen out after Farah's death and now just grows in white patches over her scalp. She pulls a blanket over her eyes.

Kawsar opens one eye. Hodan is asleep beside her, sealed-eyed, puffy lipped, damp hair flattened against the pillow, her drool seeping onto her hand and thin snores whistling through the gap in her front teeth. Kawsar wipes the saliva away and pulls her child against her chest. The light through the window is the skin of a golden apple. In a moment Hodan will stir awake and look cantankerously from the floor to the ceiling and across to the window, trying to place herself, her soul settling back into its tight frame. The siesta sky framed in the window is pink and mauve in places with thin slivers of cloud stretched languidly across it, their edges metallic from the low rays of the copper sun. If only it could be spread out, cut up and stitched, she would make a quilt from it for Hodan to spread over her on cold, dark nights in the cemetery.

Kawsar wakes to find the room dark and stars brightening through the iron bars of the window above her bed.

There are a few wispy clouds trailing across the sky, the night breeze cooler than usual, playfully rifling through the prescriptions on the table. She pulls the blankets up to her chin, closes her eyes and breathes in the jasmine, honeysuckle, moonflowers and the desert flower *wahara-waalis* that she had planted long ago in the orchard behind her bungalow. This is the only contact that she has with her precious orchard now – the frail caress of its scent when the wind is blowing in the right direction. The pomegranate, guava and papaya trees are left to Nurto's crude mercy; Kawsar knows that she will only throw a bucket of dirty water at the gasping roots. Maryam reports that the tomatoes have withered, the green chillies yellowed, the okra been consumed by lizards. Only the trees have survived. Her spirit is tied up in those trees; she feels her roots contracting as they die.

Nurto has been seduced by an Indian trader, thinks Kawsar. New, musky perfumes come from the girl and she spends a mysterious amount of time in the washroom, the slosh of water and the smell of soap penetrating the bedroom. The *Singhe-Singhes* are an accursedly lustful lot with their winking, kohl-smudged eyes and rough, turmeric-stained hands groping at girls in the *suuq*. Their women had left along with the British at Independence in 1960, departing as swiftly as they had arrived in one big throng like birds, jewel-hued saris flying behind them like tail feathers. The husbands – fabric merchants, *suuq-wallahs* and civil servants – who remained in the Indian Line quarter, play cricket on the bare, cracked earth and chase Somali girls with the tire-lessness of tomcats.

'Whose benefit is all this for? A trader?' Kawsar asks, as Nurto skips across the cement floor, leaving thin, wet footprints.

'Can't I even wash without you making a fuss?' Her hair is a damp rope untwining against her left breast; she squeezes the end and wipes her hand on her leaf-printed *diric*. She is filling out, blooming into woman-hood, hips, breasts and bottom grown full with *halwa* and dates.

Kawsar feels a misplaced pride while admiring her maid; it is a rare luxury to be able to hand over the run of a kitchen to a poor child and watch her blossom. 'You look good, that is all I wanted to say.'

Nurto's face contorts; she was primed for another verbal assault, had steeled and armed herself for it, her shoulders and feet squared. 'You think so?' she asks af-ter a moment. 'How have I changed?'

'You look like a *gashaanti* now, your skin is glowing, your hair has grown, you have curves when before you were like a tree in the *jiilaal*. You smell better too,' Kawsar smiles.

Nurto smirks. 'And you think I would go to all that trouble for a *Singhe-Singhe* market trader? I have my sights set further than that.'

'Oh! Tell me more.'

Nurto laughs, 'This American wants to take my picture. He says people would pay to put me in magazines.'

Kawsar raises her eyebrow, remembering the lewd photographs taken of Somali girls by Italians in Mogadishu. '*Naayaa*, guard yourself, I will not have people saying that you were corrupted while in my care. Say your *ashahaado* and protect your shame.'

Nurto's face falls, she was wrong to have lowered her shield, 'It's not like *that*, he just wants to help me. He says that another Somali girl is famous in New York and Paris just for walking and showing off the clothes.'

'New York, my rear end. Don't let yourself be beguiled. When I was young Italians would put naive girls in their dirty photos and films.'

'So what? Is that worse than being a servant all your life with someone calling you every name they can think of? As if they own you?'

'The way I was brought up there was no shame in clean, Islamic work of any kind. All a girl has of any value whether she is born to a *suldaan* or a pauper is her reputation, don't be simple-minded enough to throw that away.'

'To hell with reputations!' Nurto flicks her rope of hair over her shoulder, dives onto her mattress and buries her nose in a magazine with a blonde cover girl; unable to read the words, she studies it photo by photo.

The sun breaks through the leaden, grumbling clouds and slips through the barred windows, stitching crosshatches of light and shadow across her bedspread and feet. Kawsar wriggles her toes and scratches her soles with their hornlike nails. She has asked Nurto to make her a whole thermos today; she is in the mood to listen to music and sip sweet spiced tea with condensed milk. The boulder pressing down on her chest has lifted a little, allowing her to take deeper breaths without wincing; she stretches her neck to the left and holds it there before stretching to the right. She can feel the tips of her fingers and toes again, her scalp tingles; she has not taken a pain-killer for more than twelve hours and her body feels like a city coming back to life after a long night. She clicks the radio on – it is set to Radio Mogadishu in case of a police raid, and the station relays a live performance by the Waaberi national troupe in Khartoum.

Nurto is on her mattress, concentrating on the large dressmaking scissors in her grip. Kawsar has never noticed the girl's left-handedness before; maybe it is part of the reason she seems so awkward, as if she is taking life on from the wrong angle. She is hacking old cotton dresses of Kawsar's into rectangular pieces to fold up and use as sanitary pads; the older woman had noticed a damp red flower blooming on the back of Nurto's thin *diric* and offered her the long-unused clothes. She had also pointed out other garments, some of them of expensive cloth and unworn, that Nurto could take to wear, but she didn't want them, even wrinkling her nose as she rummaged dismissively through them.

Kawsar pours out her first cup; the bones in her back creak as she bends over, but it feels good in a strange way.

'I can teach you how to sew properly, if you want,' she offers, blowing steam and milkskin gently to and fro.

Nurto leaves a long pause before answering, 'I don't think I'll be any good at it.'

'Who is to say what anyone will be good at until they try?'

'Well, you for one. You tell me I'm a bad cook, that I can't clean, that I leave soap powder in the laundry, that I've killed your plants. I'm not going to give you one more thing to criticise me for.'

Kawsar laughs. 'I am just trying to challenge you, make you pay more notice to how you work. What is it that you want to do in your life, anyway? Carry on as a maid?'

Nurto lets out a snort of derision.

'Get married? Herd goats? Set up a trucking company?'

Nurto raises an eyebrow.

'What will it be then?'

'I told you, I am going to move abroad and become a fashion model.'

'Why don't you take advantage more while you're here – buy vats of ghee and stick your fingers in and lick them until your jowls and belly and buttocks vibrate with every step?'

Nurto laughs and Kawsar smiles in triumph; it is hard to make this girl lose her scowl.

'They don't like women like that over there. They like them my size with small chests, long legs and no fat whatsoever. They are not like the stupid men here who want Asha Big Legs huffing and puffing into their beds.'

'Your photographer told you that, did he?' replies Kawsar doubtfully.

'Yes, but it's obvious anyway, I read the magazines.'

'*Read?*'

'Look at, then, same thing. The pictures speak for themselves. Why are you always going on as if you are some kind of professor from Laafole University, anyway?'

'I'm no professor, I am as unlettered as a child, but I just can't stand misplaced pride.'

'It's not misplaced. I will learn to read, I will make something of my life. You old women take pride in your ignorance – that is what I call misplaced.'

Kawsar is calm, she has got into a bad habit of riling Nurto, but it has an irresistible, cathartic effect on her. 'I am a simple woman with no shame or regrets,' she lies. 'I have lived a blameless life.'

'Blameless and pointless,' Nurto spits.

The words cut deeper than Kawsar expects. She shifts away a little, as if dodging a thrown object; she has been felled by her own arrow.

'Just leave me alone.' She turns her back on Nurto and faces the wall, the familiar chips and cracks in the plaster filling her vision once again. 'You would never dare to speak to me like that if my husband was around,' she says softly.

'And you wouldn't dare taunt me like you do if my family had money.'

The girl is like a cobra, so quick to jump to the offensive. She is right about her own situation and Kawsar feels a begrudging envy that she can fight so viciously for herself. It had taken her a long time to see power and powerlessness so clearly.

They do not speak for the rest of the day. The room darkens around Kawsar, the snips of the scissors eventually cease and they clatter to the ground. Their music brings back the memory of her college: the pads of her fingers sore with needle punctures, the ache of her hand after cutting through fabric for hours, the pretty quilts and hangings and skirts she made faster than anyone else.

A child runs a metal cup along the bars of the window but Kawsar doesn't look. Unknown children have begun to peek in; they are tentative, unsure if the rumours of a witch who never leaves her house are true. They catcall through the bars and run away, spit and throw pebbles at the window. They are reincarnations of all the children who are begotten to harass old women, a fresh regiment of them born in every generation to extinguish the will to live in the already despairing; yet they are condemned in their own way, to always be eight years old with big, new teeth cramming their mouths, their hearts brimming with confused spite and fear. She does not believe they are her neighbours' children – they could not have turned against her so easily; they have to be children from other quarters, who do their mischief far from home and run away before their mothers miss them.

She remembers the widow in rags who lived in a

wooden shack behind her childhood home, her garru-
lousness in spite of the isolation in which she lived, the
little boys who taunted and threw stones at her, thinking
the muttering was a sign of madness or possession. The
only thing that possessed her and now Kawsar are memories, scenes from infancy to the last few days rising up
unbidden.

'*Naayaa*, Kawsar, let us in!' Dahabo bangs the door.

'Open it!' Kawsar calls quickly to Nurto in the kitchen.

Nurto speeds to the front, her hands covered in tomato
flesh, her bare feet making a slapping, sliding noise. She
flings the door open and spins back to the kitchen, stubbornly avoiding Kawsar's eyes.

Dahabo bends down to kiss Kawsar's forehead. 'Look
at all these papers in your window.' Dahabo points above
her head.

'They are offerings, prayers. Don't you know that I am
the local saint.' There are maybe fifteen chewing gum
and lollipop papers rolled thin and prodded through the
wire mesh as if her room is a saint's shrine.

'Little scoundrels! They have nearly torn the damn
thing apart!'

'Let them have their fun.'

Dahabo pulls out those wrappers she can reach. 'You
know that the curfew has been brought forward to four
in the afternoon now, while it is still bright outside?'

'When did they say that?'

'Yesterday, announced it in the market before we
shut up.'

'And what reason did they give?'

Dahabo scrunches up the papers in her hand. 'From what people are saying in the *suuq* it looks like the NFM will be attacking the cities before the month is out.'

'That is just talk, people have been saying it for years.'

Dahabo sits on the edge of the bed. 'No, Kawsar, it's different now. There are rebels rising against him in every region. If he goes down he will take the country with him, he'll want all of us buried alongside him, like one of those pharaohs in the Kitab. My daughters are panicked, they want to get their children out,' she says quietly. 'Jawahir's husband has arranged visas for us all to join him in Jeddah.'

Kawsar doesn't trust her ears and asks her to repeat what she just said; again that 'us' lands on her like a small incendiary. 'Why do you have to go?' Kawsar asks, almost dumbfounded.

Dahabo turns her face to meet Kawsar's eyes. 'What would be left of me without them?'

Kawsar will not let her go without a fight, without laying claim. She will scream, scatter her possessions on the floor and rend her garments. 'And what will be left of me without you?'

Dahabo holds Kawsar tenderly by the chin. 'Come with us. Leave this box prison behind and come with us. You are my family too.'

Kawsar imagines the one-bedroom flat in Jeddah, the mattresses stowed against the wall during the day, the mess and rush of children, arguments between three or four generations echoing from the kitchen. She cannot spend her last months as silent and unwelcome as a toad in an outhouse, looking out on all of that.

'Can't I just have you, Dahabo?'

'You have me, but what can I do?'

'Stay. Don't let anyone chase you out.'

Dahabo exhales and sinks down deeper into the mattress. 'Remember Asiya from college?'

'What of her?' Kawsar remembers the girl she had bullied in class, a bundle of bad teeth, bad hair, bad clothes who had encroached on their friendship.

'Not one of her children remain with her, either dead, missing, in jail or with the NFM. We will all be like that soon.'

'I am already like that, Dahabo. Don't ask me to sympathise with her.'

'I am afraid. I am afraid to wake up in the morning, to think about what will happen next week, next month, next year. I feel frayed, I cannot hold myself together anymore.' She beats her heart with four fingers.

'I will hold you together, come live with me. I will tell Nurto to leave.'

'My children,' Dahabo says firmly before putting her shoes on. 'I can't be separated from them.'

They look at each other long and hard before Dahabo silently leaves the bungalow.

'Stupid. Stupid. Old. Woman.' Kawsar hits the heel of her fist against her head with every word. She doesn't recognise the person she is becoming: an old crone who can't admit that her time is over, that children and grand-children must come first. What was she thinking? De-manding that Dahabo stay behind with her, two old women counting each other's grey hairs, is that what she wants? Shameless and unnatural, that's all it is. Next, when she hears laughter behind her back, will she be placing curses? Casting evil eyes? Wishing misfortune on those that deny her or have their families around them? So this is how old women become witches – just one or two tragedies and green poison pours out of them.

Kawsar takes one reptilian breath an hour, the distant sun beating down on her head, her yellow eyes swivel-ling in the hollows of her skull, cold brown blood curdling in the dry furrows of her veins. She has lost count of how many pills she has pushed down her gullet, but it is enough to mute the pain, enough to strip her vision of its loud Technicolor until her room appears monochromatic and brooding through the thin slits of her pupils. She presses her palms into her eyelids and replaces the torpor of her life with shooting amber stars and exploding electric galaxies. She learnt to do this as an indolent little girl, whiling away dead time by voyag-ing through the quiet, almost-black world behind her eyes. She has not aged much as a soul, still thinks too much, loses herself to dreams and nightmares, her body hiding – no, trapping – what is real and eternal about her, that pinprick of invisible light in this dark shroud of hers. She is doomed to beat about, fluttering against her skin, desperate for release into the world, as frantic as a firefly in a child's jar.

Release. That is all she has ever wanted. At one point she thought she had found it. Sitting on the low branch of a strange tree along the River Juba, crocodiles' eyes peering at her over the scum of the water, twenty-foot palm trees alive with a chorus of black-tailed monkeys, hippos yawning downstream, and thousands of butterflies emerging from cocoons above her head, their creased purple wings stirring the afternoon air, Kawsar could feel light streaming through her. She was open, skinless, born to witness this everlasting moment. Farah had searched the car for his camera, tried to name the butterflies, to explain their presence on this particular tree, but she had covered his mouth and told him just to watch, to feel; she wanted them to be as mute and ecstatic as those newborn butterflies.

Kawsar's eyelids unstick and light filters through her stubby lashes. It might be sunrise or four in the afternoon, unmoored in the undulating waves of time she just opens her eyes and accepts what she is told.

Nurto leans over the bed. 'Dahabo brought these things for you.' She places the basket beside Kawsar on the bed.

'Why didn't she wake me?'

Nurto shrugs and turns back to the kitchen.

'Listen when I'm talking to you, you little whore.'

Nurto stops short at the insult and slides her eyes back towards Kawsar, the rest of her body immobile.

'Take this rubbish back to the kitchen.' Kawsar grabs the basket and skims it across the floor, upsetting its contents – dates and mincemeat set in ghee – over the dusty cement.

'Have you lost your mind, old woman? Throwing good food over the floor for me to sweep up. You think I'm your slave or something?' Nurto snatches one of the handles, shoves the basket against her hip and slams the door behind her.

'Bitch,' Kawsar spits out.

Behind that green door she doesn't see Nurto but Dahabo.

It is such a distant thing to do; as if they barely know each other she has left a basket and skulked away. This behaviour from a woman whose birthing sheets she had washed and who had washed hers in return. What next? They would need to make appointments to take tea like the English women used to. The old Dahabo would have nudged her awake or sat on the bed and just started talking. What good was a basket without conversation? Had she become a beggar overnight? What need of alms had she who had once had Dahabo's own mother as a servant in her family home?

Kawsar's face flushes with anger. The saliva in her mouth is bitter and cleaves to her gullet; she finishes the water left in the cup on the bedside table.

She wants to throw herself out of the bed and bar the door, nailing planks across it until it is impassable, a warning and rebuke to those who pity her, who dare mistake her for a beggar, a destitute, a woman without name or reputation.

Darkness spreads over her eyes like black oil. She has woken up with tears running greasily down her cheeks, her head tense as if she has been crying for a long time but with no recollection of why. Nurto has left the paraffin *feynuus* on and the room stinks of the burnt wick. How many homes have burned down just because of simple mistakes like that?

Nurto snuffles against her pillow, muttering incomprehensible but defensive-sounding words. She argues and bristles even in her dreams, thinks Kawsar. The silhouettes of great moths flit through the room, beating against the mosquito screens on the windows like prisoners; they are eerie creatures that search for light just so they can immolate themselves with it. On full-moon nights when everything is bathed in bluish-white light and even the leaves on the trees are clearly outlined, the face of the moon is obscured by millions of flying specks, jostling with each other as if they are in a race to reach the heavens; they have a hunger, a single-mindedness that approaches devotion, reminding her of the *sura* in the Qu'ran that compares Allah to a lamp and his worshippers to moths. Maybe the fabled tree on the moon is the moths' destination and the bright light is just to mark their route; that singular tree grows a leaf with every birth and when it drops so does the life attached to it. Her own leaf must be hanging by the most fragile of strands that even the beat of a moth's wings would be enough to break its hold.

In her orchard the trees had been born from deaths; they marked and grew from the remains of the children that had passed through her. She never picked the fruit that fell from them, believing it a kind of cannibalism, but out of those soft, unshaped figures had grown tall, strong, tough-barked trees that blossomed and called birds to their branches and clambered out over the orchard walls to the world beyond. The infants in the orchard all had names, the genders sometimes distinguishable and some-times imagined. The largest of them was Ibrahim, a nearly perfect boy with pale hair thick on his curved, rubbery limbs. Seven whole months he had survived in her harsh womb. He was tired, with wrinkles furrowed deep across his brow, and she thought she had seen him take one deep, resigned breath in her arms before he put down his clubbed hands and surrendered the fight. It had been difficult to bury him; he had toes, fingernails, a good head of hair, puffy eyes that clearly would have taken the shape of her own. Farah was hostile towards the shrouded bundle; he refused to look, refused to touch. Kawsar remained in bed with him snuggled against her breast while Farah called for a doctor to stem the blood flowing from her. By the time the Italian obstetrician had appeared at the door, she was drained yellow, her clammy skin as cold as the child's, so disconnected from her senses that she dropped her legs open without a murmur and revealed everything to the foreigner. He prodded and cut and stitched while Ibrahim appeared to snooze open-mouthed beside her. When the Italian went to examine him she refused and pressed him against her breast, her nails breaking through his skin. She remembers hearing wails and screams but she herself was silent. Two days later, while Farah was out, and when the gloss of blood and fluid had dried into Ibrahim's hair and his lips had set to a dark grey colour, Kawsar gathered the stained sheets around her waist and padded to the yard in bare feet. She clawed the earth with her hands, her nails split and shredded by the gritty soil, only stopping when she had created a narrow, two-foot deep trench. She filled a bucket from the kitchen tap and washed Ibrahim clean, wrapped him in the multi-hued blanket she had knitted, and then laid him gently down. She read the prayer for the dead and then gently smoothed the earth over the blanket; it took a long time for the purple and red and pink squares to disappear under the brown earth.

Farah had returned late in the afternoon. He glanced towards the bed but didn't ask what had happened; he sat in his chair in silence and read a newspaper while she pretended to sleep with her face to the wall. He warmed up a beef stew bought from the dirty men's café he frequented and placed a bowl beside her. His fingers grazed her upper arm. 'Kawsar, you should eat to replace the blood you lost, you need iron,' he said, trying to turn her face to him.

She pulled back, mumbled something, the smell of the stew made her stomach turn. Her own raw flesh had so recently been cut up; she could imagine it diced, tenderised and seasoned. She recognised the dense smell of abattoirs on her stiff, floral-patterned sheets. Farah kept his distance but the room was thick with green-eyed flies. A pad of cotton between her thighs oozed with dark, blackened blood and once every few hours Farah tentatively reached in and replaced the pad, rushing away with it and washing his hands for a long time in the bathroom, his fingers reeking of antiseptic when he returned. He must compare her to other women, she told herself, clean women who delivered healthy, thick-jowled babies one after the other and jumped to their feet within a few hours to cook the next meal. The spectre of a second wife seemed more real with every miscarriage and stillborn. His relations must be whispering words into his ear, pointing to beautiful, young girls with ripe breasts and wide hips and saying, 'Why not? Why not?' Why not, indeed. Maybe she could help with the teenager's child – bathe it, sit with it while she went to the *suuq* with friends, stroke its fat cheeks when it whimpered in sleep.

After Hodan had died and been buried in the formal, desolate cemetery in town she had turned maniacally to her orchard, forcing life into every spare inch of it, her nails broken and lined with dirt, the knees of her *dirics* stained brown. She had planted every flower she could name and taken cuttings from some that she couldn't, had helped herself to the gardens that the English had once established; neighbours brought her seeds instead of mourning gifts thinking she was unduly concerned with supporting herself in her old age, only for them to marvel at the ripe, swollen fruit rotting where it fell. Her orchard was a spot of colour visible from the sky; it perfumed the winds of the *jiilaal* and sent its scent from house to house on October Road. When she had begun weeding, digging, sowing, watering beyond her own land and into the trash-strewn roadside bordering her house, Dahabo had pulled her inside, sat her on the bed and told her it was time to stop.

Even now a perimeter of fire-red flowers rings her exterior walls, reminding her of that time. Her orchard has become a mark on the local map, the canopied alleyway beside it a place for late-night romantic assignations. It marks the central point of Guryo Samo, the heart from which arterial roads lead away to the extremities of the neighbourhood. What mysterious animals must be nosing through its undergrowth at this hour, she wonders; she has never seen it this late and feels a sudden stab at the realisation that she never will. She could wake Nurto up and demand that she carry her over but there would be no pleasure then; it needed solitude and unhurried time to watch the night-blooming flowers quietly yawn, and for the rustle of the grass to be heard over the owls, dogs and cicadas. She would wait until all those delights could be felt in her bones through the earth.

The rains had spit their last and now it was time for the *jiilaal*, the harsh dry season that lasts from December until March. It only sends sand devils through the streets in Hargeisa, but for the nomads it is a time of thirst and suffering. Nineteen eighty-seven fades to a close and the new year slides in, as grey and lifeless as the censored comedies on the radio. Each night Kawsar prays that Oodweyne is dead before the dawn and that her own leaf then gently drops too. But each morning he is still alive, unaffected by old age or her curses.

It is weeks since she last saw Dahabo, but she still stubbornly ignores her knocks on the door when she turns up at the bungalow. She hears Dahabo's voice sometimes from the courtyard when she waylays Nurto on her return from the market and they whisper conspiratorially about her, Nurto occasionally sneaking things out to her and denying it afterwards. It is easier to not see her again than to see and touch and speak with her knowing she will soon be gone. The prophesied siege of the town is yet to come but Nurto reports that Dahabo has closed her shop in the market and sold her home. Kawsar feels more jealousy and possessiveness towards Dahabo than she ever did towards her husband; she wants to be able to walk around the market with her again, holding hands and leading each other safely across the roads. If that cannot be then she will cause Dahabo as much pain as she can for deserting her.

She has sent Nurto to the market to have new clothes made and while waiting for her return Kawsar stares at her hands, wondering why it has been so long since she put them to work. She might still knit, sew or weave to occupy the minutes, hours, days, weeks and months she still has left. Closing her eyes she imagines taking a square of indigo calico and with silver thread in tent stitch creating a nightscape with an almost full moon at its centre obscured by the shadows of clouds. She is startled from her musing by a cacophonous rush of voices and feet from the street, hears Maryam English calling out, 'Get back here now . . . Fine then, wait and see what happens to you when you get back!'

The stampede fades away and Kawsar raises her body up to the window above her head and shouts, 'Maryam, why are you hollering?'

A moment's pause and then Maryam pushes open the door looking dishevelled and aggrieved. 'My stupid son has run off with the others.'

'Where to?'

Maryam sighs. 'To the theatre. The *Guddi* called all the neighbours to come and watch the trial of some poor men the soldiers captured.'

'It's the theatre now, is it?'

Maryam laughs derisively. 'Well, I guess we are all just actors and all of this a stage. I don't know about you but I wear these torn clothes as costumes and drop false tears into my eyes when I weep.'

Kawsar smiles. 'And when there is no audience I get up and dance to the radio.'

'We all know about that.' Maryam points a finger in mock castigation.

'Do we know the men?'

170

'No, I didn't recognise the names, but maybe they're actors too, playing their parts.'

'I hope for their sake they are.'

'I'm going to go on a protest tomorrow with the students.' Nurto breaks the silence later in the evening with this declaration. 'To make them stop the executions at Birjeeh.'

'You are not going, Nurto. I forbid it.'

'I'll go whether you like it or not.'

Kawsar points her cup at her. 'If you go there tomorrow, don't bother coming back. I will ask Maryam to pack up your things and leave them outside.'

'How can you say that? I am trying to help!'

'You don't know the danger you are putting yourself in. I do, and while you are under my roof I am your guardian, whether *you* like it or not,' Kawsar says vehemently, spilling hot tea onto her thighs.

'Everything I do is wrong in your eyes, it's like you want the ground to eat me up or something.'

'That's not true, Nurto. If I didn't care I would let you go. Just trust me when I say I know more about this than you, I have learnt bitterly what can happen.'

Kawsar turns over the sequence of events that had led Hodan from the classroom to the graveyard, unsure which portion if any to divulge to Nurto. 'Am I not proof enough of what they are capable of?' she says eventually, leaving her pain undisturbed.

Nurto shrugs, aloof, and then takes the dirty dishes to the kitchen.

171

Kawsar rests her cup on the bedside table and rubs the wet stain on her blanket with a shawl. It was strange now to think that this bland little bungalow had once seen so much drama, that life with Hodan towards the end was like a Hindi film, full of fateful misunderstandings and tragedy. The first scene would have been that last morning of normality in February 1982, when Hodan left for school in her pink uniform and Kawsar watched her walk alone down the wintry street to Guryo Samo Middle School. The fact that the Hargeisa hospital doctors were about to be sentenced at the courthouse that day had meant little to her; her mind was preoccupied with errands she needed to run before her daughter came home for lunch at noon. When Kawsar had returned from the market with new school shoes under her arm she had found all of her neighbours on the street in a knot. They were talking loudly and incoherently, hands on hips, until Maryam shouted to her, 'They have sentenced all the doctors to death and now the students have gone wild.' Kawsar shook her head in disbelief – there must have been some confusion or exaggeration. How could they execute ten doctors for organising a clean-up of the hospital? At most they would be fired for making their superiors appear inefficient. As the morning progressed the news from her neighbours got steadily worse: protestors had been shot and killed near the courthouse; hundreds of schoolchildren were abandoning their classrooms and massing outside the police station to throw stones; soldiers were being drafted in to support the police.

Kawsar left her half-peeled vegetables in a basin and marched to the school to bring Hodan home. The single-storey building was deserted, the teachers' canes redundant in their hands. 'She has gone with the other rebels,' her teacher kept saying, but Kawsar checked all the classrooms expecting to find Hodan reading quietly by herself. By the time she reached the town centre it was hard to see any students in the crush of anguished relatives, the police station gate was shut and a barricade of soldiers pushed the crowd back with sticks. Later, much later in the afternoon, she heard that the girls were all locked up inside the police station while the boys had been taken to the military head-quarters, Birjeeh.

The police station gates remained closed all day and night, and the parents were not allowed to see the children or bring food. The anger on the policemen's faces, spitting as they yelled at them to go away, made Kawsar wonder what they were doing to the girls behind the walls. Kawsar staggered home in tears, dragged away by Dahabo whose children had all left school years before. 'I don't blame them. We adults have been too docile,' she had said. 'You should be proud of her, Kawsar.' But there was nothing to be proud of. Kawsar knew that Hodan wasn't interested in politics; she must have followed her classmates to change how they saw her – the old woman's daughter who was never allowed to play outside.

For the three nights Hodan was in prison Kawsar did

not sleep. She rose at dawn to wait outside the prison gates as one by one girls were released into their mothers' arms, and as she walked home alone each day at sunset, she would hand the bowl of cold *iskukaris* in her arms to a beggar. Her life had no shape without her daughter. She waited obediently outside the station, craning her neck over the barbed wire to try to see through the narrow windows.

Eventually, Hodan was spat out, looking no better than a street girl, her face filthy, her hair matted, her uniform grimy. Kawsar hailed a taxi and bundled her in before anyone could take her away again. Hodan hid her head in her mother's lap and didn't utter a word. She rushed into the shower at home, not bothering to heat the water on the stove, and then fell asleep in the bed they shared. Kawsar crept in beside her, slid the sheets gently away and checked her body for injuries. There were small bruises on her thighs, four on each leg the size and shape of grapes; she replaced the sheets and squeezed her into her arms, hoping against hope that what she feared hadn't happened.

The morning after her release, over a breakfast of liver and *canjeero*, Kawsar edged the conversation to what had happened to Hodan inside the station.

'Nothing,' Hodan said, not looking up from her plate.

'Nothing at all? Didn't they interrogate you?' Kawsar kept her voice soft, on the right side of curious.

'Just a few questions, not much . . .' She seemed to stuff her mouth to stop the words.

'They were furious with us for even waiting outside. I was scared for you.'

Hodan left the plate half-finished and washed her hands clean.

'Have a rest today, you can return to school tomorrow.'

'I'm not going back to school.'

'Why not?'

'I don't want to see any of them.'

'But they all went through it too . . .'

'Leave me, *Hooyo*, leave me be,' she snapped, before hiding in the bathroom.

After a week's absence the teacher came to speak to Hodan but she refused to see him. He then sent around three girls from the class who brought her a tin of *halwa*, and they conversed secretly in the orchard and tore the sweet slab apart with their fingers, while Kawsar strained her ears from the kitchen. She couldn't gather anything from the few intelligible words she heard, but watching their backs through the kitchen, she noticed how small Hodan was in comparison to the other girls, how much her birdlike spine had stooped from reading too many books. Ethiopian bombers were still flying over Hargeisa, reminding the government and population that they had lost the war even years after it had ended, and she called the girls inside in case one appeared, as if the bungalow might save them.

The girls left without having convinced Hodan to return to class. Kawsar watched her daughter wash her sticky hands again and again in the bathroom and felt all language leave her. The relationship between them, which had been so intimate and supple, was now brittle. From the minute Hodan was born Kawsar had breathed in her scent as if it was the air that kept her alive. Her beauty and fragility made something contract inside her mother. Kawsar had even been jealous of Farah when she watched Hodan on his knee, following the sentences on the page that he was reading with her finger. It felt as if he was stealing time from her but when Farah passed just after Hodan's ninth birthday Kawsar proudly watched her take his place in the chair and carry on reading his books. Mother and daughter had always communicated through touches and kisses and slept huddled in the same bed, but had lost that easy communion in a single moment. If she said the word they had both left unspoken it seemed as if everything would break, that the pretence of calm would be eternally lost, that shame would replace everything else in their lives. Hodan simply refused to leave the house and Kawsar acquiesced rather than force the words from her lips.

The first sign of Hodan's illness had been the silent speech, like prayers spoken under the breath but disconnected from any purpose. Not a simple *bismallah* before taking the first bite of a meal or an *ashahaado* at bedtime, but long, hurried sentences that seemed full of dread, her eyes squeezed shut as if she was making gut-deep declarations of innocence or blood-soaked oaths. Kawsar pretended not to notice, but her eyes slid away from the stitching in her hand or from her ironing to her daughter, huddled in a corner as distant as the furthest, coldest star in the sky. Then came her questions, always smelling faintly of accusation, her eyes now wide open, as watchful as an owl's. Not even the smallest twitch or reaction could escape her notice and she paid greater attention to these involuntary movements than the words that she seemed to believe were all lies anyway. Some of Hodan's questions seemed benign, banal: she just wanted to know why Kawsar had waited so long before having a child. But no answer seemed to satisfy and the question would be rephrased and repeated the next day, the next week, the next month.

Then came the obsessive cleaning, her hands scrubbed until the skin began to blister and peel. Kawsar would lay out a plate and spoon before lunch and Hodan would wash both again before she ate with them – that is while she still shared cutlery with her mother, before that dawn-blue tin bowl appeared from the back of the cupboard with a separate spoon to go with it. The little girl who was weaned on meat softened in her mother's mouth now seemed disgusted by her touch, but remained too pampered to cook for herself, the charcoal stove too cumbersome for her to bother with.

Kawsar accepted it all, pretended not to see when Hodan hit her own temple with a furious fist as if trying to knock difficult thoughts out of her head. Her first concern had been to protect Hodan from predatory boys, those stray dogs that could sniff out vulnerability from the other side of town. She was growing into her body faster than she was developing in her mind. Kawsar began to understand why those Arab women in Mogadishu covered their daughters all in black with only a slit for the eyes; it could serve as a chrysalis until their girls were ready for the heat of men's eyes. Hodan still seemed too young; her breasts looked ridiculous on her narrow chest, and she had the brown-glazed teeth of a child who couldn't keep their fingers out of the biscuit tin. It would take another decade for her to appear anything like a grown woman, but still boys in uniform lingered outside the bungalow gate after school trying to watch Hodan through the windows. One day Kawsar lost her composure and threw a shoe at one of those dogs, aimed the wedged sole at his face, hoping to blind the scoundrel, and he in return had thrown a stone back at her, hitting her in the ribs. That was the beginning of the end, the transition from control to anarchy, from hope to despair, from decency to shame.

It would have been different if Hodan had been a more aggressive child, one who could turn her anger and pain outwards towards others. In the playground at Hodan's school the boys wore steel-capped shoes and before class they would gather into a knot and kick each other's shins, the winner being the boy who survived the longest in the fray. It was not unusual for eleven- and twelve-year-olds to settle a squabble with a razorblade secreted under their sleeve. The teachers could whip, kick and punch their students as much as they pleased, but if they went too far then a parent would come in and square off with them. Violence was an article of faith nowadays, accepted and rewarded at every level; there wasn't room for the gentle or thoughtful. Just amongst her neighbours, Kawsar witnessed toddlers being pushed into fights by their older siblings; Hodan was once jumped by a group of girls for no other reason than they envied her new shoes. She ran home with a tear in her shirt, her hair ripped out of its braids, a bleeding scratch from her nose to her cheek, but what upset her most was the state of her exercise books, which had been torn and stamped upon. She didn't want Kawsar to replace the books or find the girls' mothers so that they would be punished, she just shook with grief for her once immaculate books; there was no vengeance in her, but that magnanimity was perceived as weakness, as bloodlessness by adults and children alike. She was 'cowardly', 'not right', they said. Dahabo had tried to teach her how to argue, to cuss, to fight, because Kawsar was just as meek as her daughter. Dahabo cuffed and teased Hodan to fire a reaction but it didn't work, the girl just hid behind her mother and waited for Dahabo to leave her alone. When she did succumb to violence it was against herself.

Nurto returns after washing the dishes and doesn't mention the protest; instead she sits calmly on her mattress and pores over photographs in an Indian magazine given to her by a market trader. She examines the hair, eyebrows, make-up and henna of the actresses under the glow of the *feynuus*, furrowing her eyebrows as if hard at work, wondering how she can recreate these looks with her sparse equipment. She tears out the pages with the most beautiful women in the magazines and keeps them under her pillow, as if she hopes their splendour will seep into her as she sleeps, her dreams probably tinted red and gold like the pictures.

A new moon has just been born, fragile and slender in its nursery of stars, and Kawsar gazes at it as she whispers a prayer for Hodan's soul.

She remains awake long after Nurto has turned off the lamp and fallen asleep. She only succumbs to drowsiness when she hears Maryam English's children leaving for school at seven, the crunch of their sandals loud in her ears, their reddish hair gliding past her windowsill. Kawsar falls asleep with her cheek bathed in a ray of sunlight.

The front door swings on its hinges; Kawsar likes it open for a quarter of an hour in the morning, to sweep the fetid smell of her bandages and old breath from the room. The wound from the compound fracture of her hip is still festering, itching away under the cotton gauze, and she scratches it with the end of her *caday*, the tooth stick bumping over glossy, stitched skin. In quiet moments like these she often feels her heart skip a beat as she remembers the soldier's distant eyes as she beat her to the floor.

'You can't hurt me,' she says repeatedly, her breathing slowly returning to normal.

The strip of street life visible from her bed is dreamlike, rushing past like film spinning wildly from its spool: dogs, goats, infants with bare bottoms, the speechless extras of life appearing within the frame of the door and then deliquescing into the world beyond.

From the window opposite the video hall she sometimes hears the older neighbourhood children talking in hushed voices, and in secondhand *whodead* clothes their younger siblings re-enact the dramas that their parents try to hide from them. Kawsar once – in her upright days – had watched as a girl in overalls arrested a cowboy, while a bridesmaid and diminutive nurse barked orders at her, sticks pointed in place of guns. They watch videos for ten shillings in Zahra's little cinema and come pouring out afterwards, imitating the flourishes and facial acrobatics of Amitabh Bachchan or throwing karate moves stolen from Bruce Lee. She can hear them now, scuff-kneed boys and girls organising the rescue of uncles from Mandera prison, planning heists of Midland bank so their parents can pay their taxes, and swearing vengeance against the policemen who ransack their homes. The NFM is full of the older versions of these children, leaving town hidden in the boots of cars when sticks can no longer stand in for guns. The whole country has ceased to make sense to Kawsar – policewomen have become torturers, veterinarians doctors, teachers spies and children armed rebels.

Nurto is in the bathroom; the price of her not attending the student protest is that she has a free morning, and so far she has used it to paint her nails and apply henna to her hair.

The four walls of Kawsar's bedroom seem to close in a little each day. Holes in the roof let rainwater trail down the blue paint leaving ghostly tears, as if the room is mourning all the deaths it has witnessed. First, her mother had curled up into a small ball of pain and within days of moving from her own bungalow had become mute and helpless, dying with her eyes clenched as if she had wished it herself. Farah, at an august fifty-five years of age, had died within hours of complaining of chest pain, too quickly for the doctor to finish his shift at the hospital and attend to him; sweat pouring from his face and back, he clenched at his heart and arm and begged for water, cup after cup. Hodan had witnessed these deaths, her huge eyes picturing every detail as she hovered around Kawsar's legs, intermittently squeezing them as if to say 'be strong, *Hooyo*, be strong'. Kawsar had been strong but then her child had taken a knife and cored her.

The shock when Kawsar woke to an empty house and couldn't find Hodan in the orchard or courtyard was melded with relief that she had remembered a world existed beyond their walls. She waited happily until lunchtime for Hodan to return, expecting her to have left for the market to buy the day's supplies. When the sun passed its zenith and began to drop, Kawsar's mood sank with it. She asked the neighbours if they had seen her but they were ignorant of her whereabouts; she ran

182

to Dahabo's stall to see if Hodan had visited her but left disappointed. Returning home, she opened the wardrobe to discover a holdall had disappeared along with some of Hodan's clothes, and she realised that the falling night would find her alone in the house. Dahabo escorted her to the police station that same evening to report Hodan as missing, all the while assuring her that her daughter would be home by morning. Throughout that clear, full-moon night Kawsar had waited, ears pricked for footsteps, until the sun lit up neon lights in the slats of the shutters.

Hodan did not return for ninety-two days. She did not tell Kawsar or anyone else where she had been or what she had seen, but two weeks later she took a can of gasoline and a box of matches into the bathroom and set herself on fire. The image of her bald head, marbled skin, and grinning, skeletal face will never leave Kawsar. It was with anger that she had buried that husk when those accursed fluttering eyelids had finally stilled. What sin had she committed to deserve such punishment? Even if Hodan had become a whore selling her body in the street the humiliation could not have been greater. It was years later that Kawsar had learnt young girls were doing this to themselves nowadays, torching themselves in washrooms and courtyards before their lives had even begun.

She had given away all of Hodan's clothes and possessions, and most of the gold jewellery that Kawsar had collected for her marriage was sold and the money given to the orphanage. The sheets that still smelt of her body lotion were thrown out and replaced. The anger dissipated slowly over months but never left, burning under her like a bed of coals.

Kawsar wakes slowly from her drug-induced slumber and listens for Nurto's movements to fix the time of day. There is silence until Nurto slams open the door from orchard to kitchen and dumps the shopping on the floor. Kawsar hears her footsteps rushing to the wet room and then the roar of water and banging pipes as the water tank empties into the tap. Appearing later wrapped in a towel and dripping water from her nose and ears, Nurto shivers uncontrollably.

'Wrap yourself properly.' Kawsar throws a blanket to her.

Nurto scrunches the blanket in her hands and holds it to her chest 'They . . .' she says through chattering teeth.

'Who?'

'The soldiers . . . to see . . . so everyone could see them.'

'What do you mean? Who hurt you?' Kawsar shouts, already imagining Nurto stripped naked in the street.

'Not me, not me. Nomads.'

Kawsar falls back on her pillow slightly. 'In town?'

'They dumped eight dead men down by the market, I saw one with intestines hanging out of a hole in his stomach.' Nurto looks bilious and huddles on her mattress.

'Did no one come to claim the bodies?'

Nurto shakes her head.

Kawsar can imagine the discussions of the wives and

mothers of the nomads as they seek out the whereabouts of their loved ones, asking first the neighbours, then acquaintances and eventually the police. But what distances must those women contend with? Their little homes surrounded by nothing but mountains and rocks, each *reer* a planet of its own. She used to meet the men on the minibus to the *suuq*, carefully counting out the shillings of their discounted fare while exuding a pride that the townsmen had lost. The old turbaned men were often straight-backed and hawk-faced, with robes that fell off their delicate bones; they hadn't had to contend with the *Guddi* or curfew or forced parades, but now the regime had turned its attention to them too.

'Have a rest, let it pass from your mind,' Kawsar soothes. Each day there is another outrage and it frightens her to see Nurto's reaction.

After an hour Kawsar sends Nurto to Zahra's video hall to watch a Hindi film and to take her mind off what she has seen. She sits propped up in bed and cools herself with a black lacquered fan that Farah had given her once, strands of her fine hair stirring in its draught. The air outside is heavy, still, static with compressed electricity. The *Gu* rains are approaching, belatedly making their way from the rainforests of Congo over the highlands of Ethiopia to fall on the parched, burnt land of Somalia. The sun up beyond the mauve clouds is hidden away but its heat is still capable of drawing sweat from the creases in Kawsar's skin.

The rainstorms so far have been half-hearted, rushing

away just as they start; when the real rains come they are relentless, pouring through the roof and flooding the streets until it appears as though the bungalows are at sea. They are a manifestation of a year's worth of prayers, a deluge of nomad's wishes. Only such a violent country could deserve such violent rain; it doesn't dapple against waxy leaves, it churns up the earth like artillery, destroying roads in a few hours. Children are sometimes swept along with the torrent, their bodies found miles away alongside drowned cows and mangled bicycles. From desperate drought to desperate flood, it seems as if Somalis can only expect disaster.

The flood she had seen in the far south in the sixties had seemed like divine punishment: water deep enough to submerge palm trees, minarets, telegraph poles, and within it swam crocodiles, water snakes, whole families of disgruntled hippos. She recalls standing on Farah's Land Rover on a hill looking down on villages where maybe only one or two straw roofs were above the water, men, women, children marooned on them. All across the agricultural areas fed by the Juba and Shebelle the scene was repeated, a year's harvest rotting underneath the invisible soil. It was the first time the young country had needed to beg the former colonial rulers, and since then the government hasn't stopped asking; from floods to famines to tractors and X-ray machines, prayer mats turned to the west and knees bent in supplication.

Ever since the Italians and British had gone, the country had seemed besieged by difficulties, whether natural, economic or political. The Europeans must have left a bone-deep curse as they were departing, raising long-dead *jinns* like Oodweyne in their wake to turn everything to sand and waste. Kawsar remembers meeting him briefly in Mogadishu while he was still a junior officer and Farah was Deputy District Commissioner of Baidoa, and he had been completely ordinary, no sense of promise or even malice about him, balding at a young age – that was the only thing she noticed about him. How time plays its jokes. It raises dwarves and hobbles giants – how else could Farah be in the ground and Oodweyne on a throne? He had slipped into power almost unseen following the assassination of the last elected president and his voice when it appeared on the radio was always ominous to her; it took her back to those five days in sixty-nine after the President had been shot dead by his bodyguard and Radio Hargeisa broadcasted Qu'ranic recitations non-stop, the schools and offices closed in mourning while she recovered in bed from one of her miscarriages.

The surprise she had felt on the sixth day when at nine a.m. a jaunty announcement declared a military coup and a new name for the country, the Somali Democratic Republic, had never left her but lay at the bottom of all the other bewildering events that succeeded it: the imprisonment of the Prime Minister, the abolishment of both parliament and constitution, the takeover of the country by the Supreme Revolutionary Council with Oodweyne as its chairman. Farah had been one of the few to voice his opposition; he called the new leaders 'cuckoos' and cut off contact with friends who said they preferred military rule to the chaos of democracy. Kawsar, a typical woman in Farah's eyes, just wanted peace and for the situation to be as stable as possible.

The junta introduced a Somali alphabet, organised volunteers to build schools, hospitals, roads, repair the stadium in Hargeisa, told people to forget their clan names and call each other comrade. Then they lost the war and revealed their true nature. She wishes she could speak to Farah and tell him, 'You were right, I admit it, they're intolerable,' but that would mean him seeing how everything had fallen apart in his absence: Hodan gone, his wife old and crippled, the house dirty and decayed, his old friends either dead, in jail or lost to *qat* and alcohol. The resistance that he had called for was now led by children, and in the lapsed time the regime had grown such deep roots, like the weeds in the ditch, that she feared everything would have to be torn up to remove it.

The signal from Radio NFM is suddenly stronger, the voices crisp in the night air; no longer are they ghosts speaking from a world beyond, their snappy Hargeisa accents clear and confident. Kawsar turns down the volume until they are barely audible. Nurto is dressed in one of Kawsar's old floral nightgowns, a chaste long-sleeved thing that becomes completely transparent when the light is behind it; Farah had bought it for Kawsar and she imagines his eyes consuming her body the way hers now consume Nurto's.

There is a different atmosphere at night now; they are like roommates rather than mistress and servant Comfortable in each other's smells and habits, they don't turn their backs on one another anymore. They foray into small intimacies, nibbling away at the distance that yawns between their ages and circumstances. What Kawsar really wants to know is if Nurto has any plans to marry soon. The girl seems ready, has the small pimples that teenage girls get when their bodies are ripe for love, her sighs at night heavy with lonesomeness.

'Did you hear any more from your American friend?' Kawsar asks after the radio programme has slipped into static, empty air.

'No, he is at Saba'ad taking pictures of the refugees. I haven't seen him in weeks.'

'Are you interested in him?'

Nurto turns her face away. 'I don't think he is serious.'

'He will return to his own country, you shouldn't let him get under your skin, you are better off with someone of your own culture and language.'

'What was your husband like?'

'Clever, tall, stubborn, honest, always trying to learn something . . .'

Nurto cuts her off. 'Was he rich?'

'He worked hard and became rich, those wardrobes are full of the clothes he bought me.'

'Hmm. That's the kind of life I want.'

'It's certainly good for a while, but shopping is not enough to build a life on.'

'Those women in the *suuq* with maids behind them carrying their bags seem happy to me.'

'Of course, you expect them to tell you about their jealousy of a second wife or their worry that they will never deliver a son for their husbands.'

'That can all happen if you're as poor as mud. I'd rather have worries like that with cash in my pocket than have ten sons and nothing to give them but black tea.'

'Be careful what you say, God is always listening and he will test you.'

'Let him test me with money, that's a test I will happily take.'

'Did you only have black tea at home?'

'Sometimes, when Mother was sick. It got better when we were pulled out of school and each had jobs.'

Kawsar has never known that kind of life. The only hunger pangs she felt were self-inflicted, when her mind turned away from food to focus on other concerns; she enjoyed the pleasurable light-headedness she found in an empty stomach, but maybe half of that pleasure was knowing that a fully stocked kitchen was only a few steps away. From childhood onwards her meals appeared each day at the same time to demand her attention and she fought stubbornly against their tyranny. She ate what she wanted and only when she wanted it. When street boys begged at her mother's door, she would thrust her plate out and offer them the contents as if *she* could live on air alone.

'How did *Aabbo* die?' she asks Nurto.

'How does anyone die? He became sick and a few weeks later died in his bed.'

'And that was when you stopped going to school?'

'No, we went for a little longer but then *Hooyo* couldn't cope anymore.'

An idea came to Kawsar as if a cloud had cleared. 'Nurto, if you want to go to school, I can help.'

'Oh no . . .'

'Or you could have someone come here and teach you. You have too much free time in the day and you should use it.'

'Me and school are finished. I can read as much as I need to; the only school I would like to attend is beauty school.'

'What would you learn there? How to put kohl on someone?'

'You learn everything – make-up, hairdressing, henna-painting, hair removal.'

'How would that help you?'

Nurto gave her look as if she was blind. 'I could open my own business!'

'Are people really willing to pay for someone to put lipstick on their own face.'

'For weddings and things, of course, you go to an expert.'

'Times have certainly changed.'

'They have,' Nurto replies firmly.

'And you could make a living doing that?'

'Yes, I think so.'

'So you want to go to this beauty school?'

'If it was possible . . .'

'You should sign up then, I will pay the fees.'

'*Wallahi?*'

'Yes.'

Nurto rushes to her feet and kisses Kawsar's forehead. 'God brought me to you.'

Kawsar closes her eyes in embarrassment, the kisses making her skin sing.

The moon is full and bright outside, shining like a searchlight over the neighbourhood, the wind rustling through the trees. Kawsar is open-eyed, awoken by her own laughter; the sensations she has in her dreams are so real, but when she tries to remember their substance she can't. The images have the watery, unreal quality of the old films screened outside by Radio Hargeisa on long-gone summer evenings. They are washed out and rippling, the voices uneven as if spoken by men drowning in air.

The room glitters. A girl similar in height and appearance to Nurto but with the speed of a sand devil has swept through, a cloth in each of her eight hands, leaving not even one mote of dust or stray hair behind. The sheets are laundered properly and piled tidily on the chair, all the dirty cups and glasses collected, the grime that gathered in every crevice has been gouged out, windowsills swept clear of dead flies and mosquitoes, the floor washed with Dettol, the light bulb above polished until the glass gleams. Every surface chimes with forgotten cleanliness. The air in Kawsar's nostrils is sharp and new, the small space around her expanded tenfold.

Two donkey drivers rush past the window behind her, speaking their secret language to their animals, whips flicking as their charges attempt a gallop but struggle with heavy loads of raw goat and mutton. A buzzing cloud of flies chases after them, as do the curses of the old man from New York who lives half the year in a bungalow next to the hotel.

'Take your filth somewhere else! Find another street to cut through with that tripe,' he yells.

'*Whodead*! *Whodead*!' they reply, spitting the nickname they have given him back in his face.

Nurto gently pushes open the door and pokes her head through, a bright smile radiating from her face. 'Can I make you a cup of tea? Would you like coffee? I bought fresh beans today, they're already roasting.'

This is the first time she has offered Kawsar coffee. 'Yes, but what has come over you?'

'Everything is going to change, Kawsar, how can I not be excited? I enrolled at beauty school today. Should I bake a cake? It will be nice with coffee.'

'As you wish.' Kawsar smiles softly. It will take the poor girl hours to bake a cake on the charcoal stove but it wouldn't hurt her to try.

'Are you comfortable? Warm enough?'

Kawsar raises her hand in satisfaction. 'Did you buy the painkillers this morning?'

Nurto disappears into the kitchen for a moment and then returns with a brown paper bag. 'Here they are. I bought you two packets so you don't run out so quickly.' She places them gently on the bedside table.

'Good girl.'

'Do you mind if I go over to the video hall later?'

'No, what are they showing?'

'A Hindi film, an old one called *Pakeezah*. I've seen it ten times before.'

'I know it, the one with the dancing girl who meets a man on the train. I thought it would be too old-fashioned for you.'

'There isn't a Hindi film that I haven't seen, fifties, sixties, seventies, all of them. My father, God rest his soul, worked in the cinema before it closed down and he would let me sit in the projection room with him.'

'You would make a good actress; your face is never still.'

Nurto smiles. 'I think I would be a great actress. I just need to get out of here and then I can do whatever I please.'

The clock prods time onwards in the silence, the weight of Nurto's yearning sagging the mattress when she rises.

A scent tickles Kawsar's nose and excites a sneeze.

'Allah!' Nurto races barefoot to the kitchen as the smell of burnt coffee beans grows stronger.

By four p.m. the curfew is firmly in place and, as if the sun is also under its tyranny, the sky darkens prematurely, menacing clouds hiding the moon and stars that have rushed into position. The blacked-out town seems nothing more than a stage set for the soldiers to swagger about in, the bungalow a cave beyond which there are bears and monsters and mysterious shrieks, and Kawsar and Nurto huddle like children from fear of what the darkness might bring. Nurto returned punctually from the video hall, dragged her mattress near and sits with her back against the bedframe, her hair only a few inches from Kawsar's fingers, the curls at the nape of her neck fine and red in the paraffin light.

The radio is on at the lowest volume, and the government station speaks of attempts to stop desertification around the Banaadir area, genteel visits by the President to foreign potentates, the tidy, clockwork mechanisms of a state at peace; the rebel channel, Radio NFM, reports the events in a different country, one in which water reservoirs are destroyed, foreign weapons used on unarmed nomads and prisons attacked to release the innocent. It is hard to imagine either place; from her bed all Kawsar can believe is that there is a dark, empty street outside, a few bungalows and a world that has aged, decayed and will soon end.

Kawsar wakes the next morning with a start as the door shakes in its frame, bang bang bang, a pause, then another bang bang bang, Nurto shoots up from her mattress and stands in the middle of the room, dazed, waiting for instruction. The heavy knocks on the door continue.

Trembling a little, Kawsar tightens her head cloth and gestures for Nurto to open it.

Hiding behind the door, Nurto turns all the locks and pulls it open slowly.

Dahabo pushes it fully open and enters.

'What are you trying to do? Scare us to death? We thought you were the back-breakers,' Kawsar shouts.

'Well, if you won't open the door to me, I have to do what I can.' She strides over to Kawsar and pulls the blankets roughly off her. 'You're coming with me. There is a car waiting outside to take us to Mogadishu, from there we will fly to Jeddah.'

Kawsar flings the blankets back over her legs. 'You must be crazy!'

Dahabo pulls the blankets down again. 'I have delayed everyone's departure trying to get an exit visa for you, Kawsar. Don't make a fool of me.'

Kawsar leaves the blankets at her feet and folds her arms tightly like a little girl being chastised. 'Who gave you my passport?'

'Who do you think?' She nods her head towards Nurto who is hiding in the corner. 'Believe me when I tell you it is time to leave. If you could get up and walk you would see all the soldiers outside, the half-empty market. Bring what we can't replace later and let's go.' She takes Kawsar's hand and gently tugs her forward.

Kawsar wriggles her fingers out of her grip and folds her arms again. 'No one is keeping you behind, Dahabo. Go if you want.' Her heart is racing but her mind feels numb, unable to cogitate at all; her warm bed seems the only safe place to cling to.

'In the name of God!' screams Dahabo. 'When will you change? When will you lose your damned pride and vanity and stubbornness? Am I supposed to beg you to save your own life? When are you going to change? When are you going to change? Look at you! Look at how you're living! You want to be left behind like this? Because she won't save you.'

'I don't expect her to. Nurto, go and put the kettle on.'

Nurto scuttles to the kitchen.

Dahabo twirls around the room looking for things to pack on Kawsar's behalf. She opens the wardrobe and throws things out randomly. 'Where do you keep your photographs? What about your wedding gold?'

A car horn beeps from outside.

'They are waiting, Kawsar! This isn't the time to play your games.'

'Leave it alone, you are making a mess, Dahabo. I'm not going with you. Listen, turn around. Listen to me!'

Dahabo finally turns around and reveals her watery, bloodshot eyes. 'You are the one deserting me, Kawsar, not the other way around. I will carry you out on my back if you let me.'

'I know you will, but I don't want you to.'

'So you're just going to die here?'

'I will live out my life in my own home, Dahabo. There is no tragedy in that.'

Dahabo begins to sob for the first time in front of her – terrible, awkward cries that catch in her throat.

Kawsar unwraps her arms and holds them out.

Dahabo walks unsteadily to her and then wraps her arms around Kawsar's neck.

'I am sorry for how I have treated you in the last few weeks. I didn't want to lose you. Go with your children, Dahabo, and put your feet up and don't think about anyone else anymore, you deserve every good thing.'

Dahabo's tears seep through Kawsar's scarf and onto her skin.

'Remember when your mother brought you over to my house for the first time and we hid her cloth and her mop and her detergents on the roof and she spent the whole afternoon either looking for them or chasing us. I thought I had met my own spirit in another body.'

'Stop it, stop it.' Dahabo pulls away, allergic to outpourings of emotion. 'So you will not come with me?'

The car horn sounds again, this time longer and more irritably.

'No.'

Dahabo nods. 'I accept your decision but I will never stop thinking about you.'

'And me you.' Kawsar holds Dahabo's head and kisses her hard on each cheek and then her forehead. '*Nabadgelyo*, witch.'

'*Nabaddiino*, hag.'

* * *

The day passes in a blur. Kawsar feels drugged, numb, as if she has just had surgery, an amputation. She can still smell Dahabo's scent on her clothes, can feel her presence nearby, but she is already on the road, on the one decent tarmac strip that leads to Mogadishu. She doesn't cry but just stares at the door, wondering if some strange event might bring her back, and in the evening takes enough painkillers to force sleep.

Deep in the night Kawsar opens her eyes. Something isn't right. The stray dogs are quiet; usually they bay and yowl while tearing apart the rubbish dumped along the road- side. She can't even hear the rumble of water tankers driving along Airport Road. The soldiers are not banging on any doors.

She looks over at Nurto on her mattress, her legs stretched out over the cement floor, her head hidden under the blankets. Kawsar opens her mouth to call her name and ask that she look out of the window but resists the urge. She will stay awake herself and keep an eye on the window above her bed.

Pressing a hand to the regular bouncing beat in her ribs, she remembers how her father, mother and husband all succumbed to their weak hearts. Farah took his last breath in this very bed, his skin clammy, his mouth agape, his eyes bulging out of their sockets. Deep within the pillow was his sweat, that from his life and from his dying, commingling with hers. Her own organs appear to be at war with her now; her urine when it dribbles out into the bedpan is as dark as tea and the solid waste is sheathed in mucus and blood. Only her heart seems distant from this skirmishing, its beating muted but insistent; it has suffered so many shocks that its exterior has thickened, padding it like gauze from further hurt. When the end comes her heart will be the strongest part of her, trying to drag the rest along like a mule with its load. She wishes she could give it a sugar cube and say, 'Well done, you have served me well, but it's time to retire now.'

Drifting between wakefulness and sleep, Kawsar sees herself pulling the bolt of the wooden door leading from her austere kitchen into the walled orchard. The screws in the upper door hinge have worked themselves loose and Kawsar has to lift the door by the handle for it to swing open. She hears a sigh, whether it is her own or the orchard's she cannot tell. Beyond the kitchen door awaits her Eden: the trees, plants and fruits of her labour, a small patch of earth that she has ruled benevolently. Branches stretch from one end of the crumbling mud wall to the other, creating a net of leaves sifting sunshine and moonlight.

She takes a deep breath and sucks in the scent that exudes from these children of hers: the tamarind, guava, pomegranate, bougainvillea and jasmine that she's dreamed into life. If her neighbourhood with its old bungalows and wide streets made of fine, gold sand seems unlike anywhere else in Hargeisa, she doubts there is anywhere like her orchard in the world. It is a place in which time moves differently; it whooshes backwards to her youth rather than plods forward to her end. Within these four walls there is nothing to tell her she isn't a young girl biding time in the fresh air until her laden mother returns to drop the day's shopping onto the kitchen floor. Here, her joints are supple, her spine straight, her thoughts as clear and wide as the horizon. She will leave arrangements to be buried under this mica-flecked soil, where she's certain she will still be able to feel the rain on her bones, as warm and slick as blood. Her mind stumbles forward, scouting for the spot for her grave. Somewhere quiet and unobtrusive that won't spoil the view over the orchard.

She creeps over to the far left corner where the tamarind tree stands like a woman shaking her hair in the breeze, weaver-bird nests dangling from the top branches; it provides both shade and birdsong. Beneath the tree is a scrappy patch of wild grass, dry and yellow, and she tears at it, not wanting something so untidy on her grave. She stretches out between tamarind and back wall and, as if preordained, the length is perfect, like a good shoe with a little room beyond the toes. The earth is busy beneath, seething with insect life, whole cities, whole tribes reproducing, breathing, dying in a timeless panic. What will they think of her when she falls into their world? A heavy, dumb, dark intrusion? Or manna thrown down by anonymous benevolence? More likely there will be no thought, just the desire to get to the eyes, the tongue and the other succulents before something else does. Kawsar's skin prickles at the idea of tiny mouths sucking and nibbling at her, her ancient remains nursing strange bodies.

'Let it come. Let it all come,' she murmurs.

Waking while the sky is pink and still bejewelled, she prays that Dahabo has reached the capital safely and that she is not afraid when she boards the plane to Jeddah. Neither of them has ever flown before and it seems incongruous, ridiculous to fling themselves into the sky at this age. Kawsar lies back on her pillow and notices the bed gently vibrating underneath her; she enjoys the sensation at first, thinking it is a figment of her imagination, but then the shaking becomes more violent, grinding her bones against the bedframe. The walls of the bungalow seem to moan before they too start to shake, clanking the tin roof above and sending the framed textiles to the floor.

'What's happening, Nurto? Is it an earthquake?'

Nurto tries to spring out from her mattress but her legs become entangled in the sheets; she rips the blankets off and throws them to the floor. She is at the front window in seconds.

'Tanks. The street is full of tanks and soldiers.'

'Allah, it's started.'

The turrets on the tanks adjust into position, whirring like giant cicadas, before clicking into place. Then they hear the first distant gunshots of the war, a feeble ping like that of popcorn jumping off the pan, but followed by screams and wailing.

Nurto ducks her head below the window. 'They have gone into Maryam's house.'

Kawsar takes a deep breath, tries to think of something to say to calm Nurto, but her mind is blank. Terror burns her thoughts as they form.

Nurto inches her head back up to the corner of the window. 'They have dragged her out into the street.'

Kawsar watches her as the minutes drag by: Nurto seems transfixed, perfectly still apart from the fine strands of her hair stirring in the breeze.

A burst of automatic fire clatters out and Nurto turns around and crumples onto the floor, her knees pressed against her chest, her head in her arms. The soldiers shout to each other in a rapid dialect that Kawsar barely understands. They sound confused, overwhelmed by the magnitude of what they are doing. Kawsar picks out a few phrases: 'When is the PM gun going to arrive?'; 'Hassan, which house next?'

'She's dead. I have to go see if *Hooyo* and the children are safe.' Nurto stands up, avoiding Kawsar's eyes, slowly straightening her bed sheets and folding blankets.

'Please bring me a jug of water, a cup, painkillers, the leftover *canjeero* and the radio,' Kawsar replies, suddenly swept by a wave of calm.

Nurto shoves the table closer to Kawsar's bed and neatly organises the items on top. She has filled the plastic jug till it is nearly brimming over and balances it delicately as she carries it from the kitchen.

'Poor Maryam.'

Nurto shakes her head but doesn't reply.

'Take this.' Kawsar removes a roll of notes from under her pillow.

Nurto kisses the back of Kawsar's hand as she takes the money. No tears come to their eyes. She wedges a chair under the handle of the front door, picks up her canvas bag full of clothes and toiletries, and leaves through the back door in the kitchen. Kawsar knows that she is brave enough to climb over the high orchard wall. She regrets the shards of glass she has embedded along the top to deter thieves. Nurto, bleeding or not, will have to creep through the bushes and farms beside the ditch until she reaches her family's shack in north Hargeisa.

The tanks start to fire, a blast of heat accompanies every mortar. Kawsar puts her fingers in her ears but the rattle penetrates her skull. A plume of dust billows in from the windows, carpeting everything in plaster and sand. Kawsar stretches a hand over the jug but still the water is contaminated.

The tanks blow their way down the street cloaked in a white pall of smoke. Kawsar props herself up on her elbows and looks through the side window. Her neighbours try to flee, hidden in a haze of cement dust, but bright sandals and dresses give them away and the soldiers drop to their knees and shoot at the ghostly figures. Overhead there is the groan of a plane's engines and then sweeping down from the direction of the airport she sees a MIG with the Somali flag on each of its wings. Kawsar feels the air swarm about her and steal the breath from her lungs as missiles peel off the clanging tin roofs of the neighbourhood.

She collapses back onto the bed and pulls a blanket over her face, fearing that a bomb will explode through her roof in a matter of seconds. Both she and Guryo Samo have reached the end of their time; the soldiers will return the street to the desert, unplug the stars, shoot the dogs and extinguish the sun in a well.

FILSAN

Filsan spends her days in Hargeisa but the nights in the city she misses so much that she wakes with its spicy marine scent in her hair. Mogadishu the beautiful – your white-turbaned mosques, baskets of anchovies as bright as mercury, jazz and shuffling feet, bird-boned servant girls with slow smiles, the blind white of your homes against the sapphire blue of the ocean – you are missed, her dreams seem to say. The memories cleave to her ribs like barnacles. She feels an exile but doesn't understand what keeps her here: ambition, a desire for change, a need to escape from her father – it doesn't seem enough to make her stay away.

Filsan is alone, untouched, forgotten. She opens her eyes with her hand on her stomach, imagining the hand is someone else's. There is no use shaving her underarms, legs or privates because there is no one to see them; only her own fingertips run along her thighs. Once upon a time men had called for her and made their intentions known to her father, but he had ridiculed them, and she too had nothing but contempt for their preening flattery; they had no interest or knowledge of her as a human being, just that she was his daughter. She wanted someone who wouldn't ask his permission but would strip him down to the old, insignificant man that he was, who would just take her away, but it was becoming too late for anyone to want to spirit her anywhere; things like that happened to seventeen-year-old girls, not women with frown lines deepening on their foreheads.

Filsan rises and takes her uniform from the peg on the door; she is up ten minutes before the alarm but doesn't want to remain with her thoughts, simultaneously mulling over everything and nothing. She pulls her tunic over her head and her trousers over her legs. A quick visit to the bathroom and then she is beside the stove in the communal kitchen, the wall above her blackened with soot, the smell of meat and ghee still in the air from the previous night. Water boils in her saucepan, tea leaves, cardamom pods and cloves shivering on the surface; as it's about to bubble over she grabs the handle and pours just enough to fill her enamel cup. She tips in three spoonfuls of sugar and then washes and dries her saucepan before locking it away in her cupboard. She is naturally untrusting, but has become obsessive about securing her possessions in these barracks; the other women have no shame in stealing underwear from the clothesline, dishes from the kitchen, and soap from the sink. Their rations are reduced not by rats in the storeroom but by fellow soldiers who cut into the rice sacks or tap holes into the vats of oil. Filsan wishes she could report the culprits, but they are hidden behind a culture of venality; in the local police stations wealthy prisoners are allowed to 'rent' a cell, paying the guards to let them spend their days free and only returning at night for a snooze. They have no concern for the country or the revolution; it is simply a case of what they can get for themselves.

She drinks the tea immediately, its heat scorching her throat in a way she finds pleasant. This is the entirety of her breakfast. She has never been taught to cook; her father preferred her to concentrate on her studies and leave the domestic work to the maids, but now she wishes that she could rustle something up rather than depending on take-out food. Looking around the dark kitchen and hearing the gurgle of her stomach, Filsan feels like an orphaned child rather than just a motherless one. Back home, her housekeeper Intisaar would have covered the dining table with a vinyl sheet decorated with small yellow flowers and laid out a flask of black tea; a jug of orange juice; a fruit salad of mangoes, papayas and bananas; a plateful of *laxoox* hidden under a domed fly guard; and if her father had requested it the night before, scrambled eggs and lamb kidneys.

The other women – there are about fifty all together in the barracks – drift into the kitchen while Filsan nurses her empty cup and gazes at the view beyond the window, a bare yard crisscrossed by poles and clotheslines in the foreground with the two domes of the central mosque behind. Breeze blocks abandoned when the nearly completed hotel was commandeered by the military form another kind of barracks for cooing pigeons beneath the window. She ignores her comrades as they ignore her, but what would she say to them if she could? She would tell them that she has never been good at making friends, that Intisaar's children had seemed kind but had not been allowed inside the house by her father, that the neighbourhood kids had scorned her, that she found it easier to talk to her father's friends, that her face was closed because she didn't know how to open it. Silence takes the place of all those words and her loneliness remains as dense and close as a shadow.

She rinses her cup, locks it away and returns to her room to make the bed before departing for the offices of the Mobile Military Court. The scheduled assignment to the Regional Security Council had vanished the minute she had been thrown out of Haaruun's car, and instead she was told to investigate returned sailors and café owners suspected of anti-revolutionary activities. She hears laughter from the kitchen as she turns the handle to her room and knows it is aimed at her; it is hard to tell whether her comrades find it ridiculous that she would reject Haaruun, or if it is just funny to them that anyone would want her.

As she enters and bends down to pick up a sock, she is overwhelmed by an urge to wail, her blood suddenly darkening with self-loathing, with anger that her life should be so small and inconsequential, that this two-metre-by-two-metre cell should be the span of her world. Her father had locked her away, had told her she wouldn't regret the decisions he had made for her, that she would be a new kind of woman with the same abilities and opportunities as any man, but instead she lives the celibate, sterile, quiet existence of a nun, growing nothing but grey hairs. All her life she has been left to gather dust, as unseen as a picture on the wall, and to wail and roar and strike out sometimes seems the only way she will ever be heard.

The offices of the Mobile Military Court are in an old colonial complex. The brick chimney jutting out from one of the rooftops is something she had not seen in Mogadishu, where the weather was never less than sultry; here the wind is so cold and fierce at times that it is not hard to imagine an Englishman dozing by a fire with a long-haired dog at his feet. In her Spartan office there are just two desks, one for Captain Yasin and a small, scratched one for her, Corporal Adan Ali. They coordinate a string of bureaus across north-western Somalia which, since the fierce NFM rebel attacks on Sheikh and Burao were put down in 1984, have jurisdiction over civilians as well as military personnel. On her desk is a multi-coloured pile of reports, warrants and court transcripts; her eyes are immediately drawn to the two green documents that represent two more death sentences handed down by Colonel Magan, court

prosecutor and judge. The Colonel works in an adjacent
building and rarely visits them, but his brutality comes
across clearly in the red-inked words he leaves on the
margins of her transcripts: 'He is a buffoon and liar';
'Why haven't we got rid of this one yet?'; or more
commonly, 'Track down his friends'. He has already sent
more to their deaths this year than the National Security
Service or Regional Security Council. It is like sitting in
the middle of a spider's web, pulling in tendrils to see
where flies have been caught, everyone related by clan or
by marriage, one rebel leading to dozens more and
requiring more ink for her typewriter.

She is an office worker within the military, neither
noticed nor commended by the gold-braided men above
her, and it galls her that despite two years of enlistment
in the Women's Auxiliary Corps and five years working
for the green-uniformed enforcers of the regime, the
Victory Pioneers, her chief tasks are still those of a secre-
tary. Had her father been dreaming or lying when he told
her that she would make the ground shake in Hargeisa?
Had he been drunk? Or just desperate to remove her
from Mogadishu in case the suspicion around him
became something more tangible and sinister? In the
notes sent from the agents to her desk she sees how difficult it is to interpret someone's actions, intentions, words;
if she had to create a dossier on her own unknowable
father, where would she even begin? He had shown her
both tenderness and contempt, cruelty and honour, a
glimpse of the world through the bars of his love. She

sees him now pacing the flat roof of their three-storey villa in Mogadishu, a strip of the Indian Ocean visible between two slender minarets, watching over the neighbourhood with binoculars, scanning east and west for the spies he believes watch him.

Captain Yasin arrives, tall and elegant in his black beret. With just the two of them in the office she cannot help but watch him all day: his regular strolls around the office and into the corridor, the private calls he makes on the only telephone line in their department, the menthol cigarette butts slowly filling his dark glass ashtray, the tin of mints he rattles absent-mindedly when frowning over some problem.

Filsan stands up and salutes him but he smiles and holds up his hands, palms outward.

'Now don't get too excited, Miss Corporal, but I spoke to Major Adow a few days ago and he asked me if I could recommend an impressive graduate to go on a mission to educate those troublesome nomads at the border. I looked high and low and then I remembered you, crouched over your little desk. Such efficiency! Such honesty!'

Filsan looks up at him with both contempt and desire.

'To Birjeeh with you, on the double!' He points dramatically to the door and she laughs despite herself. As she leaves the room, his eyes track her with an interest she doesn't find unwelcome.

Birjeeh Military HQ has the unexpected presence of an enchanted castle perched on a barren hill, partially hidden behind high crenellated walls with watchtowers; the wide arched entrance only needs a portcullis and moat to finish the picture. Filsan has escorted prisoners to the concrete armoury that now functions as a detention room, but can imagine long-forgotten prisoners with scraggly beards hidden in secret underground cells.

The logistics officer, Lieutenant Hashi, ushers her to the Major's office with a scowl on his tight, foxlike face, already aggravated by something.

The room is crowded with thirty muscular commandos from the locally garrisoned 26th Infantry Division. They stand in a crescent shape around Major Adow, but between their bodies she can see snatches of the brown, khaki and gold of his jacket, a black pen held between his fingers like a wand.

'Come closer, Comrades,' he says before standing up. Filsan notices that his height remains the same.

Lieutenant Hashi unrolls a map and pins its corners to the felt board behind the desk. It shows the north-western region of Somalia in minute detail: waterholes, reservoirs, dry riverbeds, dirt tracks. There are three blue circles on the map over villages near the Ethiopian border; enclosing the blue circles are red semicircles.

Major Adow points his pen at each blue circle and names it in turn. 'Salahley, Baha Dhamal, Ina Guuhaa. We have solid intelligence that NFM rebels are fed, watered and sheltered in these villages. Ever since the secessionists moved their headquarters from London to Ethiopia they have been getting bolder and bolder, and it is places like these that allow them to think they stand a chance in hell of defeating us.'

Filsan stands at armpit height to the soldiers; she finds herself enjoying their smell, the musk of their sweat mixed with hair and gun oil.

Lieutenant Hashi catches her gaze, his bloodshot stare intended to intimidate her, but it is nothing in comparison to her father's.

'You are charged with demolishing the water reservoirs of Salahley. They have been building one every year for more than ten years now and have given some over to the rebels to use. Corporal Adan Ali! Where are you, my girl?' Major Adow shouts.

Filsan pushes forward until she is a metre away from the desk.

'It is your duty to communicate our anger and ensure that it is understood that further punitive measures can and will be enforced. We need an educated comrade who can articulate the principles of the revolution. That's you, isn't it?'

'Yes, Major,' replies Filsan quickly.

'They will have water trucked in monthly and they can use their traditional wells.'

'I will tell them, sir.'

'The exact date and time of the operation will be confirmed by Lieutenant Hashi. Baha Dhamal and Ina Guuhaa will be dealt with by the Fourth and Eighteenth Sectors simultaneously. Are there any questions?'

The soldiers shift nervously but don't reply. Filsan has

an urge to speak but fears appearing too arrogant. She clears her throat and all faces turn to her. 'Will we be taking prisoners?' she almost whispers.

Major Adow smiles broadly, the same kind of smile he would give a dog riding a bicycle. 'Good question, *Jaalle*. We have yet to confirm that detail but well done for speaking up.'

Filsan sees the other soldiers smiling condescendingly, even though they were too cowardly to raise their own voices.

Hashi gestures to his watch and Major Adow nods. 'Comrades, let us end this meeting.' He raises his fist in the air and bellows, 'Victory for the Party. Victory for the National Army. Death and defeat to the rebels.'

Filsan shouts the slogan in unison with the other soldiers, pumping her fist in the air.

Filsan's eyes snap open. Damp sheets twist themselves around her legs. Fragments of songs circle her mind, love songs that she knows the surface meaning of but not the deepdown; in the pitch black they sound taunting and nightmarish. The Salahley operation will be her first in the field, the first time she has left Hargeisa since arriving, and excitement prevents her closing her eyes for long. She is living a soldier's life while her father sits in front of the television watching Egyptian soap operas.

The call comes two days later. They are scheduled to leave Hargeisa at five in the morning and arrive in

Salahley by nine if they drive at full speed. The truck will pick them up at Birjeeh and then head for the west. Filsan had hoped that her period would wait until after the operation, but as if to spite her it comes early, blanching her face and nearly doubling her over with cramps. She gulps back black tea after black tea and avoids eating anything that might worsen her nausea, but by the morning of the attack she is curled up, sobbing at how diminished she feels. Taking a deep breath she unfurls her limbs and forces herself through her morning routine. She arrives at Birjeeh before the others, the sky still dark but birds flapping and shaking each other awake in the branches. The compound looks even more imposing now, its walls blending into the darkness beyond to form a citadel of ether and stone.

The unit of thirty men and Filsan leave Birjeeh in a convoy of four large trucks of the type the locals call 'the fates' because of their involvement in dozens of fatal traffic accidents. Filsan rides in the passenger seat of the first truck, the pain in her abdomen and back lulled by the gentle reverberations of the engine. The driver had held out his arm as she struggled to clamber into the tall vehicle, but apart from that there is no exchange between them.

'Morning, Corporal.' Lieutenant Afrah twists his neck into the cab from the bench behind.

'Good morning, sir.' Filsan salutes awkwardly. The Lieutenant has the strange-coloured eyes that some Somalis possess, brown around the pupil with a thick halo of blue as if he is going blind.

'Are you nervous?' He smiles and reveals the sweet gap between his teeth.

'No, I just want to do a decent job.'

'It will be easy, in and out before the engine's even cooled. I have a rifle here for you, an FAL automatic. The recoil isn't so bad on them, better for you than the Kalashnikov. Major Adow said you have had arms training?'

'With the Women's Auxiliary Corps, but that was some time ago. I don't know . . .'

'You won't need it; it will just be a deterrent if there are any troublemakers in the village.'

'Yes, Lieutenant.' Filsan takes it from him; the stock is relatively short while the barrel scrapes the roof of the lorry. She holds it across her chest with the strap over her back; she never hit the targets well during practice in Mogadishu but it feels good to hold a rifle again; a gun makes a soldier even out of a woman.

She presses the cold butt against her stomach and leans back, eavesdropping on the muttered conversation between two commandos just behind her. They are talking about a woman one of them has had sex with in a way that makes the woman sound like some kind of animal he has caught and killed.

They sail through the last urban checkpoint and leave the messy, compacted town to shrink and disappear in the rear-view mirror. A rim of light is developing all around them, as blotchy and bright as overexposed film, the horizon broken up by lopsided pyramids of granite.

She has seen a landscape like this only once before, as a fourteen-year-old on her way to Dhusamareb during the Somali Literacy Campaign. *'Haddaad taqaan bar, haddaanad aqoon baro*. If you know it, teach it, if you don't know it, learn it' had been the slogan, all the schools, colleges, universities emptied of students and professors for seven months so they could be sent to fight against illiteracy in every town, village and encampment. Radio Mogadishu broadcasters described the conflict in the most passionate terms: the weapons were pens, books, chalks and blackboards, the heroes simple teachers and teenagers who gallantly battled ignorance throughout the country. Filsan had set out from Twenty-first October Square in Mogadishu during *Eid* in August 1974. The President had delivered a magnificent speech and she could still recite parts of it: 'The battle you engage in with your forces has more honour than the ordinary one, and has more value than anything you have known.' He was right; if she could go back to that time she would. She missed living with the blacksmith's family, teaching in the mornings and late afternoons, learning country songs and dances from the daughters, sitting by the stream at dusk, drinking milk straight from the cow. The whole campaign had been paid for by civilian donations, and even as a fourteen-year-old she had been treated with respect because she could read and they couldn't. She wrote down the poems of old men in the new Somali script and they folded her scribblings and tucked them into their clothes like talismans. It was a dreamtime – they were full of love for the country and one another; now there seemed to be only rebels and thieves and soldiers fighting each other. She felt that she was the last one to still believe in that old Somalia, the one she grew up with.

The tarmac road ends abruptly and the truck slows to deal with the stony, broken track. In the south of the country there would be ostriches, antelopes, occasional lions or leopards, but here the only wildlife to pass them has been an old tortoise dawdling by the side of the road. It is a barren landscape, hard and dull, made for nothing other than mischief. There are no signs or obvious landmarks; the driver seems to know by intuition which forks in the road to take.

Filsan asks how people navigate on moonless nights in these desolate areas, and he points to the sky. 'Maybe God tells them or they still know the old maps of the stars and find their way like that.'

Her own ancestors were merchants on her father's side and sorghum farmers on her mother's, sedate accumulators of land and wealth; she has no family history of crossing deserts or camel caravans. It seems as if this wild terrain had determined the character of the people or had attracted like-minded spirits to dwell upon it. As the lorry approaches the border with Ethiopia it begins to climb slowly but steadily, the air fresh and scented by the yellow flowers of gum arabic trees. A young shepherd hides behind a thicket of acacia trees as the convoy passes, his small figure just visible between the scrubby crowns, his black-headed sheep grazing across a vast distance.

Filsan turns back as Lieutenant Afrah calls for attention.

'We are approaching our objective and I demand that each of you act according to the training you have received. We do not expect to engage the enemy today but as always maintain vigilance; we will conduct brief house-to-house searches and if you find villagers with arms, bring both weapons and offenders to me. The explosives crew are in the last truck of the convoy and are experts. It should take no more than half an hour to destroy the reservoirs. We want a smooth, calm operation. We will be in constant contact with Birjeeh by radio; anything out of the ordinary must be reported to me. Do a final check of your weapons now.'

It is a *tuulo*, barely even a village: a few beehive-shaped dwellings with old cloth hanging over their entrances, a tea shop with kettles resting on open fires, one solitary stone building with a tin roof, goats, stray children, a cleared space under a tall tree for religious lessons and clan meetings. Filsan feels that she has stepped back in time, that she is staring at a scene that has hardly changed in centuries: Bedu women peer out of their *aqals*, their attention fixed on her, on her trousers in particular – this alien, this neither male nor female curiosity in their midst. In her eyes they are just as peculiar: short, hunched, toothless, like children prematurely wizened.

The elders have been summoned and Filsan remembers her role in this theatre. She steps forward to intercept the three men, but they ignore her and continue on their sticks and bandy legs to a conscript behind.

She grabs the man on the right by the arm. '*Jaalle*, it is me you need to speak with.'

He is a thin, wiry man but he shakes her off with surprising force. Filsan pursues, not willing to ask for anyone's assistance in dealing with him; she wants to drag him back by the long tufts of grey hair skirting his bald pate and make him kneel at her feet. She catches up with him and shoves the barrel of her gun in the small of his back. 'Stop!'

He freezes and turns slowly to face her.

She withdraws the rifle but holds it tightly, still aimed in his direction.

'We want to speak to the commander. What reason have you got to come here? What wrong have we committed?' His eyes are clouded with glaucoma, his ears as large as a desert fox's.

'My commander has delegated me to speak with you. We are here with the full authority of the revolutionary government. There is strong evidence that you have been assisting the outlawed National Freedom Movement, and to prevent further collaboration the *berkeds* surrounding this settlement will be destroyed.' Filsan speaks in a rush, not stopping to breathe. 'You are still entitled to use your traditional drop wells and will be supplied with supplementary water once a month by the local government.'

Another elder steps forward, wagging his rough-hewn

cane at her. He is a broad man with henna-dyed hair and he expects her to take a step back; she doesn't. 'Those *berkeds* are our personal property, we paid for the materials, built them, we maintain them . . .'

The whole village seems to have crowded around Filsan. The other soldiers have disappeared into the shacks.

'This is government land,' Filsan raises her voice and gestures to the expanse beyond them, 'and you do not even deny that you use the *berkeds* to support the terrorists.'

The third elder, younger than the other two and still possessing a full head of black hair, joins the conversation. '*Jaalle*,' he says mockingly, 'we use those *berkeds* to water our camels, our goats and sheep, to perform ablutions before prayers, for a cup of tea in the mornings. We have nothing to spare for anything else. We are in the middle of a long drought; do you think we would give water to rebels?'

As he speaks, a huge plume of water, mud and stone flies into the sky to the west of the village. Detonations every three minutes radiate around the village, the bellow of the dynamite echoing against the limestone hills. The villagers run towards the explosions, the elders in the lead, children yelping in excitement and fear behind them.

Filsan pursues and catches up with the crowd just as Lieutenant Afrah orders the final detonation. The rectangular cement walls of the nearest *berked* have been blown into fragments that jut out like headstones from the mud.

The destruction silences the elders but she can sense their anger in the same way she had learnt to read her father's: the set of their jaws, the tension in their shoulders, their bodies angled away from the subject of their hate.

The commandos begin to filter into view, smiling and relaxed, unconcerned by the reaction of the villagers. These kinds of raids are welcome to them, bringing minimal risk and potential loot. Filsan pants after her chase and presses her palm against the stitch in her ribs. The villagers are rooted to the soil, their heads turning from crater to crater, false rain dripping from the acacias. She marches towards the elders, intending to explain the necessity of the action, the benefits they could enjoy if they only shunned the rebels, the projects that they might partake in to diversify the local economy.

The red-haired elder swivels at her approach and swings his cane at her face. She doesn't notice her finger squeeze the trigger of her rifle as her whole body recoils from the blow. The knock of the rifle against her chest surprises her, as does the sudden pop of bullets. When the elder falls back onto his behind she assumes that he has lost his balance trying to strike her, until points of blood spring up over his shirt, turning the white cloth a red that darkens before her eyes. Then the two other elders drop to the ground, their open eyes still watching her. Movements at the periphery of her vision blur so she does not recognise the grey shadows as her comrades advancing on the prostrate men.

'Hold fire!' shouts Lieutenant Afrah.

Filsan looks down at her feet and sees bronzed beetles scuttling over them; she presses one boot on the other, and the beetles are stilled, transformed into empty bullet shells.

The elders are slumped over each other like drunks; a howl sweeps over the plain as first one woman and then another rushes to the dead and dying bodies.

Filsan tries to step forward but her boots feel cemented down.

Lieutenant Afrah aims his Kalashnikov at the young men in the crowd. 'Get back! Back! Back!'

A group of soldiers corner the youths and force them back to the cleared space at the centre of the threadbare settlement. Filsan notices how thin their calves are for the first time, just shafts of bone below their frayed sarongs. They are hustled away, hands on the back of their afros, to squat in the sun until the soldiers depart.

An old woman pulls the wives off the corpses and shrouds the men's faces under a shawl; she says nothing, but turns to Filsan and points a finger, whether to lay blame, mark her out for retribution or curse her, she cannot decipher.

'Get in the truck, *Jaalle*, we will secure the area,' Lieutenant Afrah orders.

Filsan peers down at her distant boots. 'But I can't move.'

Afrah clicks his fingers and a conscript no older than fifteen comes to his side. 'Escort her back to the truck.'

The conscript takes her elbow gently, like he would his grandmother, and leads her forward as she stumbles over the broken ground.

'You did well, *Jaalle*,' he keeps repeating in her ear as they trek the half-mile back to the vehicles.

'But what happened? Who killed them?' she whispers.

In the dark cocoon of her room Filsan watches scenes from the day flash across her mind: three corpses hitch-hiking back to Hargeisa with her, the smeared viscera of flies wiped back and forth over the windshield, a line of vultures silhouetted against the midday sun, the quick untruthful briefing to Major Adow back at Birjeeh, the soldiers gathered around her in the canteen describing their own killings, the smack smack smack of the type-writer as she wrote a report of the operation in Salahley.

The alarm clock buzzes angrily at four a.m., drowning out the soft hiss of rain from the yard. Filsan slaps the contraption off and curls up to enjoy the warmth of the narrow bed.

She notices her heart pounding under her crossed arms; it thuds as if she has been fleeing something or someone, yet she is safe, barely awake, in the comfort of her own room. Disquieted, she rises and washes in the communal wet room, the cold water tightening the skin of her breasts and scattering large goose pimples over her arms.

The washroom smells foul, the one small window in the wall not enough to dry the damp walls or remove the stink of the blocked toilets: twisted hairpins, broken combs, rusty razors, stained underwear all gather abandoned behind the door. Girls who had been trained to clean their homes from an early age rebelled, became slovens, leaving the mess for someone else to worry about while pampered Filsan finds herself obsessing over dirty floors and full sinks. There is no point reporting the lazy private assigned to cleaning duties as no one would care enough about the women's quarters to discipline her. She ekes out a tiny amount of the imported shampoo she had bought in Mogadishu and scrubs her scalp with her fingernails.

Swirling thoughts in her skull refuse to coalesce and she scratches harder and harder to uncover the cause of the continued hammering within her ribs. As she bends down to rinse her hair under the tap, she begins to cry, unstoppable tears that sting her eyes. The thoughts that had buzzed around each other now fuse and spell out m-o-n-s-t-e-r in glowing letters across the blackness of her mind. The letters dance and mock her. She is in every way a monster and the weight of that recognition weakens her knees and bows her head; in prayer pose she rests her cheek against the slimy floor and lets the flowing water rush over her.

Slowly Filsan's heartbeat quietens, the word dims, she hears footsteps in the corridor, knocks on the door. Prising her body from the cement, she turns the tap off and wraps a towel around her body before grabbing her nightdress and shampoo and scuttling back to her room. In the corridor she is forced to squeeze past a girl waving and blowing kisses to her lover in the yard. Filsan glances through the window and catches the man tucking his shirt into his trousers and waving back. Her modern father had spared her, but this girl and the others are probably all circumcised, and yet keep lovers as if it is their prerogative. It was only her who listened to the rules, who feared breaking them – no one told her it was fine to steal or fuck or kill as long as it was kept quiet. She had taken every lesson so seriously, absorbed them in her heart, desperate for a pat on the head, and now she is unsuited for the real world, a freak.

Returning to her room, it appears more cell-like than ever, a criminal's lair more than a soldier's quarters. A small oval mirror on the opposite wall traps her reflection. The white of her towel, the brown of her skin, the black of her hair form abstract shapes; she is anonymous, innocent, just a human silhouette. Filsan steps closer, the nightdress and shampoo still clenched in her wet arms. The face of her mother stares back, cold and strange, the face that her father can't stomach looking at. He doesn't understand that she didn't choose to look like that woman; the high forehead, the wide-set eyes, the small nose and chin were imposed on her. She dislikes looking at her face as much as he does. If she had had a decent mother she would not be here, nearly thirty years old, unloved and unlovable, wishing the mirror would crack into a thousand pieces.

Filsan sits heavily on the low bed as another cramp

squeezes her abdomen. Her body is ripping itself from her control, trying to get away from her, or so it seems.

She had felt a similar sense of disintegration before, when she was just fifteen and growing timidly into this womanly body. Her cousins, Rahma and Idil, were visiting for the second time from Washington DC along with her diplomat uncle, Abukor. While their fathers went from one hotel bar to another, they traipsed along Mogadishu's wide boulevards, avoiding the grasping hands of Vespa-riding bachelors and the dangerously driven Beetles and Fiat Unos of the voluptuous import/export ladies who sweet-talk lucrative trade licences from government officials. The sisters would scream as Filsan rushed them, arms linked, through the chaotic, beeping traffic circling the Ahmed Gurey roundabout, towards the beach, where they might paddle fully clothed or sit on the seaweed-strewn white sand licking runny ice cream from their fingers. She watched as Rahma and Idil made friends with four lanky boys playing football near the surf. It didn't matter how badly they spoke Somali, the girls' flared jeans, red lips and cocky expressions were enough to get the boys crowding around. They met them day after day from then on, Filsan slowly relaxing in their boisterous, play-fighting company.

One boy, Abdurahman, with glasses and thick, lamb-like curls, caught her attention by asking what books she liked reading; she didn't expect him to know of *Eugene Onegin*, *The Master and Margarita* or *Slaughterhouse-Five*, but he nodded approvingly and asked if she knew that Pushkin was part Ethiopian. One afternoon they left the beach for Dervish Park to watch a government rally; they could hear the chanting and drums as they walked down Via Makka Al-Mukarama, and she fell in step with Abdurahman. He lent her his sunglasses when he noticed her squinting against the bright sunlight and she swept her hidden gaze over the bronze silhouette of Mohamed Abdullah Hassan on his horse, over the tall, weeping trees pulled away like theatre curtains by the sea breeze, and over the wasp-waisted boy beside her with the face that came from somewhere distant and exotic. Somali Revolutionary Socialist Party banners drifted from poles at the entrance to the park. Filsan was at the highest point of the sand hills that separated the coast from the main town, beside the whitewashed Hotel Bulsho, with which she shared a view over the antique, lightless lighthouse and the ancient district of Hamar Weyne, founded a thousand years before by long-bearded Arab and Persian traders. She felt like the song sung by Magool, 'Shimbiryahow' – languid, soaring and free: '*Oh bird, do you fly? Do you follow the wind?*' She heard the question in her mind and answered 'I will.' A carnival was already in full swing: men juggling with red and green peppers, fake woollen lion manes around their faces; drummers pounding goatskin drums and making bizarre, head-jerking expressions at the crowd of teenagers and university students; girls in traditional red-check wraps swinging their hips from side to side and sweetly singing revolutionary songs. She lost her cousins and the other boys in the scrum and reached out for Abdurahman's arm before he disappeared too. She pinched the cloth of his shirt between thumb and forefinger and held on loosely like that. There were more banners above their heads, written messily in blue paint, declaring 'Death to tribalism', 'Comrades not enemies' and 'A new dawn'.

A bearded Party member with a megaphone spelt out the new philosophy: you don't ask what clan anyone is from, you do not talk about high-class or low-class tribes, you do not give advantages to those related to you. He was preaching to the converted; the boys had not asked about the girls' clan and nor would it occur to the girls to care about the boys', that was for old-timers and losers. The music died down apart from a drum roll and then, just as Filsan reached the centre of the huddle, an effigy made from scraps of cloth stuffed with grass, bearing 'tribalism' on a sign around its neck, was strung up over a tree branch, a real noose around its fraying neck.

'Burn it! Burn it! Burn it!' the audience chanted.

While the activists dithered, a long arm reached out from within the crowd and held a lighter to the effigy's foot. It went up in a burst, scattering burning confetti over their heads.

Filsan squealed and ducked away as the incandescent flakes landed on her bare skin. Abdurahman threw his shoulder over her arm and ran with her back to the entrance, holding her close in the stampede. Rahma and

Idil ran past laughing. Filsan reached into the flow of bodies like a fisherman and caught Idil's wrist.

'Man, this country's crazy!'

'*Ramshackle* is the word,' corrected Rahma.

'How can you guys live like this?'

'This is your country too.' Filsan exchanged a knowing look with Abdurahman. The girls seemed to be constantly disparaging something: 'Look at that *naaasty* man eating with his *naaasty* hands'; 'Look at that *naaasty* bread sitting on that counter'; 'You expect me to sit on that *naaasty* hole?' Everything was so '*naaasty*', and sometimes so *najaas*, if they felt like speaking Somali. They turned the flowery written English she learned at school into a harsh language only intended for criticism.

'Hey! Sharmarke, Farhan, Zakariya, we're here,' Abdurahman shouted to his friends.

They joined together in a group of seven and headed back to the street. It was already four in the afternoon and Filsan wanted to return home to Casa Populare, put her feet up and read one of Rahma's stupid romance novels before dinner.

'We can't go back yet,' wailed Idil. 'We sit in every goddamn night. I'm bored, Filsan, bored!'

'We have to be home before it gets dark,' Filsan replied softly.

'They are never home before late and there are still *two hours* until it gets dark,' she spat.

'As you please.' Filsan held her hands up in submission.

'Let's go to the cinema, there is one nearby in Ceel Gaab, we'll catch a film and walk you home before it gets dark.' Abdurahman ushered them in front of him before rolling his eyes at Rahma and Idil's backs.

They followed Via Makka Al-Mukarama down to Ceel Gaab, covered their noses against the dark clouds of exhaust fumes at the bus terminal, crossed the old Italian square and stopped for a moment as a funk band – bass guitar, lead guitar, organ, saxophone, drum set and male vocalist – jammed in a storeroom open to the street.

'Now *this* is what I want to see. Africa gone funky, baby,' shouted Idil, clicking her fingers and twisting her hips.

'We are not all so hopeless then?' Abdurahman asked teasingly.

'Not every last one, no,' she replied flatly.

They reached the Ceel Gaab cinema, sandwiched between an Indian jewellers and an Italian café with an extravagant espresso machine on the counter. A street urchin lurked by the entrance and pulled at their clothes until they bought a few bags of roasted peanuts from him.

'I hope there is a Kirk Dabagalaas film showing, Kirk Dabagalaas burns the other actors off the screen,' Abdurahman said, and immediately Filsan knew what her cousins would do.

While Idil fell into a burst of hysterics, Rahma dropped her chin, looked at him over her eyebrows and repeated 'Kirk Daba-ga-laas?' in disgust.

Filsan thought she could see beads of sweat rise along Abdurahman's hairline. 'That is his name.'

'His name is Kirk *DOUGLAS*, not Dabagalaas, DOUGLAS.'

'Who cares, Idil? Who CARES! Why don't you stop pretending you're American for once? You were born in the same hospital as me, weren't you?' Filsan was centimetres away from her cousin's shocked face.

The sisters went silent then and stayed far away from Filsan as they climbed up to the wooden balcony seats. A revolutionary song played before the feature, and Filsan and the boys stood and sang, 'This blessed government, this blessed work . . .' while Idil and Rahma chewed their peanuts. It wasn't even an American film in the end but a Chinese picture, in which an imperial spy was caught by bandits in a distant province and forced to fight his way back to the Forbidden City. Filsan enjoyed the first half but then felt the time drag. She adjusted Abdurahman's watch to the light and saw it was already past six; it would be nightfall in a few minutes. She fidgeted in her seat, afraid the sisters would not come with her if she got up to leave, so she forced herself to wait, no longer paying attention to the film, just hearing the violent sound effects as she looked yearningly at the exit.

The lights finally came on at ten past seven and she hurried to the door and down the steps to the street. The sky was black and moonless, the palm trees lit up like giant pineapples in the square.

'Let's hurry,' she shouted to Rahma and Idil, as they hauled their feet out of the cinema.

'Don't worry, we will see you home.' Abdurahman

gestured towards the bus station, where ten-seater Fiat buses waited for customers.

They left the centre of town in an old bus that had most of the stuffing exploding out of the chairs. A teenage conductor with three missing fingers squeezed around their legs to collect the five-shilling fare in his good hand. Filsan watched the city through plastic flower-garlanded windows; as they approached the suburbs the roads were sandy and the villas modern, sharp-edged, protected by club-carrying watchmen at their gates.

'Would you like to visit Hamar Weyne tomorrow? I can take you and your cousins to the market, there is a good Yemeni Café where we can sit and have a juice . . .'

She didn't turn her face from the window. 'That's not going to happen.'

'She is too hard, leave it,' Sharmarke whispered.

'Here!' shouted Filsan as they passed the Coca-Cola advert near her corner of Casa Populare.

The bus screeched to a stop and the whole group disembarked. Filsan turned to Abdurahman, 'It's fine, you can leave us here.'

'We'll just walk you up a little further,' he said, following her.

He was trying to be polite but Filsan was in enough trouble already without risking her father seeing them with a gang of boys.

She saw him then, or at least his silhouette, lit up by the veranda light as he stood in the street. The shadow he cast on the ground was huge and terrifying.

'Please . . . just stay here.' Filsan waved Abdurahman back and walked the last ten metres to the house as if she were a mountaineer battling Arctic winds and altitude sickness; she felt the blood drain from her head to her ankles, and heard nothing but the scrape of her feet on the sand.

It was almost a release when the first blow came, a backhanded slap to the side of her head that pulled out the Minnie Mouse clips her cousins had bought her. She heard their screams from far behind.

She was limp, like a doll, as he took her arm and threw her up the steps to the veranda.

'Throw the devil off your back, Adan,' called her uncle from the doorway. 'Let the girl go.'

'*Aabbo*, stop him!' one of the girls shouted.

'She did nothing wrong!' a boy's voice yelled.

Filsan couldn't tell them apart anymore, her senses were shrouded, as if parts of her mind were shutting down, faculty by faculty.

Uncle Abukor tried to pull her away from her father's grip but he shouldered him out of the way.

Rahma and Idil were inside the house now too, all five of them struggling in the narrow hallway. Intisaar watched from the kitchen door, her eyes wide as she wiped her hands repeatedly on a cloth.

Her father's hand was wrapped in her hair. 'Where have you been?' His spittle landed on her neck as he shook her head from side to side. 'Is it time for you to follow in your mother's footsteps? I shouldn't have kept you! You scorpion, you whore, you don't deserve to carry my name or my father's. You were going to bring those boys, those dogs into my house? You thought while your uncle was here that you could do what you liked? Idiot! I should throw you out! Let you live in the gutter with your filthy mother.'

Filsan saw her uncle's podgy little hands trying to beat back her father, his brown shoes doing a desperate shuffle on the tiles, but it was no use; he had to ride out his rage, it was worse if it was truncated.

She saw a glimpse of Rahma and Idil clinging to each other by the wall, their mouths twisted as they howled; they looked ridiculous.

His blows were losing their force and he turned to sharp slaps instead, his untrimmed nails sometimes catching her skin. 'Get up to your room,' he panted and pushed her up the stairs. 'Intisaar! Check her underwear. If you find anything pack her bags and put her out.'

Filsan scampered up the stairs like an animal on her hands and knees and crawled into her dark room, too afraid to switch the light on. Intisaar's heavy steps followed her upstairs, boom-boom, boom-boom, boom-boom, in time with her pounding heart.

The door creaked open and before Intisaar had to say anything, Filsan reached under her pleated skirt, pulled off her high-waisted cotton underpants and scrunched them with trembling fingers into her housekeeper's outstretched palm.

'Oh, what a life,' Intisaar sighed before closing the door.

It was two days before her bedroom door was unlocked and she hadn't moved from the crouched place she had found on the floor. When she finally stood up her eyes darkened and her knees gave way. Intisaar hooked her under the arms, kicking away the untouched plates of yoghurt-soaked rice she had made for her, and guided her to the bathroom where she gently washed her bruised body. The house was silent; her uncle and cousins had moved out to the Al-Uruuba Hotel in protest, Intisaar said, and Filsan was relieved she wouldn't have to see their faces again or deal with their pity.

Waiting for her on the desk at the Mobile Military Court office is an envelope embossed with the governmental crest. She opens it delicately and slips out the card. It is from the propaganda office instructing her to go to Radio Hargeisa where she will be interviewed. Major Adow must have informed them about the Salahley raid. Filsan throws the card onto the desk; she has waited so long to be noticed but now wants to hide in the corner, slip into the darkness with the cockroaches. They expect her at the radio station at three p.m.

Her report on the events in Salahley is at the top of a pile of documents, covered in a garland of signatures and stamps from different offices.

Captain Yasin enters the office. 'I hear you're a real soldier now.' He makes a pistol of his fingers and pretends to pull the trigger at her.

Filsan hides her face in a file and murmurs nonsense words in reply.

'You'll get promoted now they've seen what you're capable of.'

She lifts her head. 'Really?'

Captain Yasin smiles. 'Of course, they can parade you around like a prize camel, show you off to the foreign journalists who are always criticising the government.'

'They want me to go on the radio.'

'There you go.' Yasin lights his first cigarette of the day. 'Next you will be receiving a summons to Brigadier General Haaruun's office to get a star on your epaulette.'

Haaruun's name chills her. She will never receive anything good from him. It is better to stay here, underneath the radar, than risk more humiliation at his hands.

'You owe me in a big way. I can imagine you as the President's number three wife, reciting his own sayings back to him!' He guffaws at his own joke.

'Why are you not on television, Captain? Your talents are wasted here,' she says, finally rising to the bait.

Filsan skips lunch and arrives at Radio Hargeisa half an hour early. The studio stretches along the whole top floor of the building. The British had built it just as they were preparing to leave and it's now an institution within Hargeisa, the broadcasters as familiar as relatives to the city's population. Filsan waits behind the microphone as Ali Dheere reads the news: thousands reported dead after a massacre in a Kurdish village in Iraq, Soviets report a build-up of arms by Afghan rebels, Archbishop Tutu has been released after marching on the Cape Town parliament with two dozen church leaders. As she listens to the news Filsan feels a brief moment of solace. The whole world is aflame with conflict; what she has done in Salahley pales into insignificance compared to what is commonplace in Iraq and South Africa. Saddam Hussein is rumoured to be poisoning his dissidents, while the Afrikaners take their opponents to quarries and kill them on makeshift electric chairs.

'We have joining us this afternoon a very special guest,' Ali Dheere begins. 'A Mogadishu girl who is serving her country in the armed forces, a remarkable young lady, in fact, who has put aside the usual desire to settle down with a family of her own . . .'

Filsan takes a sip of water from the glass beside her.

'. . . and has taken up arms to defend the country. Her name is Corporal Filsan Adan Ali and she is the first woman to engage the enemy in battle since the Ogaden War. Corporal Adan Ali, welcome.'

'Thank you,' Filsan says softly into the circular microphone.

Ali Dheere gestures for her to speak up. 'So, Corporal, what made you want to become a soldier? It is an extraordinary occupation for a woman, isn't it?'

'Uh . . . I . . . my . . . father is in the military and I always wanted to follow in his footsteps, that is the main reason, I think.'

'*Haa* . . . so it is a family tradition passed on from your father. What do you think are the particular challenges of being female in the army?'

Filsan takes a minute to think, to censor opinions that are better left unsaid.

Ali Dheere winds his hand in the air as if to speed her up.

'It is really no different. We experience the same training, are given the same responsibilities, face the same dangers as our male comrades. There is no special treatment.'

'I see, but there are still very few of you, aren't there? Why is that?'

Filsan is now on autopilot, reciting the lessons she has been taught from junior school onward. 'The revolution is still in its early days, slowly combating and defeating reactionary traditions and superstitions. The Comrade has shown us that men and women are equal and we can both play a part in improving our country.' These are the words of her year-six textbook.

'This isn't the first time you have made the news, Corporal. We have a copy of the *October Star* from March nineteen seventy-five, and here is a picture of you receiving a medal from the President. How did you manage to obtain a medal at such a young age?' He laughs.

'I taught rural workers in Dhusamareb during the literacy campaign and my students passed the state literacy test at a higher rate than any others in the district.'

'And how did that feel . . . meeting the President?'

Filsan tries to remember the moment, but it is in a haze, captured fuzzily by her father's camera. She was on an assembly line, given ten seconds before an official shoved her along, but she recalls that he had wrapped her hands in his as they greeted, patted her shoulder and held her gaze. He seemed genuinely proud.

'It was the greatest moment of my life.' Filsan hesitates in case it sounds an exaggeration. 'I knew then that I would dedicate my life to the revolution.'

'Excellent. You are a woman of your word too, because you recently put yourself on the front line to tackle the insurgency threatening the stability of the nation. Could you tell us more about that?'

Filsan takes a deep breath; she just has to stick to what they put into the report. 'We were sent to Salahley to discourage civilians from harbouring terrorists; we had intelligence that a few naive individuals had been induced to give material aid and shelter to the agents of Ethiopia, and as the political officer it was my duty to express the government's wishes.'

'There was a confrontation with the rebels, wasn't there? In which you were caught up?'

'Ah . . .' Her fingernails rap on the table as she wonders how much to give away.

Ali Dheere points to the table and wags his finger.

She places her hands in her lap and leans forward. 'We were ambushed by three rebels who had been sheltering in the village. They were dressed as civilians but armed. I was the first to engage them but then my comrades

provided support and the attack was brought to a posi-
tive conclusion.'

'Never let it be said that a woman is weaker than a
man. We have lionesses in Somalia ready to jump to our
defence. Corporal Adan Ali, thank you for your sacrifices
and we are honoured to have you within our military.
Comrades, let us keep our eyes and ears open so that
young patriots such as Corporal Adan Ali are not put in
unnecessary danger.'

The first strains of a political anthem and a wave from
Ali Dheere let her know that she is free to leave.

Filsan jogs down the stairs of the station, almost tap-
dancing with nervous energy. The interview had been a
kind of ambush, a flurry of questions that she was too
obedient not to answer, but Filsan likes the image created
of her by Ali Dheere: it is heroic and martial and imper-
meable, a woman apart, giant yet ethereal, a *jinn* with a
sword clutched to her breast. A *jinn* that wouldn't
suddenly remember the sandals of the one she had struck
down, the sweat-stained strap under his calloused foot,
the loose latticework of leather over his toes. Filsan has to
drag the alternative version of events she had recounted
to Ali Dheere into her mind to rub out the real flashes of
memory. Lieutenant Afrah had said as he tried to calm
her down in the truck back to Hargeisa that thoughts of
the man would eventually sift down and settle beneath
other events and concerns. Filsan would wait it out but
there seemed to be parts of the jigsaw to put together

first: Why couldn't she remember firing the gun? What happened in those seconds just before and after? What hole had she slipped through?

Captain Yasin makes an aeroplane from a card and throws it towards Filsan's desk. It glides just short and lands beside her feet; it is her request for leave stamped with 'APPPROVED'. In just six weeks Filsan will be back in her yellow room with the cherry-print curtains. She craves Intisaar's cooking, her crispy lamb *sambuusi*, the grilled fish served with spiced and sweetened vermicelli, and hot oily *bajiye* dipped in green chilli sauce. Intisaar the maid, paid a thousand shillings a week, has been everything a mother should be to her; while Intisaar's own children were raised by their grandmother, she laboured in the malign atmosphere of their silent house. Filsan writes down a list of things to buy Intisaar from Hargeisa, things that show she knows her and has been thinking about her – a silver necklace, or even a gold one if she can afford it, imported Taarab records, support bandages for her swollen knee. The last item might be the most appreciated now that Intisaar has crossed the border from middle age into old age; at fifty-seven the marrow starts to dry up, she had said in her musical Bajuni accent, and from then on you are just waiting for your bones to turn to dust. She would hold Intisaar's bones together with splints and tape if she had to rather than lose her. How much better would her life have been if she had been born to her? Sleeping huddled with her siblings in a mud and stick *cariish*, falling into whichever arms lay nearest, tasting love in her mother's milk, when she returned smiling at night.

'I heard you on the radio. I didn't know you had met the President,' Captain Yasin's voice startles her.

'It was a long time ago and there is no reason for you to know.'

Filsan opens a window to clear the room of the Captain's cigarette smoke and stands idly for a moment watching the wind shake desiccated leaves into the yard.

'You want to come to Saba'ad with me?' Captain Yasin asks. 'I'm going to check on the state of the militia there, see if there are more than five of them this time. I have to write another report.'

A report *I* will end up writing, thinks Filsan as she sinks into her chair.

'Come on, it will be good for you to see them.'

'What about these files?'

'They're not going to walk away, are they?' Yasin pulls her up from her chair. 'Come on. It's an order.'

Filsan scribbles a note on her desk with her whereabouts and follows him to the jeep.

Saba'ad is twenty miles north-east of Hargeisa. The largest of five refugee camps in the north-western region, it has grown and established itself as a kind of satellite town and stretches as far as the eye can see. Twenty thousand Somalis from the Ogaden region of Ethiopia scratch out a living here, having first fled the fighting between seventy-seven and seventy-eight and then the subsequent famines in Ogaden.

The camp's residents live in a mishmash of dwellings scrabbled together from donated tarpaulin, acacia twigs, old cloth and scavenged metal. Dust blows up in large gusts from the eroded, denuded landscape. Filsan covers her nose and eyes against the sand and keeps close to Captain Yasin. At different points of the camp various charities maintain schools, clinics, community centres; German, Irish and American aid workers mark out their own fiefdoms with flags and acronym-heavy placards. Looking down on the camp brings home just how great Somalia's humiliation was in the war; these people have land, homes and farms just a few miles away, but subsist here on gruel. At one point in late 1977, victory looked certain, and the violence it took to turn them back from their ancestral lands was so great the nation had still not recovered and maybe never would.

Captain Yasin had told the militia leader to meet him by the burial ground to the west of the camp and the men are waiting, around fifty or so, squatting between the rocks placed to mark graves. The fighters are ragged teenagers in sarongs and vests; they are armed with long sticks and wear sandals made of tyre rubber. They rise as Captain Yasin and Filsan climb towards them.

'Is this all of you?' Captain Yasin asks.

The militia leader is tall and skeletal, a green cap obscuring his eyes. 'No, we have more but they are tending what animals they still have.' His voice is grainy, dry.

'This is Corporal Adan Ali, she will be working with you too.'

They squint in Filsan's direction.

'We need to know how many of you there are before we can arrange proper weapons.'

'When we have our weapons then we will come out into the open. Not before.' The leader scrapes pictures into the sand as he speaks: straight lines, suns, hills, curved horns. 'We are waiting for you to tell us what you want from us.'

The teenagers watch Filsan with benign interest, their arms draped over each other's shoulders; they have the lean limbs of marathon runners but are penned into this prison of sand and rock.

'You must gather as many men as possible. Organise them. Discipline them so that you can work alongside us in keeping this country together,' Captain Yasin replies.

'It will happen.' The leader hawks and spits into his drawing. 'What will you give us for the time being? And when are you going to help us get our own lands back?'

The teenagers lean forward to hear the response.

'Be patient. We will set aside more rations for you, but there is little we can do until we receive all the hardware we need.'

Filsan looks up quizzically.

The leader nods defeatedly. 'We will just wait then. The Ogaden is going nowhere.'

'Within the month you will have rifles, RPGs, transport. This girl will make sure of that,' he gestures to Filsan.

She doesn't understand what he is referring to. Why would they give RPGs to these refugees when Somalia already has one of the largest armies in Africa? What is he promising these men, and why? She wonders if he has drawn her into weapon smuggling or some kind of conspiracy. She imagines what her father would say if she were court-martialled over something so squalid. Turning on her heels she abandons the gathering and traces the route back to the jeep. Captain Yasin is soon beside her but she speeds on, ignoring him.

'What's wrong?' He pulls her arm back.

'Let me go!' She wrenches it free, not caring that he is her superior.

'Wait, Filsan! What's the problem?'

'I will report you! You can commit whatever crimes you like but you won't take me down with you.'

'What crimes?'

'Don't think I'm stupid. I may be a woman but I can't be fooled so easily.'

'What are you talking about?'

Filsan stops abruptly and lowers her voice, 'You are selling arms.'

He bends back with laughter. 'You're crazy! Selling arms? To them? And what would they pay me in?'

'So why are they receiving rocket-propelled grenades meant for the army?'

He pulls her close. 'Because that is what the government wants. We can't talk about this here.' He takes her
arm again and marches her to the car. 'Get in the jeep,' he
orders. 'I can't tell you everything but I will tell you what
I know.'

They drive away from Saba'ad in silence and only when
they have reached the long, empty road to Hargeisa does
Captain Yasin feel comfortable talking. 'The government
has decided that the situation as it stands is untenable. If
the NFM continue to attack a village here, a battalion
there, other clan militias will become emboldened and
soon we will be fighting on twenty fronts.'

Filsan has never seen him so serious before. She watches
his sharp profile and feels that old desire for him creeping up on her.

'They – all of the leadership in Mogadishu and Hargeisa
too – have decided that there has to be a change.'

'What kind of change?'

'An end to it all. The whole population has to be resettled to stop the terrorists taking over.'

'Empty Hargeisa?'

'All the towns – Hargeisa, Burao, Berbera – anywhere
the NFM might gather.' He wipes sweat from his upper
lip with his wrist.

'When will this happen?'

'Not confirmed.'

It seems unbelievable, too final, but it might be an
improvement on this constant, draining game. The local

population could live more freely in an area controlled by the government; it is an extreme solution but these are extreme times.

'How do you know about it?'

Captain Yasin smiles. 'Ahh, don't you know that I am in the inner circle?'

'When will the rest of us be told?'

'When it is absolutely necessary, and Filsan, please, you cannot tell anyone about this or we will both end up in jail.' He holds her gaze in the rear-view mirror.

'Don't insult me. I am not some market gossip. I take my work more seriously than anyone else in the department.'

'I know that,' he nods. 'That's why I told you.'

On returning to her room, Filsan is overwhelmed by the urge to put things in order. She remakes her bed, pulling the corners tight, sweeps the linoleum floor and wipes a cloth over it, tidies away the dirty clothes piled on the chair, dusts the windowsill till it is free of dead mosquitoes, collects the cassettes littered under her bed and shoves them in a drawer, jumps up onto the bed and polishes the bare light bulb and, finally, opens the window and sprays a few squirts of perfume onto her bedclothes.

She emerges from her frenzy a little calmer but still restless. Thoughts fight for attention. She feels giddy, spun around; for so long she has wanted something to happen to her, anything that would penetrate the film that separates her from the outside world, and now event follows event in a flood, leaving her bobbing along with waves tight around her chest.

The pile of books beside her bed – academic treatises on counter-insurgency and a hardback copy of Machiavelli's *The Prince* – demand her attention. The Machiavelli book was a leaving present from her father; she picks it up, wipes the dust from the renaissance portrait on the cover and opens it. It makes her smile that her father has autographed it as if he wrote the five-hundred-year-old book. No dedication, no message, just the flourish of his signature on the title page. He had handed it to her wrapped in the plastic airmail package it arrived in and told her that it articulated all she needed to know about people. She has not read it but places it beside her pillow as a kind of holy book, a totem of her old life. She is still unwilling to find out what terrible secrets about humanity it contains and puts it back. She wants to read something dry, neutral, technical, and hopes *The Primary Manual on Counter-insurgency* will focus her mind.

She turns on the bedside lamp. The densely packed words and convoluted diagrams hurt her eyes, but she forces herself to read its sentences again and again. Small boxes introduce examples of the theories put forward by Mao, Marshal Bugeaud and others. She enjoys these histories – every known human problem and conflict seems to have antecedents, however ancient or distant; modern communists were emulating biblical acts of vengeance.

The book helps, her thoughts less disordered now. Captain Yasin sinks to the bottom of her concerns. She detests what women become when men enter their lives. Love seems to make fools of women infinitely more than it does men; in university the girls let their boyfriends copy their homework and sat morosely in the canteen deciphering the merest comment or act, cheapening and changing themselves, throwing away their futures to marry men who would become little more than taxi drivers. Filsan suspects that she is too rational to truly love someone; it embarrasses her just to see canoodling couples – it is as if they have had lobotomies – but if the opportunity presents itself to slip into a relationship with Captain Yasin, she won't refuse it. She tries to avoid the term 'last chance', but it is there in her mind unbidden.

She moves the Machiavelli book off the bed and a piece of paper flutters out, a blue-lined page from a notebook. She picks it up off the floor and recognises her own handwriting. 'Dear *Hooyo*,' it begins – she had written it on the bus to Hargeisa, in the hope that now she was living her own independent life away from her father she could start again with her mother – 'I have been promoted to a new position in Hargeisa and am looking forward to seeing how people live in the north.'

Filsan cringes at her words; she can imagine her mother laughing at them and shouting, 'Who does she think cares?'

'I have been thinking about you a lot and wondering if it is not time that we changed the way we behave towards each other. I know that you have not had an easy life and that you believe I have but that is not the case. In my own way I have suffered and paid the price for you and *Aabbo*'s divorce.' The note ends there, just as the recriminations would have started. Filsan remembers tucking it away in the book to finish at a calmer time. She grabs a pencil from her drawer and rests the note on her textbook; she treats it like an exercise, listing the pertinent points first:

- You married *Aabbo* out of your own volition.
- You decided to leave him for another man.
- You have done nothing with your life but live off one husband after another.
- You should not be surprised that I take after my father when you are the one who left me to him.
- I am ready to forgive you.
- I want a mother who I can sit with and talk to in a nice way.
- I will help your children with their education.
- When I am with you I don't want to talk about *Aabbo*.
- When I am with you I don't want to talk about the past at all.

It has been four years since they last met. Filsan had caught a bus to the Wardhigley district. Nothing had changed. The house was still filthy, crammed full of the fruits of two failed marriages and the most current one. Filsan could feel crumbs underneath her on the chair, surfaces were sticky to the touch, and children drooled over her knees and hands. It disturbed her to see her own reflection – older, fatter, but still recognisably her – living in these conditions. After placing a glass of carbonated orange and a saucer of biscuits in front of her, her mother had retreated to the kitchen with a neighbour, but her voice carried through: 'His hostage looks at me exactly the way he did'; 'You would think she would come here with money at least'; 'She doesn't look like the marrying kind, face like a shoe.'

'His hostage', that is what her mother had always called her. Filsan's father had only given her mother a divorce on the condition that she left Filsan to him, for him. She had accepted his condition, but from then on the child had become their Ogaden, their little piece of disputed earth. Deputations of clan elders visited one house and then another to negotiate access, to encourage compromise, to drink tea and pontificate. Filsan's father did not budge: from the time Filsan was five to when she turned thirteen, she was his alone. But as she got older and began to grow into her mother's face and body, he started to send her away for days to that messy, mud brick house. The way he looked at her hardened, he stopped embracing her, became impatient with her hovering around. She stopped being his and became nobody's.

She scribbles over the points; it is easier to leave her mother to the past, that wound is mostly healed and there is nothing to gain by picking at it.

* * *

The next morning there is a gold-wrapped sweet on her desk. Captain Yasin keeps his head down, tapping at a typewriter, his fingers stiff and awkward. Filsan hides her smile and takes her seat, resisting the urge to ask him what has brought him to work so punctually. She has consciously not applied any make-up or changed a single thing about her appearance. If he wants her he will have to take her without embellishment or artifice. She peeks surreptitiously at the top of his head and the bald spot germinating on the crown; the gold sweet is infantile but touches her nevertheless.

'I've got bad news for you,' he says.

She looks at him directly.

'Leave is cancelled. The rebels shot down a plane over the border last night; they have found ground-to-air missiles from somewhere.'

'That's terrible.'

He shrugs his shoulders. 'The end is nigh.'

Captain Yasin leaves for lunch alone, but at the close of the day, when her fingers sting from the impact of the typewriter keys, he mooches over to her desk and asks what she plans to do with her evening.

'Read, Captain.'

'Poor girl, is that the extent of your life?'

Filsan sits rigidly. 'I am not here for fun. I want to make something of my life.'

'Life is to be enjoyed.'

'For layabouts and street boys, maybe.'

'No, for you and for me too. Let me take you out to dinner.'

Filsan's eyes sweep down to her hands. 'I don't know.'

'I don't know? Are your books really more interesting than me?'

'I have work to do.'

'As do I. Let's discuss it over a meal.'

Captain Yasin waits under an electricity pole a hundred yards from the barracks. He appears thin and angular in a white shirt that glows fluorescent in the dim light. She has changed into a pair of flared jeans and a loose red tunic with a shawl over her shoulders. They meet awkwardly and shake hands under the light of a nearby tea stall, her hand tiny in his.

'Roble, pleased to meet you,' he smiles. It is the first time he has told her his name.

'Filsan, likewise.'

Walking beside him, Filsan feels a static charge as if the cables above are lightly electrifying them; it surprises her how good it feels to stand beside a man and know that he has picked her ahead of all the other women.

Roble leads the way with his hands in his pockets and makes small talk about the restaurants he likes, the hotels that serve alcohol, the best places to meet senior officials.

Filsan nods politely and wonders if he has heard about her incident with Haaruun. She knows that news of it has spread through the stares and nudges in her direction, but hopes dearly that it has somehow missed his attention.

He draws her away from the road as a truck passes perilously close; the curfew is imminent and civilian vehicles rush to their destinations despite the derelict condition of the road.

They turn right at a checkpoint, he raising a hand in greeting to the group of soldiers behind the barrier, and enter the Lake Victoria, an open-air restaurant with tame wildlife roaming the grounds.

It is packed with men in uniform, seated on white plastic chairs around tables set unevenly into the gravel beneath; red light bulbs hang in a chain from one corner to the next and the drone of a generator masks the music from two large speakers.

The men glance up from their card games and meals to judge the woman in their midst.

'Is this OK?' Roble asks, pointing to a dark table under a bougainvillea bush.

Filsan knows what the stares mean. That she is a whore to be seen in public with a man she isn't married to. Their eyes are still on her as she slips into her chair. A waiter in a black bow tie and shoes with the soles slapping free appears quickly beside Roble. He orders two colas and a lamb platter.

Slowly attention drifts away from Filsan back to the red nucleus of the restaurant.

'Bedus,' Roble smiles. 'You would think they have never seen a woman before.'

'Uneducated, that's all.'

'Or jealous.' Roble strokes her little finger with his knuckle.

'Don't do that.' Filsan snatches her hands from his reach.

He raises his palms in acquiescence.

A fawn barely a foot high creeps close to their table, shivering nervously; Filsan takes a pistachio from the bowl on the table and holds it out on her hand. It comes nearer and nearer and sniffs Filsan's palm. It is a thing of sublime beauty, the large black eyes and extravagant eyelashes, the caramel coat, the delicacy of its bones. It refuses the pistachio and skits over to another table.

'Why are you not married already?' he asks.

'No one has wanted me.'

'Do you know the reason why?'

'No, why?' Filsan smiles with surprise; she decides to be candid tonight, to not hold back for once.

'Because you act like you don't need anybody.'

'I *don't* need anyone, but that doesn't mean that I don't want certain things.'

'And those certain things are?'

'Someone by my side, on my side, who I can share my thoughts with, I guess.'

Roble lights a cigarette, adding another pinprick of light to the dark. 'Thoughts about the organisational budget of our office or other thoughts?'

'All kinds. You wouldn't guess how far and deep my thoughts reach.'

'Ahh, so you are philosophising up there in your little room.'

The waiter returns with a tray piled high with rice and a lamb shoulder, and two cola bottles rough with reuse.

'Sometimes, and other times I am just wishing something good would happen in my life.'

'Something like me?'

Filsan raises an eyebrow. 'That is very arrogant.'

'Accepted, but is it wrong?'

'I don't know yet. Why have you suddenly become so attentive?'

'Time. We have much less time than we realise, especially as soldiers, and I don't want to wait for anything.'

Filsan lifts the bottle to her mouth to hide her smile. 'That is very dramatic. But our office is pretty safe, isn't it?'

'For now, but don't worry, you have me to protect you.'

'I think I would be better at protecting you.'

'You would type them into submission, I'm sure.'

Roble walks Filsan back to the barracks. The curfew has shut the civilians inside their homes, with only faint smells of charcoal and spice and paraffin lights hinting at their existence. The street is dark and deserted, apart from the squeak and rustle of stray cats chasing mice and the soldiers at the checkpoint talking softly over the hiss of a radio. Filsan looks up; the sky stretched over them like a dome is alive with stars, thin black clouds with haloes of white and silver pass over the half-moon – it is a city up there, teeming with life.

'You know that on clear nights you can spot satellites?'

'I've heard that. In Mogadishu there are too many lights to see anything like this.' Filsan carries on staring at the heavens and stumbles over a stone.

Roble catches her by the waist and rights her; for a moment her hands rest on his and then she pushes them away.

They stroll slowly to the barracks, unafraid. Filsan remembers reading once that the night was made for lovers, each pair invisible to the rest. It was in a romance novel she had found under her bed, left behind by Rahma.

A sharp wind runs through the street, billowing out Roble's cotton shirt and forcing Filsan to wrap her shawl tighter. They are nearly at the barracks.

'You should stop here in case anyone sees you,' Filsan says, turning to him and holding out her hand. 'See you tomorrow.'

Roble chuckles at her formality but shakes her hand.

He waits for her to pass the sentry gate and enter the compound. Out of sight in the stairwell, Filsan watches him turn and walk away. She feels a pang in her chest as he strides, head bowed, into the dark; he seems so lonely, so vulnerable, prey to whatever ghosts or beasts might assail him. Filsan begins to blow a kiss at his back but feels ridiculous and just follows his white shirt as it disappears into the night, like a ship's sail surrounded by high waves and low clouds.

* * *

Instead of the dreams she expected – tender, candlelit, sublime – Filsan sinks into a nightmare. She stands on a dark plain, just her and the elders, their backs against the wall of an intact *berked*. The wind howls all around them, whipping away the words that emanate from her mouth; she carries no rifle or pistol but a great serrated knife that shines in the grey light. The white pilgrim robes of the elders flick and snap against the bluster but they are silent. Filsan raises a leg and steps forward, gravity disappears, her step becomes a jump, a flight and she pedals desperately down. Floating past the tallest elder she grabs his arm and anchors herself to him. His skin is frigid and in his empty eye sockets are distant twisting whorls. Filsan touches his chest but there is no heartbeat, no exhalation or inhalation; the body is a hard shell, perfectly preserved by the sterile moon air. The *berked* behind is full to the brim with powdery white dust. The abyss beyond is starless, featureless, and seems to reach into eternity. Filsan sees that the only shelter to be found is inside this body. She saws at the elder's neck with the knife, the skin clinking like metal against the blade, spitting out bright sparks. Arduously, Filsan draws the knife back and forth, raising blisters on her palms, until the metal jugular is slit open. Holding onto the elder's robes, avoiding the void of his gaze, she lowers her arm and rotates her aching shoulder. She lifts the knife once again and turns to the incision she has made, a trickle of liquid slowly seeping out from the hollow within; pressing a finger into it, she scrutinises the stain. It is thin, bright blood. Seeing no alternative, she continues to force her way inside him, blood smearing the knife, her hands, her cheek. The head creaks back and falls to the dirt. Filsan tries to squeeze through the aperture but can fit no more than an arm inside, blood splashing through her fingers. There is nowhere to go but the abyss that pulls at her.

She starts awake in her bed and switches on the overhead light, certain that her slick, cold hands are covered in blood. She holds them near her eyes and they are clean, with the same brown lines on the palms and plump fingers as always. She rests her cheek on the pillow hoping for the dread to pass.

'We will not be forgotten so easily,' the elders seem to say.

'I will outrun you,' she replies, and throws the sheets away from her.

She leaves the barracks without visiting the bathroom or kitchen, and washes her face once she has got to the office. The sun rises through the barred windows and slowly the elders recede from her thoughts. She starts on the pile of reports she was too distracted to complete the day before. One particularly thick document contains sightings of a rebel commander, spotted in Ethiopia but also within Somalia itself, inside the Oriental Hotel if the *Guddi* were to be believed. Filsan has noticed that the *Guddi* act as if false information is better than no information at all, but their constant machinations against one individual or organisation makes her job ten times more difficult.

Outside a convoy of police cars streams past, sirens screeching. Filsan leaves her chair and stands by the window. A fire is burning in the direction of the Regional Security Council headquarters in the old District Commissioner's house; the shouts of protestors are muffled under the sirens. A column of black smoke stands in the sky like a giant *jinn* escaped from a bottle. She picks up the phone and rings the number for Birjeeh; a busy tone wails back at her and she returns to the window. In that column of smoke she sees weeks of work and investigations; whoever set the council building on fire has thrown a gauntlet down to the government: if they can reach such a secure site there is nowhere they can't penetrate.

Roble enters alongside Colonel Magan, the Mobile Military Court prosecutor. Filsan thinks she can see a hint of a smile on the Colonel's face as he sits briskly behind Roble's desk. A failure at the Regional Security Council could be a victory for him.

'Do any of these damn things work?' Magan shouts as he stabs at the buttons on the telephone.

She tries to catch Roble's eye but he is staring down at the Colonel with a furrowed brow.

'Dead.' Colonel Magan replaces the earpiece, pulls his chair further in to the desk and gestures for them to stand before him. He has the face of a bird of prey: small-eyed, hooked-nosed and menacing. He winds his sinuous fingers together and rests his chin on his knuckles.

Filsan stands to attention in front of him and holds her hands nervously behind her back.

'We need to get this situation under control. The fire at the council building is just a diversion. The real disaster was last night at Mandera prison,' he taps his knuckles against his jaw and breathes in deeply, 'where the rebels attacked and freed most of the prisoners.'

Roble finally glances towards her and she meets his gaze eagerly.

'The roads to the east are closed for the time being and every infantry unit in the area has been sent to the border to stop the NFM smuggling their comrades out of the country. You will have patrol duty seven times a week and will be given additional instructions as soon as I receive them. I will be in meetings at Birjeeh for the rest of the day. I want you, Captain Yasin, to identify as many collaborators as you can and find out what they know about the prison escape.'

The creaky, unwieldy machinery of the Somali National Army cranks up a gear after the prison attack. Within four weeks the Saba'ad militia receive their grenade launchers and an instructor to teach the use of them, more militias are raised in camps across the desert, and Filsan makes arrangements for divisions of troops from Beledweyne, Kismayu, Merka, Galkayo and Mogadishu to be quartered in government buildings across Hargeisa, including in their own office. Roble talks incessantly on the telephone, a pen behind his ear, organising the smooth transfer of heavy weapons from Mogadishu to Hargeisa. The only respite they enjoy is the security patrol they conduct in Guryo Samo neighbourhood between three p.m. and six p.m. every day. The security organisations have been broken up into fragmented units, competing against each other to dig out the roots of the NFM, information hoarded like treasure rather than exchanged. Three hours they spend in solitude, wandering up and down streets so sandy their boots sink up to the laces, ignored by everyone apart from the children who flee at their approach. It is the first time Filsan has carried a rifle since Salahley and the weight of it seems ominous, the power inside the barrels and coils and hammers harder to ignore as she shifts it constantly to the side.

The neighbourhood has a somnolent atmosphere; they joke about falling under a sleeping spell, but sometimes they yawn so much it seems possible. They buy soft drinks from a stall under a willow tree using government-issued vouchers, to the bald shopkeeper's evident but silent displeasure. After each patrol they stagger back to the barracks in the watercolour light past an overgrown orchard, frail flowers tumbling over the wall and nodding their translucent heads with almost synchronised timing. Roble picks at the red and pink blooms sometimes and gathers them into a limp bouquet for Filsan, which she then hides under her tunic and retrieves in her room, pulling out the crushed, damp stems from between her breasts.

Four hundred of the rebels from Mandera prison are caught within a fortnight, mostly toothless old men who intend to keep their secrets locked in their rattling bones. Filsan and Roble are instructed to interrogate a man, Umar Farey, from Guryo Samo, who is suspected of organising anti-revolutionary meetings inside his hotel. In the former armoury of Birjeeh, Roble reveals a flair for violence that Filsan hadn't expected. While she sits in front of a typewriter, volleying question after question at the hotelier, Roble stalks around aiming punches with precision. At one point Filsan begins to giggle. She covers her mouth and lets the feeling pass, but the detainee reminds her of a concussed cartoon character; she can imagine tweeting birds circling his head. Umar Farey tries to appear indifferent to the knocks, his head swivelling back rigidly each time to the front, his blank, bloodshot eyes focussed on her. She can feel the elders leaning over her shoulder to peer at the typed pages she has written, their breath on her neck tickling to an infuriating degree; she turns around and shouts, 'In the name of God, leave me alone!'

'What's the problem?' Roble snaps.

'Sorry.' She drops her head.

The interrogation lasts another hour but they gain no valuable information from it. The prisoner is escorted back to his cell with a bleeding nose and Filsan wraps Roble's swollen knuckles in her handkerchief and buys him a bag of ice from a hawker to press against it. She nervously touches him, brushing dust off his shirt and checking his damaged hand regularly, but he is unusually taciturn.

'Who were you talking to in there?' he says finally, as they walk back to their office.

Filsan blinks rapidly and smiles a false smile. 'No one.'

'And why were you laughing?'

'He looked ridiculous. The prisoner.'

'It didn't exactly make us look professional though, did it?' Roble says sternly. 'And it's not just that. I catch you sometimes, staring into space for minutes at a time, your mind somewhere else completely.'

'Do I?' Filsan feels her face burning, almost as if a mask has been ripped away.

'You're not like any other woman I've known.' He smiles, but there is no softness to his words. He looks at her as though she is crazy.

Filsan trots obediently beside him, head down, wondering how long he has been thinking this about her. She steals glances at him, trying to read his expression; his eyes are narrowed and his lips set in a firm line, but this has been his normal look recently. She keeps quiet, hoping his mood will change; maybe it is the interrogation that has soured it and he just needs time to forget about the stubborn hotelier and his lies.

Roble barely exchanges any words with Filsan all afternoon and hides behind a barricade of papers on his desk. By early evening the distance between them lessens and he agrees to walk her home. They reach the checkpoint closest to her barracks after nightfall; the soldiers are clustered around the radio, slender young men in woollen greatcoats made for stout Russian or German fighters. The only light comes from a weak torch that sends out circles of diminishing white light. The group unfurls at their approach; they salute Roble and look Filsan up and down, up and down.

'There has been an attack on Burao, Captain,' says the boy with the torch; his face is in shadow and all Filsan can see of it are his crooked teeth and pointed little chin.

'When?' barks Roble, snatching the radio from a soldier's hand; there is only static coming from the speaker.

'It's not clear, sir, maybe a couple of hours ago. There is serious fighting, hundreds of rebels have besieged the town.' His voice sounds like it hasn't fully broken yet, or maybe he just can't find the words to describe the situation he has been thrown into.

'Where is your commanding officer?'

'He was called to Birjeeh. They believe more rebels are on their way to Hargeisa and he's organising reinforcements to secure our area.'

Filsan clenches her rifle tight.

'I have to stay until their officer returns.' Roble pulls the strap of his rifle over his head and clicks the radio to another channel, where faint voices speak in acronyms to each other.

'I'll stay too, Captain.' Filsan takes position behind the metal bar of the checkpoint.

'Corporal, go back to your barracks and wait for further orders.' He turns his back on her and holds the receiver to his ear before asking a soldier, 'What kind of numbers are we talking about exactly in Burao?'

'We have no idea, sir, communications keep failing.'

Filsan approaches Roble and whispers in his ear, 'I want to stay with you.'

'Just go, Filsan, this is serious.'

Meeting his eyes she feels a sudden surge of hatred towards him. What makes him think he is better than her? 'I'm going, Captain.'

'Walk her home,' he orders to no one in particular, but she marches on ahead without waiting.

The road is a pale strip surrounded by black trees, black walls, black absences where lives should be. It is only seven p.m. but there is not a sound apart from the thud of her boots.

She checks over her shoulder, sees a soldier from the checkpoint following her half-heartedly at a distance; his presence irritates her more and she speeds up, promising herself that she will never even look at Roble again, that she will teach him a lesson for humiliating her. She knows she will see him at his desk the next day, excitedly describing how the rebel assault was bloodily put down in Burao.

She doesn't pay attention when the bushes beside her seem to whisper and shift, her eyes are fixed on the side turning to the barracks and do not register the shrubs lifting up off the ground. She pushes a strand of hair away from her forehead and adjusts the rifle strap to stop the gun knocking against her thigh. All she wants is a shower and then to fall asleep.

Filsan ascribes the crack of a twig breaking behind her to a stray animal, the scent of musty sweat to her long physical day, but a fluttering doubt makes her stop and turn around.

Stretched across the road are *jinns* with tangled branches growing from their heads and arms; she reaches out to touch one of the silhouetted figures and is surprised to feel real flesh against her fingers.

'Raise your hands,' the *jinn* demands in a Hargeisa accent, before drawing a Kalashnikov up to her face.

PART THREE

Kawsar's door withstands five heavy bangs before smashing open. She turns to find an adolescent soldier dressed in a camouflage jacket in her room; their eyes meet for an instant before he retreats. The door clicks back into place but the bar lock is broken, swinging from its screws.

'Well?' says a voice behind him.

'Ransacked, nothing in there. Let's go.'

She wonders if he saw her or if he thought it was a corpse that met his gaze. How would she even know if she had died? There is no one to wail or weep beside her. No neighbour has come to check on her and from that she knows they must be either dead or gone.

Her head is pounding and her throat sore. She pours a glass of dusty water from the jug and checks the packet of painkillers. Only five left. She swallows them down. There are still footsteps outside her window, heavy boots on concrete. The soldiers are laughing, the mysterious delight of boys at play. They are probably going through the undergarments in Maryam's bedroom.

Kawsar rests a cheek against her damp acacia-print pillow case, tears hanging from the thin branches like leaves. She feels woozy, sepia images and sunken sounds washing up from the seabed of her mind: the thud of policemen's laced boots as they paraded before the District Commissioner in Salahley. She had loved that sound when she was young, remembers bringing the breakfast dishes in a bowl to the veranda so she could listen to the thump of her husband's feet on the grit; it flew to her over the birdsong, clinking metal plates and the British sergeant's screamed commands. The policemen then were beautiful, their hair glossed and parted sharply to the side, their uniforms smelling of detergent and soap. Kawsar had dressed her new husband Farah as if he were a doll, washing and ironing his clothes every day, polishing his boots at night with Kiwi wax. She had taken pride in his appearance as well as her own. They planned to take their country back from the British and look beautiful while doing it.

She takes another sip of water and recites the prayer for the dying. She can accept a simple bullet – there is no need for them to waste their time on an old woman – but she fears they will pull her out of the bed or try to make her stand up. She intends to offer them the gold and cash under the mattress if they promise to not move her. It is a pathetic vigil. She places the radio next to her ear, turns the volume down and switches it on. For years the airwaves have been a front line in the war between the dictator and the rebels, but now Oodweyne's voice crackles out of the speaker, crisper, clearer and more triumphant with every word.

'Citizens, we have been driven to extreme but decisive action. We appealed to our comrades in the north to seek peaceful means of resolving our differences; we begged them to not allow our sovereignty to be undermined by enemies of the Somali people and their collaborators. Our forbearance in the face of terrorism has earned us the sympathy of the world, even the President of the United States is sending aid to eradicate the threat we're facing: a US Navy ship is expected to arrive imminently in Berbera port to deliver necessary supplies. We have the means and will to achieve a victory never seen before in our history and all anti-revolutionaries will learn bitterly what it means to defy authority and progress.'

Before the announcement is repeated Kawsar kills his voice. It is not so painful to die when all that she knows is dying around her. It seems as if the world had been built just for her and is being dismantled as she departs. Late one night towards the end of the sixties, in Mogadishu's National Theatre, Kawsar had sat waiting for Farah to return to their table. She had pleaded with him to take her out while they stayed in the capital for his police training, but everywhere they went his attention was stolen by his Somali Youth League friends. She had watched forlornly as cleaners swept the floor and stagehands took apart the city that had seemed so alive only minutes earlier. Smooth-faced apprentice carpenters, who pinched almonds out of golden bricks of real *halwa*, dragged the comedian's confectionery stall off the stage. A painted sunset backdrop fluttering with inky birds was rolled up and eased into a cardboard tube by another boy. Kawsar, who had been the first to build a bungalow on October Road, would see it forced back to its original state too, the homes levelled to the ground so that the juniper trees and baboons could return.

Deqo's eyes snap open inside her barrel. It sounds as if men with hammers are smashing on its exterior. BANG, CRASH, BANG. She rises on her haunches and looks out but there's nobody there, just the usual silent circle of trees. Still the blows continue and Deqo steps out of the barrel to investigate. She hasn't seen another soul for weeks, having avoided the town and market in case the old man found her. The hair on her head is wild and hopelessly knotted, and her skin shows through the holes in the now-ragged dress she had fled Nasra's house wearing. Her mouth is raw from her diet of hard, unripe fruit and she has lost every ounce of weight she had put on in Hargeisa; now taller, lean and spare, she doesn't hear her footsteps when she walks, but rather seems to float over the earth, leaving no imprint. The flashes in the sky are welcome, the more rain that falls the greater her store of drinking water in the bucket that she has appropriated from the rubbish heap under the bridge.

As she squints up, she notices how oddly the lightning strikes; it seems to shoot up from the ground rather than downwards, and the thunder is guttural and metallic at once. A plane swoops deafeningly overhead and she stumbles into the bushes in fear. As she approaches the concrete bridge over the ditch, the ground rumbles from the procession of slow, dark green tanks crossing from north to south; she imagines there must be another parade taking place in the stadium, another day of soldiers, speeches and dances. After the tanks pass, the bridge is empty and she climbs the embankment up to it. She checks south to the airport and north towards the theatre: pillars of smoke stand irregularly here and there and everything is eerily quiet, apart from the mysterious blasts she could hear from the ditch.

Curious, she heads for the *suuq*, hoping to ask one of the market women what is going on. She expects it to be open like always, with the basket women on the left and the vegetable sellers on the right, hawkers her age milling between them selling snacks and individual cigarettes, the central market a dense confusion of heads and arms. It isn't until she nears the huge blue and white flag painted on the side of the local government office – the same image she has only ever seen in fragments through the crowd, but which is now revealed in its rain-bleached entirety – that Deqo realises she is in the heart of the *suuq*. Overturned tables, crates and silence replace the world she knew, the only company the emaciated, flea-ridden cats cowering under an awning and lapping desperately at a dark pool of blood.

Deqo checks the ground for a morsel to eat but there are only scattered peanut shells and trampled vegetables. Taking the alley adjacent to the municipal building, she soon reaches a checkpoint. Soldiers in yellow camouflage jackets and trousers guard it, but a woman in a khaki uniform and beret gestures for Deqo to approach. 'Put your hands in the air. Where have you come from?' she shouts.

'The market.' Deqo points behind her. 'Where are all the traders, *Jaalle*?'

'Somewhere in the hills. Who are you? Where are your family?'

'I am an orphan, from Saba'ad.'

'Put your arms down.'

Deqo drops them slowly.

'I am hungry, *Jaalle*, where can I find some food?'

The woman walks across to another soldier, discusses something and then returns with him. 'If you are willing to do something for us, we can give you food.'

Deqo shelters her eyes from the sun with her hand and nods.

'Follow us.' The woman leads Deqo and the soldier toward the wealthy neighbourhood on the other side of the ditch. Crouched and with their rifles poised, they peek around corners before proceeding further. A radio on the woman's belt crackles and she switches it off.

'You see those houses at the end of the road?' She points

to two huge villas, their gates torn open. 'I want you to go inside and see if there are any people in them.'

'Is that all?' Deqo asks.

'Just that and then we'll give you something to eat.'

As Deqo tiptoes forward, emulating the soldiers, she can see that the garden walls of the villas have holes punched out, craters as large as truck tyres. The houses themselves are unscathed and have glossy, new cars parked in front of them. Deqo glances back anxiously at the soldiers who quickly drop out of sight. She enters the compound of the slightly smaller villa and stands beside an abandoned child's bicycle, expecting someone to challenge her; birds rustle, guns pop in the distance, but no one emerges. The whitewashed villa has a tiled, columned veranda leading to a glass double door. She walks inside. She counts seven rooms not including the bathroom and large kitchen. An overhead light has been left on in one of the bedrooms but she doesn't know how to turn it off. The rooms still smell of the family they belong to, a strange combination of washing powder, spices and children.

The larger villa next door also appears empty, but there are dirty footprints on the rug. Deqo picks up a bullet from beneath the coffee table and holds it as a kind of charm as she inspects the rooms. There are two televisions in this house, one in the living room and one in the largest bedroom; her reflection is caught and watched by their black eyes. The kitchen is full of packets of food she doesn't recognise.

She sprints back to the soldiers, who beckon her around the corner.

'Did you see anyone?' the woman asks impatiently.

'No, they're empty.'

'Are you sure you didn't see anyone? Tell me the truth.'

'I checked every room.'

'What's that in your hand?'

Deqo unfurls her fingers to reveal the bullet. The female soldier takes it from her and whispers something in her companion's ear.

'I found it in the larger house. Under a table.'

The soldier replaces the bullet with a melted chocolate bar from her pocket. 'Go your own way now,' she orders before they retreat the way they came, checking every direction like thieves.

Roble said he had come running as soon he heard shouts. Filsan had been surrounded by a disparate gang; two older men – one in khaki, one in a safari jacket – and two teenagers, wearing jeans and big-collared shirts.

'Give us your gun,' the man in khaki demanded, his rifle trained on her.

Filsan stood absolutely still, unable to respond. It was as though everything that she had learnt had deserted her.

One of the boys reset the trigger of his Kalashnikov, and the sound of the metal jolted her back into her body. She looked down the barrel and, seeing her own end, roared Roble's name.

Before the young gunman had the chance to recoil his Kalashnikov, a shot from the direction of the checkpoint had brought him down, with a bullet to the back.

The rebels turned to defend themselves, Filsan's presence suddenly unimportant as she dived into the gulley they had been hiding in. The frantic exchange of fire was over in seconds, leaving three NFM dead on the ground and the man in khaki pursued into the night by the soldiers.

Roble sprinted up and pulled her away from the thorns, his heart thumping against her ribs, the moment only spoiled by the scent of dog shit on her boots. Crouched under his arm, shocked but unharmed, Filsan had marched with him back to the checkpoint, all anger between them evaporated. He was completely in shadow, just the outline of what a man should be, and she held on, pushing closer and closer against him. She felt out of herself in an exhilarated, animalistic way, all her reticence and manners stripped away; she wanted to merge with him, *become* him. But Roble had sat her down on the barrel at the checkpoint, handed her the torch and turned to the radio transmitter, shouting demands for immediate reinforcement, his eyes darting fearfully in every direction. They had been separated that very night, he assigned to a checkpoint on the hills outside of town and she to Birjeeh to help coordinate Victory Pioneers with the armed forces already in Hargeisa.

Over the next few days, each time Filsan sees a military truck careering through the streets, uniformed casualties prostrate on the back, she is chilled by the thought that Roble could be amongst them. Far from being repelled and driven out of the city, the NFM have grown in number and entrenched themselves. Hundreds of rebels have returned from exile in the scrublands of Ethiopia, from their desert lairs, carrying their scavenged weaponry on their backs. Veteran fighters, whose names and photographs pepper dossiers of wanted men, have come to wreak havoc, their apparent resurrection a call to arms to thousands of the city's angry youths.

At the checkpoint nearest to the National Theatre, Filsan oversees movement into the centre of the city. Most residents fled within the first hours of the bombardment, but stragglers remain: the crippled and elderly, the patients thrown out of the hospital when it was requisitioned by the military, street children and lunatics freed from the asylum by a mortar blow. Filsan switches on her radio and hears that the rebels have cut the water supply to the hospital and they need water to be trucked in immediately for the injured soldiers there.

Two members of the Victory Pioneers, Ahmed and Jimaale, are stationed at the checkpoint to help identify NFM sympathisers; they know everything about everyone – family, clan, neighbourhood, occupation, associates – the years of spying finally paying off. They seem invigorated, their pockets bulging with watches and money confiscated at other checkpoints; they keep asking the conscripts to give them a weapon but Filsan forbids it.

A group of civilians creeps up to the barrier, with bundles wrapped in blankets on their backs. The solitary male with them is around twelve years old and struggles to manoeuvre a cart full of their worldly possessions.

They stop beside the barricade and wait.

'Where have you come from?' Filsan asks.

'Iftiin,' a young woman says, a strap across her forehead to secure the load on her back. She seems to lead the group, while the eldest woman leans against the wall panting.

'What is your name and who are these people?'

'Nurto Abdillahi Yusuf. These are my mother and siblings.' She waves back without turning her head.

'Her father used to work in the cinema; they are a well-known *anti* family. Check that cart, they are probably giving supplies to the enemies,' shouts Ahmed, rushing to the cart himself.

'Stand back,' Filsan orders before cutting through the tethers that hold the contents of the cart in place. She rummages within it: a foam mattress, a paper bag of medicines, sacks of flour and rice, a *girgire* cooker, and then something that surprises her.

She digs the revolver out of the hole it has been hidden in within the mattress.

'There!' exclaims Jimaale. 'Caught like a cat with a piece of chicken.'

'It is for protection against bandits, we are just women and children, we need something for our safety,' pleads Nurto.

'Who gave it to you?' Filsan checks the gun over; it is an old police model.

'We have had it for years, my father bought it after we were burgled in the seventies, everyone has one, drunks and glue-sniffers were breaking in at night.'

'Liar! Liar!' Jimaale shoves the girl. 'You are an *anti*! Why not call the police if you are broken into?'

'We have seen you at protests against the government, you can't lie to us.' Ahmed kicks her to the ground.

Filsan pulls him away. 'Take them to Birjeeh. Let them discover the truth.'

Ahmed and Jimaale pull the bundles off their backs while Filsan ties Nurto's wrists and then her mother's. Her children fight Filsan's hands away, but she resists striking them and orders the two youngest conscripts to march the whole family to headquarters. As their figures recede, it strikes Filsan as ironic that they had delayed fleeing so they could take as many of their possessions as possible, but now those very possessions prevent their flight.

The crackle of the radio breaks into Filsan's thoughts; on the end of the line is Lieutenant Hashi, the logistics officer, ordering that she move to the checkpoint beside the radio station. She leaves Ahmed and Jimaale to pilfer what they want from the cart and rushes to the next position.

Kawsar hears snatches of the chaos outside: the scrape of corrugated tin as it is pulled off the neighbouring homes, the *whoompf* of deep-throated cannons firing behind the hotel, the ominous approach of footsteps in the court-yard. She senses her death is imminent; every part of her is cold and her heart beats sluggishly, hopelessly. A weight presses down on the bed and she turns her head. Farah sits there in his favourite narrow-shouldered pinstripe suit; he leans back and sighs a bottomless sigh, 'Who would have thought it would come to this?'

It is so good to hear his deep, clear voice that it brings abrupt tears to her eyes.

'*Kawsar-yaaro*, little Kawsar, you have struggled too much without me. Put it behind you now.' He smiles and she recalls the shallow dimple in each cheek. 'We have been waiting for you.'

Teasingly, Hodan steps out of the kitchen, smiling her father's smile and dressed in a satin wedding dress that pools on the floor around her.

'Take me with you.' Kawsar holds out her arms and lifts herself as far as she can.

As Hodan nears, Kawsar watches her perfect, luminous face fade until she sees nothing but dust motes floating in the air. She turns to Farah but the bed is empty. She drops her arms and cries out, cursing herself: Why can't she at least have a simple death after such a long, complicated life? What is this trial that she has been forced to endure? If she had a knife she would end it herself.

Deqo winds back to the villas. The trees are bare; all the birds have flown away, leaving an ominous silence in their wake. She wants to see those grand kitchens again, touch the gleaming copperware and empty those cupboards groaning with mysterious, exotic packages. The guttural thump of mortars booms behind her and she picks up speed, keeping close to the wall and hiding beneath the shadows of flowing pink bougainvillea bushes. Ducking into the largest villa she runs up the concrete steps and enters its cool, green-tiled reception room. A heavy wooden-framed armchair is close enough to the door to push back and use as a barricade. The overhead fan stirs at the change of air she has brought in with her, but the rest of the house is eerily still. Vast sheets shroud the other furniture, dust and dead insects already gathering within the folds on the floor.

Deqo paces through the hall and into the kitchen. White-painted cupboards dominate one wall and hide the pans, cutlery and provisions that would have crowded the floor of Nasra's kitchen. A straw mat beside the window has the dark imprint of a body clearly visible, two plastic slippers and a *caday* the only other reminders of the maid who lived and worked in this room. Instead of a makeshift *girgire* she had had a permanent charcoal-burning range to prepare meals with, four circular hobs and an oven underneath that must have shortened her labour by hours. A huge enamelled sink holds the dirty plates that the family had used before fleeing. Deqo prods the congealed red sauce on a plate and puts her finger to her tongue; it still tastes good. Two large taps drip onto the dishes and she decides to wash them as a kind of payment for the family's unknowing hospitality. With difficulty she turns the stiff taps and water gushes out, clear and abundant; a cloth and dishful of detergent are within her reach and within moments the sink is empty.

Shaking her hands dry, Deqo marvels over how all this luxury has been hidden from her. Work in a place like this isn't work; there are no buckets to lug from the standpipe or collapsing piles of pans and knives to dodge. The kitchen has a high ceiling and two wide windows that funnel the midday sun inside, pale yellow walls casting a gentle light over everything. Three giant copper pans hang from the wall and their shifting bottoms shine beams of gold onto Deqo's skin. She breathes deeply, knowing she has found where she belongs.

Opening the nearest cupboard she fills her arms with packets of imported biscuits she has seen in the market but has never eaten. Shoving a bottle of cordial under her arm she heads for a bedroom. She settles for the largest one and throws her stash onto the silken pink quilt that covers the gigantic bed; it is like reclining on a cloud, floating magically on a carpet. She extends her limbs into a star shape and then pulls them back and forth, caressing the silk and sending shudders of pleasure up her spine. Unscrewing the bottle with her mouth, she spits out the top and swigs the dark liquid, as thick and sweet as caramel. Scrabbling a hand over to the open biscuit wrapper, she draws three out and stuffs them into her mouth, letting crumbs cascade over her and flicking them carelessly away onto the bed, onto the floor. She is free to do as she pleases without punishment, guidance or scrutiny.

Waking up in a dim, strange room, full of shadows and dark recesses, Deqo panics at the wet sensation over her legs. She leaps from the bed and finds a pool of dark red cordial splattered over the quilt. Grabbing the sticky bottle, she curses herself for making this palace so filthy so quickly. She rips the cover away and to her relief the sheets beneath are still pristine: bundling the quilt up in her arms, she carries it to the bathroom to wash later.

No sound seems to penetrate the house from the war beyond the walls; it echoes and hums and ticks as if she has been swallowed by a giant and caught within his ribs. Deqo dances and slides over the tiled floor; she feels completely safe, hidden away, with only the pad of her feet for company. Light seeps from under a door and she remembers the other rooms, each of them as well furnished as the one she has slept in. She pushes the door open and discovers the room alive with shadows, fluttering, monstrous shadows that span each wall. Deqo looks up to see six white moths beating their wings between the bulb and floral lampshade. She wonders if this is the only light they could locate, if the rest of the town has descended into lifeless shade, and if like her they are afraid of what might happen in that darkness.

Approaching the window, she notices the hole in the mosquito mesh through which the moths must have entered. It is just a few moments before nightfall and a swipe of watery indigo separates the brooding sky from the sullen earth. Distant flares shoot up like stars but leave a sickly green vapour in their wake. It is an alien world being destroyed, one that she doesn't belong to or feel any ownership over. Turning away from the window and drawing the curtain across, her attention turns to the key in the wardrobe; it clicks like a stiff knuckle and the thick-mirrored doors fall open. It is packed tight with clothes, the metal pole sagging with the weight of them, the bottom of the wardrobe covered with rows and rows of shoes. Deqo takes out a pair of silver high heels and slips her feet inside, a gap the size of her fist left behind the heel. She spies sequins between the layers of clothes and pulls out the garment, a kind of short-sleeved top heavy with embellishment, a palm tree picked out in jewel-coloured beads on the front. A wide-brimmed black hat finishes the look and Deqo totters back to look at herself in the mirror; for the first time she likes the girl smiling back at her.

After a motionless couple of hours at the theatre checkpoint, another order from Hashi comes, this time telling Filsan to join Roble on the Jigjiga Road to Ethiopia. A jeep collects her and she jumps in eagerly despite the danger of the district they are entering. Hundreds of rebels are hidden in the hills around Hargeisa and the exchange of fire between them and the soldiers reverberates down into the valley. Filsan covers her nose against the acrid smoke drifting over from burning houses and rolls the side window up. She has nothing to bring Roble, not even a bottle of cola; the only comfort she has to offer is her presence and she hopes that will be enough. Small dots clamber along the hills as the jeep sweeps past; the refugees appear nothing more than bundles of multi-coloured blankets moving in columns like ants.

'Should just stay in their beds rather than dying out there,' the driver says in an accent that reminds her of home.

Filsan turns to him, suddenly interested. 'When did you arrive from Mogadishu?'

'Three days ago. I have barely slept at all, just drive, drive, drive.' He makes a cutting motion with his hand at the road.

'How are things there?'

'Difficult, the city is full of northern refugees.'

That isn't what Filsan cares about; she wants to know if any new singers have broken through in her absence, if the Lido beach café is still open, if the television reception has improved at all.

He tells her he was born in Wardhiigley but brought up in Hamar Weyne, had attended a school she has only vaguely heard of, and worked as a mechanic before joining the army. They have no family, acquaintances or interests in common and the conversation quickly drifts to an end.

The jeep abandons the tarmacked road and climbs a dirt path up into the hills. 'I can't get any closer than this, just follow the curve to the right and you will see them.'

Filsan wipes her brow, hoping she doesn't look or smell too bad. This isn't how she would choose to be reunited, but it is better than waiting.

Suddenly he is there, leaning against a boulder with a pair of binoculars to his eyes; she stops to enjoy the sight of him, calm and nonchalant, as the din of machine-gun fire hitting rock clatters only a few dozen metres away. He notices Filsan after an age, the binoculars still to his eyes but a broad smile stretching beneath his four-day stubble. He holds his arms open, despite knowing she will not fall into them; instead she rushes up and shakes his hand between both of hers.

'Welcome, welcome, *Jaalle!*' He beckons her to the others. 'This is Corporal Abbas, and Privates Samatar and Short Abdi. Tall Abdi is refreshing himself behind the boulder.'

She salutes and they jokily click their heels to attention.

'Have you brought anything to eat?' Abbas asks.

'I'm sorry, I haven't eaten myself.'

'We'll die of starvation up here, I swear,' he groans.

Filsan looks up to Roble. 'When did you last come down to the city?'

'Two days, it's a shambles! They keep telling us just a few more hours, just a few more hours, but still no one has come to relieve us, apart from you that is.'

'They didn't tell me to bring any provisions.' She makes a show of checking her pockets for some chocolate.

'It's not your fault; they don't know what they're doing!' Roble pats her shoulder. 'At least we haven't had any trouble.'

'None?'

'Nothing. We have just been watching through the binoculars – it's better than being at the cinema. Here, have a look.' Roble lifts the binoculars from his neck and passes them to Filsan.

Hargeisa looks beautiful for once, the sky an unusual haze of pink and purple, clouds tinted with smoke, tin roofs like golden pools reflecting the huge orange setting sun. The devastation is lost within deep shadows. She puts the binoculars to her eyes and scans until something comes into focus: a slice of road and the wheels of a car. The burgundy Toyota stops by the side of the road and about eight civilians disgorge from it. Other refugees run along the road and then walk a few breathless steps before resuming their flight. Swinging back to the car, she watches a father escort his young daughter – a girl of five or six in a spotty dress – to the scrub along the track to urinate; he holds her up by the arms and keeps his shoes far away in fear of splashes. A hail of mortars falls nearby, one of them only a few feet from where the father and daughter stand, and all the passengers jump out of the bushes and scurry back to the car. The father darts after them and gestures desperately for the girl to catch up. She stumbles behind, dragging her underwear up with one hand. The father jumps in just as the car begins to pull away; he holds the door open but the driver speeds off, leaving the little girl behind a screen of exhaust fumes. More missiles fall but the girl doesn't stop her pursuit until she is engulfed in a volley of Katyusha rocket fire.

Filsan drops the binoculars in disbelief that the father has just left his child to die. The car, now only a dark speck, continues up the winding road to Ethiopia.

She imagines herself in the girl's position and feels a sudden longing for her father back home, seeing him clearly in her mind's eye with a tumbler of whisky in front of the television, his right foot hitched up under his left thigh. For all his severity he would never have abandoned her like that. She had ignored the last two calls he had made to the barracks; he wants her transferred back to Mogadishu, away from the war.

The sun has set, the silhouetted hills resembling the spines on a lizard's back, and the town within the valley is lit here and there by fires. A call has come through declaring that they are all to be relieved from the checkpoint for a briefing at Birjeeh and now they wait, blowing warm air onto their chilled hands. Abbas and Short Abdi have gathered twigs and built a pitiful fire, and Roble and Filsan huddle together in silence. Tall Abdi approaches and asks for a cigarette; he is shivering and scrawny in a short-sleeved shirt. Roble gives him his half-empty packet. At last they hear the crunch of tyres on grit, and five soldiers laden with assault rifles and an RPG arrive to replace them.

They drive slowly back to Hargeisa without headlights, hoping not to attract rebel attention or the increasingly common friendly fire from jittery conscripts. Filsan knocks against Roble as the jeep hits one pothole after another; they are squeezed together in the back,

295

hidden from view and he puts his arm around her shoulder. She takes his rifle and leans it against the side with hers. A pitter-patter of tracer fire sends white lights into the sky; it reminds Filsan of the cheap Chinese fireworks occasionally set off in her neighbourhood during Eid. The whites of Roble's eyes glow for a second in the light of a checkpoint flash and then dim.

'The moon's going to be strong tonight,' he says softly.

'How do you know?'

'We old nomads know these mysteries.'

She elbows him gently in the ribs. 'You know as much as I do and that's nothing.'

'You'll see. Give it another two hours and you will think there are floodlights above us.'

'I'll be asleep in my bed in two hours, not staring up at the moon like a fool.'

'Well, I'll be joining the other fools for our midnight social club.'

The jeep brakes suddenly and Filsan hits her mouth against her knee.

'What was that?' yells the driver.

'What?'

'Something was just thrown at the windshield.'

'Don't stop, then! Drive on!'

'Go!' shout the other soldiers.

Filsan tastes blood and rubs a finger on the stinging area of her tongue.

A flash of light illuminates the red smear on her index finger. Less than a second after the flash, an elephant charges into the jeep; that is how it seems to Filsan, an angry bull elephant dashing through, flinging her and Roble out onto the street.

Splayed out, holding the earth as if it might move, she turns to Roble and reaches out. 'Get up, Roble. Get up.'

No answer.

'How many?' someone yells.

'Seven, they're all down!' cries another.

Peeling herself up from the grit, Filsan scrabbles around her and grabs the strap of a submachine gun that has been blown out of the vehicle, pulling it near her.

Footsteps run towards her, voices calling unintelligible commands, flashlights scanning the massive wound in Roble's back.

'Abbas? Abdi? Can you hear me?' she croaks.

'I'm here, Corporal,' whispers Tall Abdi. 'I'm still here. Get ready.'

The rebels begin firing before she can pick any of them out. She sprays bullets into the darkness beyond the flashlights. Her grip is weak and the force of the gun makes it jump in her arms.

'You're going to hell,' a fighter screams.

They turn off all of their torches and surge forward.

Filsan doesn't stop shooting. Her gun spits out bullets and unlike in Salahley everything feels wholly real: her heart is thumping hard, she is aware of the smallest sound, feels like an animal about to be ripped apart. The smell of burning flesh blows over to her and she holds her breath.

Somewhere beside her Tall Abdi is shooting too. Bullets ping off the frame of the smouldering jeep and hit the sand with a small puff. The rebels are around four metres away; she can't tell how many of them there are but she needs to maintain that distance, and she drags Roble's Kalashnikov closer to use when her magazine runs out.

'I've been hit!' a rebel cries.

A flashlight switches on and off but it is enough for Filsan to train her sights at the figure who has briefly appeared: a bony young man in glasses who might have been any one of the science students at her university. She squeezes the trigger and aims a barrage at him in particular.

The fire from the rebels decreases. Her eyes have adjusted to the darkness and she can make out two silhouettes, one dragging, the other limping desperately behind.

'Don't stop, Corporal, don't stop.' Tall Abdi is somewhere behind her, his voice weaker than before.

She doesn't need any encouragement. The preservation of her small, inconsequential life – the life she has so frequently wanted to end – is now all that matters.

Another layer is added to the cacophony when a vehicle skids to a stop behind the jeep.

Still firing, Filsan glances back to see if more rebels have arrived, but instead it is a unit of soldiers in an armoured personnel carrier. She continues shooting, her whole body shuddering with relief and fear.

The soldiers fan out around the jeep and soon two

rebels crumple and hit the ground; the others try to melt back into the darkness from which they emerged but are pursued on foot.

As gunfire echoes around her, Filsan crawls on her hands and knees to Roble. His eyes and lips are open as if he has been caught mid-sentence. She puts two fingers to his jugular vein and presses hard. Nothing.

After seven attempts, the television finally comes to life; alarming voices shouting from the wooden box make Deqo duck under the bed. A woman's face fills the screen; she smiles conspiratorially and talks directly to Deqo. 'We have such a show for you, between now and ten o'clock you will be regaled by comedians, serenaded by singers and moved by poets. Gather the family and neighbours, prepare a flask of tea and put your cares aside.'

'OK,' replies Deqo, peeping out.

'Our first guest is well known to all of you. Please welcome Sheikh Sharif to Mogadishu.'

The screen expands to include Sheikh Sharif, the garish orange backdrop and the heads of the live audience. Sheikh Sharif, to Deqo's surprise, is dressed like a poor nomad in a *ma'awis* and vest in the middle of the elegant theatre, a *caday* clamped between his jaws; he races on, narrowing his eyes against the lights trained on him.

'Take those things off me, I can't see where I'm going,' he hollers, holding a hand to his eyes and stumbling exaggeratedly.

Deqo laughs along with the audience.

'*Joow!* Don't I know you?' He points to a man in the front row. 'Aren't you Hassan Madoobe's sister-in-law's cousin's best friend's nephew? Sure you are! Wasn't it your mother who was trampled by ostriches?'

The camera zooms in on the audience member shaking his head with mirth.

'Sure it was! Have you brought your whole *reer* with you tonight? The place is packed as tight as the purse my wife keeps her black market dollars in.'

'What are you telling strangers our business for?' bawls a harsh voice from the wings.

The audience cheers and then an old woman, decades older than Sheikh Sharif, emerges waving a cane at him, chasing him around the stage while he pleads for help. '*Tollai!* Won't someone stop her? Ostrich boy, come and restrain her! This is what happens when you leave the *miyi*, your manhood is left behind with the camel bones.'

Between her giggles, Deqo picks up on a commotion near the window. She wriggles from underneath the bed and pushes the curtain aside.

Four men chase a lone, suited figure. 'Stop where you are!'

'I'm innocent! I swear on my faith,' the fugitive shouts, but continues to run.

'Shoot!' orders the captain and the soldiers obey.

Deqo watches as the bullets hit his back, twisting him into one wild pose and then another. His legs propel him a good distance before he falls to his knees by the villa gate.

'Swear on your faith now, dead man!' exclaims a soldier.

Deqo regards his death with the same detachment she does the television show. She has no comprehension of why these grown men are tormenting each other and is grateful for the glass separating her from them.

Returning to the programme she watches the exploits of Sheikh Sharif and his wife impassively until a singer takes the stage. She recognises the songs from the cassettes Nasra used to play, but this woman makes them sadder and slower. Deqo fetches an overripe banana and a packet of lollipops from the kitchen and watches the rest of the variety show until only white snow cascades over the screen. She sleeps with the television on, bathed in blue light and shushed by white noise.

A truck takes Filsan and Tall Abdi to the hospital, along with the bodies of Roble, Short Abdi, Abbas, Samatar and the nameless driver. The floor of the van is awash with blood, mainly from the driver's neck where a section of shrapnel from the rocket has nearly severed his head. Roble is flat on his back, staring up at the moon, which is as bright as he had predicted. The rush of adrenaline has left Filsan and she now feels the gunshot wound in her hip; she squeezes her trousers and blood oozes between her fingers.

Chains clang as the gate to the main hospital creaks open for them; an orderly in blue helps her down from the back while Tall Abdi is stretchered out. He fought the battle with a chunk of muscle blown out of his abdomen, but now wails like a child, pleading for help from God, from the doctors, from his mother. Filsan holds onto the orderly as the van trundles to the morgue, her heart imploding as if primed with dynamite. She shakes her head in disbelief, wishing for a way to rewind time by just half an hour to change this ending.

'Come on, come on, it's not safe out here,' the orderly warns.

He leads her to the emergency ward. They have to pick their way carefully through the beds and the casualties on the floor with assorted tubes attached to them. A pink-uniformed nurse directs them to a stained bed in the corner with a curtain around it for privacy. The middle-aged woman brusquely sends the orderly away and tells Filsan to lie down, then whips the curtain closed with a noise like knives being sharpened and asks what's wrong with her.

'My hip,' she winces.

The nurse yanks down Filsan's trousers and under-wear and prods the swollen wound with her bare hands. 'It's just a surface injury.'

'Please, let me have something for the pain.'

'What can you give me in return?'

'Check my trouser pocket.'

The nurse roots through all the pockets until she locates the roll of small shilling notes; she counts out the money with bloody fingers and then tucks the whole lot into her waistband. 'I'll get you something,' she whispers.

If this is how they treat the living, what must they be

doing to the dead in the morgue? she thinks. Were greedy hands searching through Roble's clothes already? Would they steal the watch he was proud of or rip the silver tooth from his mouth? The certainty that they would nauseates her. There is nothing to cover her body with so she tries to tug her trousers up, but collapses back, preferring the exposure of the unkempt thicket of hair below her stomach to the corkscrew-like pain drilling through her pelvis.

The doctor comes, his face partly hidden behind a mask like an Arab girl's, his coat dyed brown with dried blood. He stitches the wound quickly. He doesn't seem to see her nakedness and works mechanically without word or eye contact. At the end, the nurse bandages the wound and gives her painkillers and a soiled blanket to sleep under.

The ward is loud and bright all night. More injured soldiers arrive and some depart, carried out unceremoniously to make room for the living. The provincial hospital only has one operating theatre, so procedures usually done under general anaesthetic are now attempted under local right there in the ward. Wrapping a pillow around her head doesn't soften the screams and hollering from men losing an arm or foot a few feet away. At about four in the morning, still wide awake and feeling almost deranged, Filsan calls for water, and calls again, and calls again. She pulls open the curtain around her bed and squints against the fluorescent light. The doctor, surrounded by all the nurses, is arguing with Lieutenant Hashi.

'This is an order from the highest level. You have no choice.'

The doctor raises his hands in disbelief and walks out.

'Coward!' spits Hashi after him. 'The job falls on you then, nurses. Do your duty.' He beckons a group into the ward. Ten uniformed high-school students in handcuffs shuffle past, flanked by four policemen, and he orders them to follow the nurses into an anteroom.

Birds chirp in the trees outside but her thirst keeps her from sleep. Filsan waits for the nurses to reappear but they don't. Eventually, the orderly who had brought her in slouches into the ward and she taps on the metal bedframe to get his attention. She gets a good look at him this time: a bald man in his thirties, with an obsequious, fearful expression on his face. He checks over his shoulder before bending down and putting a hand on her upper arm. 'What's wrong, cousin?'

Gesturing to her throat, she manages to croak, 'Water.'

He rubs her shoulder in an intimate way that she doesn't like. 'I'll get it for you but you need to wait.'

'Why?'

'They are doing something sensitive in the room.'

'You cannot even get a glass of water?'

'No, no, no. I don't want to see it.'

'See what?' she says, exasperated.

'The children, they are bleeding.'

'They're donating blood, that's all.' Filsan wonders at the ignorance of the man. 'You don't need to worry.'

'No! They are being bled dry. The soldier said they should be used like taps.'

'Hashi?'

'That one.'

'Like taps? So they die?'

'That is the plan.'

A squabble between stray dogs wakes Deqo. They growl menacingly and she rubs her eyes and yawns loudly in frustration. She will fill a bucket of cold water, disperse the mongrels and then return to sleep. Water sloshes over the lip of the bucket and onto the courtyard but there is still enough to give them a shock. Head down, biting her lip, two hands straining around the thin handle, she doesn't notice the vultures perched on the roof until a shadow swoops over her. It drops something near her feet and she glances down. A leaf? A wrinkled piece of leather? She picks it up curiously. A human ear. She throws it and the bucket down and bolts back to the veranda. The vultures swoop and circle before settling on the mango tree. She has never seen so many in one place, the branches of the tree sag and bob under the weight of them.

A muscular white dog with brown patches enters the gate, droplets of blood hanging like dew from the hairs of its muzzle, and sniffs the track leading to the house. Deqo grasps the broom resting against the wall and charges it.

'*Bax*! Out! Out!' she yells, shoving the bristles of the brush into the dog's pink nose.

He stops in his tracks, yelping a few times, before padding out into the street. She pursues him and throws a few rocks at his rear. 'Stay out.'

Then she spots the fugitive: torn, bloodied, but still smart in his suit and tie. She hits the broom against the wall until the pack leave their feast. She avoids his face and focuses on the shiny black loafers on his feet, decorated with a gold link chain. Wedding shoes, she thinks. The dogs growl their impatience but keep at bay. His rotund stomach bulges against his shirt buttons and already there is a smell, sweet and repugnant at the same time. Deqo pulls the shoes off his feet – they are too good to waste – places them against the wall and then begins to dig a hole in the sandy earth with the handle of her broom. The dogs watch curiously but don't interfere. She will never be able to dig a hole deep enough to prevent them getting to him, but she can at least give him the dignity of a burial. About two feet down she gives up and kneels down to rest. Her eyes accidentally fall on his face as he slumps forward. The dogs have ripped away his nose and exposed the bone underneath his left cheek. The ear is gone too. The undamaged part of his face is that of a wealthy forty-something with unlined, pale skin, the kind of man who has recently returned from overseas to find a wife or maybe build an ostentatious villa near his mother with the money he has saved.

Flinging the broom to the ground, Deqo grabs his leather belt and attempts to drag him to the edge of the pit. It is like hauling stone; she tugs again at the belt but the rigid body won't shift. Stepping over him, she pushes his bullet-pierced back with her hands and then her feet; it is like the games she and Anab used to play in Saba'ad, play fights where one attacked and the other rolled up in a ball and resisted. Giggling a little, imagining that he is just pretending to be dead, she pushes his bottom. It is no good; he was at least twice her weight while alive and now has the dull burden of death on top of him. Deqo has learnt to be persistent though; there is no problem that she can't find a solution to within her own limited means. She stalks around him, wondering how best to take him the few inches to his grave. If she could only lift his torso she could use his weight to flip him. Taking hold of the broom she slides it under his side and then levers it up; he moves slowly, slowly, slowly and then rolls onto his stomach. She tries again and this time he tumbles into the grave.

Sweating and with a stench of rotting flesh on her hands, she brushes great armfuls of fine sand over him, concealing first his face, then his torso and finally his long legs. It is done. She tears a cluster of flowers from the pink bougainvillea and plants it over his head. 'There you go,' she exclaims.

The children's bodies are brought out of the anteroom in twos. A hand drops off the trolley as lifeless and yellow as an autumn leaf. Filsan watches mesmerised as the nurses go in and out of the bleeding room with barely a flicker of reaction. They hold scarlet bags of blood in their fingers – apparently destined for the operating theatre – and go around the ward with smiles for the patients. Follow orders. Follow orders. Follow orders. That is the code they have been brought up under and it endures until the burden of guilt cracks the spine. Her father would probably explain their actions as the necessities of war, but to her they seem like the cannibals of old tales: totally ordinary yet irrevocably depraved.

The orderly returns with a glass of water.

'Has it finished in there?' She gestures with her head to the anteroom.

'One more to go.'

She gulps from the glass.

'May Allah have mercy on their souls,' he says, before pushing his squeaky trolley away.

She doesn't know if he is referring to the students or the nurses.

Her mind travels to that last child beyond the unvarnished wooden door of the nurses' station. At that age she was planning on becoming a pilot for the Somali national airline, a fanciful dream that never got off the ground but which had felt real and possible and irreplaceable at the time. Her father was under too much suspicion to influence the aviation professors by the time she was old enough to apply for university. She imagines the needle going into the student's slim arm, the thick maroon blood seeping out of it, slowly, painlessly but lethally. When will they realise that life is leaving them? That for all the incandescence and noise of their short existence, death is wrapping its tendrils around them?

Filsan is both attracted to and repulsed by what is happening in that room. Is she brave enough to offer herself instead of that teenager? Or should she just submit to a future of growing grey hairs seated next to her father in their matching armchairs? The decision is made for her when the door jolts open and the last corpse is carried out in the arms of an orderly; it is a girl, her long, black plait swinging and bouncing beneath her, her wrists free of shackles, the expression on her face calm and beatific.

Filsan edges off the bed; the pills have subdued her pain enough to let her keep pace behind the orderly.

Time to leave, Deqo thinks. She does not fear death itself, but the idea of her body being eaten by the city's scavengers chases her from the comfortable solitude she has enjoyed so blithely. People – both danger and sanctuary is to be found amongst people. The newfound possessions she can't leave behind – the shoes, dresses, cans of food, compact mirror – she bundles into a scarf and knots up, away from jealous eyes. It is time to return to Saba'ad, to the lumpy porridge, dust and interminable waiting.

She tidies the various messes she has made, bidding farewell to each room and respectfully closing the doors. The vultures have left the mango tree but, on reaching the road, she sees two of them standing on the uncovered knees of the man she buried; the dogs must have unearthed his bottom half and then abandoned him, and now the birds pick vigorously at his thighs. Deqo trudges in the opposite direction.

The street is full of militiamen, dressed half in *whodead* and half in camouflage wear, stripping the homes as professionally as removal men: three short men carry a huge wardrobe on their heads to a nearby lorry, while a boy wrenches the corrugated tin roof off a samosa stall.

She avoids the checkpoints she can and talks her way through the ones she can't. Her derelict condition is enough to convince the soldiers she is who she says she is. A few tea shops and cafés are still open to cater to the military, but otherwise everywhere is deserted. She loses track of where she is in relation to the ditch and looks around for anything that might guide her out of the city, before wandering into a pretty neighbourhood with goats bleating plaintively in the yards.

The sun has passed its zenith and Deqo feels sweat trickling down her temples. She leans against a bunga-low and notices an orchard opposite with tall fruit trees waving to her over the glass-crested wall. There is a low, wooden gate. She jumps up and climbs over. It is like being back in the ditch but tidier and sweeter smelling. The ground is littered with pomegranates, tamarinds and papayas. She fills her skirt and then sits in the shade under a tree to eat a wrinkled yellow papaya, spitting the slimy black seeds as far as she can. Someone has put hard labour into this orchard; there are no scrubby, unused patches or broken hoses and scrap metal piled up in a corner. Weaver-birds sing in the nests above her head and trumpet-headed flowers blow within arm's reach.

Curious and emboldened by the peace of the orchard, she creeps towards the small, blue-painted bungalow and peers through a crack in the back door into a dark, empty hallway. The bars on the kitchen window are designed to keep out a burglar but are wide enough for her; she drops her bundle to the ground and crawls in, dropping feet first into a hillock of saucepans.

A clatter in the kitchen, a pot lid maybe, dancing like a cymbal before making its peace with the earth; Kawsar swivels her head towards the half-closed kitchen entrance.

'Come on, I'm ready,' she says with a voice that doesn't sound like her own.

The kitchen door swings gently, tauntingly, but no one appears. She had once found a thief in her kitchen and held him tight as he tried to escape out the back; she fought with him and is eager to face the soldiers now.

'*Soobax*! Come out!' she yells.

Still nothing stirs. Kawsar grabs her glass and throws it with all her strength at the kitchen door. The glass shatters against the door handle, rainbows flaring as the shards tinkle to the floor.

A hunched figure emerges as if lured out by the yellows, reds and blues that Kawsar has conjured up. It is a small and indistinct shape. A girl with frayed plaits and a blood-red smock holding her hands behind her back as if on parade.

311

'Hodan?' She is angry this time, fed up with her child torturing her.

The girl's face is downturned, her chin pressed into her neck, a fan of black eyelashes hiding her eyes. She doesn't evanesce this time.

'Answer me,' demands Kawsar, her heart beating harder. She searches the girl for injuries but there aren't any; she is only playing dumb.

'Get out of my house if you're not going to speak.' Kawsar points a stern finger towards the front door.

The girl doesn't reply or shift an inch. Her feet are bare and dusty, her long legs sprout like weeds between cracked paving, but her resemblance to Hodan is certain: the heart-shaped face, the dimples, the reedlike body all belong to her child.

'Watch your feet on the glass,' Kawsar says, her tone softening.

The girl stretches her toes, shifts her balance, but stays rooted to the same spot. Her smock is torn in places along the side.

Kawsar takes a deep breath. 'What do you want from me?'

'I just want to rest.' The voice is not Hodan's; it's deeper and wearier.

'Rest then.' Kawsar waves a hand in the direction of Nurto's mattress.

The girl treads over to the divan and tucks her legs slowly underneath her, shyly pushing her skirt down between her knees as she crosses them. She chews her bottom lip nervously like Kawsar used to as a child.

'What is your name?'

'Deqo.'

'Where have you come from?'

'The ditch,' she says, deciding that the old woman would prefer to hear that than Saba'ad.

'Where is your family?'

'It's just me.' The girl meets her eyes.

Kawsar feels a charge when she hears those words.

'How do I know you are not here to steal from me?'

Deqo shrugs her shoulders, suddenly surly and tired of the questions. She picks at the dirt underneath her fingernails.

Kawsar's eyes fall appraisingly on her, from the short toes to the dull, knotted hair on her head. She looks like one of those hardy, parasitical children born in times of famine, probably carried over from Ethiopia when only a few weeks old and nursed on rainwater and sugar, kept alive by a will already steely and adult.

The old woman's room is like a tomb, sour with stale air and dust-coated. Deqo watches her for some time before leaving the safety of the kitchen. She reminds her of those crones in Saba'ad who conduct ceremonies in their tiny *buuls*; with names like Sheikha Jinnow or Hajiya Halima, they are the ones who know how to let blood, burn sicknesses out, diagnose and remedy the myriad ailments that constantly afflict the unhappy women of the camp. Their holiness comes from pilgrimages to saint's tombs and the miracle of their own longevity. Deqo assumes this old woman must be so convinced of her closeness to God that she doesn't feel the need to flee like everyone else; she survives on prayers alone and is waiting for the dust to slowly settle and entomb her in her own shrine. Then Deqo steps into the bedroom and immediately recognises whom she has found.

Kawsar clears her throat and adjusts the bed sheets nervously. 'You should leave now; this isn't the time for tea and conversation.'

Deqo's attention is suddenly pulled up. 'I don't have anywhere to go.'

Kawsar thinks that even the most ragged, glue-sniffing beggar-child would go running back to their family in fear of these bombs, but maybe Deqo is unafraid because her family are nearby, looting the neighbours' homes alongside the soldiers.

'So what do you expect to do when the soldiers arrive?'

'There aren't any nearby. We'll be safe for a while.'

Kawsar raises her eyebrow at the presumptuous 'we' and feels a wave of mischief rise in her, 'What shall *we* do until they get here then?' she says with a smile. 'Play *shax*? Chase a *garangar* along the street? Plait each other's hair?'

'Yes, would you plait my hair, please?' Deqo replies eagerly, lifting a hand to her head as if to hide its scruffiness.

Kawsar senses a pulse of pleasure at the girl's frankness, a kind of warmth that tending to a child's needs has always given her, a sensation she has nearly forgotten.

'Get the hair oil and comb from the dresser.'

Deqo hands them to her.

'Sit beneath me,' Kawsar orders.

The girl sits lightly on the floor, holding her weight up with her arms; she smells of fruit and sweat.

'We should wash it, but never mind.' Kawsar pulls apart the old plaits, sifting Deqo's soft but dirty hair between her fingers, massaging jasmine oil into her scalp while Deqo toys absentmindedly with the bottle top.

The words of an old song play in Kawsar's mind: *'Love, love isn't fair, teardrops always chase behind.'*

'Can I stay here for a while?' Deqo asks.

Kawsar's heart is beating hard, her breath shallow and quiet. She wants time to end at this moment, for there to be nothing in the world beyond her nimble fingers and the girl's hair to spin into silk. There must be a hunchbacked, toothless sorceress somewhere who weaves all these disparate people together, thinks Kawsar, who carelessly throws this child together with me, while families are ripped apart.

Resting a hand on the girl's narrow, sinuous back, she can feel the heat of her soul through the oily palm of her hand, as smooth and alive as an egg. She doubts that incandescence can just disappear. If they are killed right here, would their ghosts continue as they are, the old ghost plaiting and the young one waiting, fidgeting? She can imagine that, the silence and peacefulness of it, a source of envy to passers-by – battling with the rage and

315

chaos of life – who happen to glance in through the barred window.

Filsan rushes through corridors behind the orderly and the dead student, disembodied voices flying past like birds, snatches of sunlight filtering through dust-specked windows. The orderly stops and she freezes. He enters a room and she can tell by the stench that they have reached the mortuary.

He returns empty-handed and she sneaks a peek through the closing door. There are no other hospital workers inside and she holds the door before sliding through. Bodies are heaped on the floor, three deep in places, in various states of decomposition. Her eyes dart around for Roble's face but she keeps returning to the young girl, her narrow body stuck on a shelf above the others. Filsan catches sight of the metal stores on one side of the white-tiled room and opens them methodically, top left to bottom right. The faces are like molten wax models: a facsimile of an old woman here, a wealthy civil servant there, a newborn baby squeezed beside its mother. She opens the last door despondently, hoping to find him and not find him at the same time, but there he is.

They have wrapped Roble decently in white cloth, leaving only a diamond shape around his face. He appears to have aged twenty years overnight; his cheeks are sunken, his lips wide and slack, his eye sockets deep and dark. There is no blood, no visible injury; she touches his eyebrow and smoothes the hair, and the incredible frigidity of his skin is the only convincing proof that he is gone. She runs a fingertip over his bottom lip and then twists her head to kiss him on the mouth, her nose grazing his chin; the first kiss of her life numbs both her flesh and spirit. She opens her eyes to the mortuary tiles, to the grime on the fridge handles, to the prettily marbled veins on the hand of a corpse waiting on a concrete slab.

'I'll be with you soon.' Filsan pushes the handle and returns Roble to his abode.

Shaking wildly, unable to withstand the stench, she strips to her bloodied underwear and shoves her uniform in a corner. She undresses a dead woman – a teacher-type with sensible, large-rimmed glasses – taking her paisley *diric*, shawl and delicate sandals, leaving the bruises on her naked body visible like emblazoned accusations.

She clambers out of the window into the bright sun of the weed-strewn hospital yard. She adjusts the scarf to cover her nose and mouth and bends her head down low. Putting one foot cautiously in front of the other, she knows that she will probably be killed before the day is out, either as a deserter or as a lone woman in the middle of a battlefield, but she cannot remain, whatever the cost.

'Just walk, just walk, just walk,' she mutters.

Beside the wall dividing the main hospital from the psychiatric ward is a tangle of bushes and discarded strips of barbed wire, beyond which is the incinerator block. She checks around her before slipping into a shadow to the side of the concrete cabin; she struggles to climb onto the low roof and over the perimeter wall in her light sandals. Losing her footing, she falls heavily on her back into the road.

The street is empty, the imprint of tank tracks visible like a giant's footsteps. Filsan dusts herself down and turns east to the neighbourhood she used to patrol with Roble. There are more than fifty checkpoints dotted around the city – she had helped decide the location of each – and even if she manages to avoid them all, there are still mortars, cluster bombs and strafing fighter jets to evade. She catches sight of a crowd of people a few metres ahead, crouched against the hospital wall, a pair of grey trousers visible here, a bold-coloured *diric* there. She hides and makes certain no soldiers are with them and then advances. The group is motionless and silent; Filsan imagines they are too wounded or fatigued to move any further towards the hospital.

A few more steps and the truth sets in: thirty corpses lie dumped on top of each other, limbs entangled and frozen into grotesque shapes. Some have fresh blood on their skin while others are already discoloured and swollen: bulging thighs, purple faces, taut, shiny skin where shirts gape open. All have multiple bullet wounds, apart from one man whose throat is cut wide open, the rigid architecture of his neck bisected and revealed.

Filsan shields her nose against the smell and the ecstatic flies. She stares at one face for a moment and then another until she recognises the family she stopped at the checkpoint; all of them are here now, the limping mother, the three little girls, the adolescent boy with his over-burdened handcart, and the sharp-chinned young woman leading them all. Filsan tries to remember her name. Luul? Nura? The woman's eyes are still open, her head thrown back in shock, her arms reaching out to her sisters. It seems from the spray of blood on the wall that they were executed here. Filsan does not feel guilt or remorse as she gazes over the bodies, rather an insatiable curiosity and desire to know when and where her own death will come and what expression she will wear to meet it. She has never been like other people, and the corpses confirm that she has no useful place on this earth; she is doomed to be nothing more than one of death's handmaidens.

She checks the sky for planes and listens for tanks. All is quiet. She turns down a narrow alley littered with animal droppings and follows it through to the next alley and then the next.

'Why did you leave me?' Kawsar asks after staring at Deqo for a long time.

Deqo chews her upper lip, looking down guiltily; she remembers that day at the stadium in snatches, no thoughts or feelings, just momentary images of dancing, then blows, then the wind in her hair as she ran away.

'I don't know, I was frightened.'

'Didn't I look after you well?'

Deqo nods.

'Was there anything more I could have done?'

Deqo shakes her head.

Kawsar exhales loudly and her eyes slowly fill with tears. 'I have missed you so much.'

Deqo pads over to her bedside and wipes the tears away. 'I'm sorry,' she whispers, delighted to have made such a deep impression on the old woman.

'You left me with nothing but an empty heart,' Kawsar sobs. 'It's too late to soothe me now.'

Deqo continues stroking her cheek. 'It's not too late, I can help you. I will get you out of here.'

In a few hours Deqo has removed the dirty sheets from the bed, fed Kawsar a can of tuna and rubbed a wet towel over her face and arms. Caring for her has distanced the war from Deqo's mind.

'It's too late,' Kawsar repeats over and over, crying bitterly.

Deqo leans against the bed and waits for the tears to pass, knowing that they always do. She learnt that from Nurse Doreen in Saba'ad: as rainstorms come quick and heavy before leaving a clear sky, so do tears.

Kawsar's sobs ebb and then stop; her reddened and contorted face seems childlike, filled with perplexing thoughts.

Deqo looks away shyly while Kawsar slowly composes herself. She sits cross-legged beneath the bed and pats the tight, stinging plaits on her head. 'I want to take you back with me to Saba'ad.'

Silence.

'We will be safe there, everyone will think you're my grandmother. Nurse Doreen will help you.'

No response.

Deqo turns her head and sees Kawsar's eyes closed. Leaping up she puts her ear to her mouth and feels a warm stream of breath on her skin.

'Sleep then.' She pats the liver-spotted hand.

Restless, Deqo watches out of a window that has a fine crack running diagonally from one corner to another; all it would take is a light press and the glass would snap in two. She sees the wind stirring the strands of a *miri-miri* tree and wants to feel that breeze on her face.

Stepping out into the street she turns right, away from the direction she came. Three dead bodies spoil the peaceful scene; the *miri-miri* and bougainvillea and juniper cannot cover the scent of their decomposition. She unties a goat that has been left tethered to a pole and the creature slumps to its knees in exhaustion, looking up at Deqo with terrified, wide eyes. She walks away, leaving it to its own fate. The local *dukaan* has been ripped open and looted, dented cans of condensed milk and kidney beans embedded in the sand. Deqo steps in and discovers the shopkeeper's bloodied body behind the counter, a prayer cap on his head and a handful of worthless military chits clamped between his fingers. She picks through the goods on the ground and gathers bags of sweets, bottled drinks and potato chips in her skirt.

Lost, parched, Filsan tilts her head against the smoke-blackened wall and pants long, ragged breaths. She staggers out into the street and into view of a checkpoint.

Their guns swivel over to her and she raises her hands in defeat. There is still about ten metres between them and Filsan thinks through what is about to unfold: one of them will recognise her and radio through that they have caught a deserter; if she is lucky they will send her to a southern jail, if not she will be executed in Birjeeh. Rejecting either possibility, she dashes into a dark alley and sprints as fast as she can, her pain momentarily lifted by the adrenaline pumping through her veins. The soldiers chase but don't shoot, probably too young and still frightened of their weapons; they are gaining on her and she turns back to see one just five metres behind. She ducks into the tiny space between two buildings and then cuts through into another alley; she races to the rectangle of bright light at its mouth and is spat out into a familiar road. Hearing the soldier's boots at her back, she continues as far as she can before collapsing behind the corrugated tin wall of a *dukaan*. A face appears in a crack in the metal and a refugee girl with a collection of looted items in her arms blinks at her. Filsan turns her back and wishes her away.

'Hey *yaari*! Where did that woman run to?' a soldier shouts.

Filsan holds her breath.

'She went up there,' the little girl says.

'Where? Show me.'

She clomps forward. 'Around that corner, you see?'

'Comrades, follow me,' he yells behind him and then their army boots bolt away.

The long-lashed eye appears back at the crack. 'They've gone.'

She gestures for Filsan to follow and leads her to the safety of a small, blue bungalow.

An old woman is buried within the sheets of the bed, the lower part of her face covered by a blanket. A smell rises from her that makes Filsan gag.

'Is that your grandmother?' Filsan whispers.

'Yes. I am looking after her. Who are you?'

'Filsan.'

'Why were they chasing you?'

'Because I used to be one of them.'

'And now?'

'I am one of you.'

Kawsar stirs while Filsan is in the bathroom. She mutters indistinct words and moans before opening her eyes. Deqo stands impatiently beside her, waiting for the moment to tell her about the stranger.

'What's the matter?'

Deqo checks over her shoulder. 'I brought a woman here while you were sleeping.'

'Who is she?'

'She used to be a soldier.'

Kawsar rises up on to her elbows and wipes her hands over her face. 'She didn't give you a name?'

'Filsan.'

'Is she alone?'

'Yes.'

There is the sound of footsteps accompanied by the swish of a long *diric* trailing on the tiles. Then Filsan appears: gaunt, dishevelled, humbled but unmistakable.

Deqo looks between the women as they exchange fixed, cold stares.

'Have you come to finish the job?' Kawsar finally says.

Filsan raises her hands, whether in denial or surrender it is difficult to tell.

Deqo notices that Kawsar's face has flushed a deep red and her eyes have a glassy film over them.

'Look what you have done to me!' She flings the blankets away to reveal her wasted legs discoloured by patches of peeling skin.

Filsan's head bows a fraction.

'Are you satisfied now that your friends have decided to send us all to hell?'

Deqo inches closer to Kawsar and holds her arms out as if to shield her. 'What have you done to her?'

Filsan's sobs are awkward, resistant, her mouth clenches to hold them in. The expression of emotion seems to cause her pain. 'Forgive me, forgive me, forgive me,' the words rock her.

Kawsar sets her jaw and watches without pity. 'Only God can forgive you.' Her voice is calm but icy. 'Why are you here? Are they after you now?'

'I've deserted.'

'So they might follow you here?'

'Maybe.'

'Get out! Don't bring more trouble than we already have.'

'Let her stay.' Deqo pleads, grabbing Kawsar's hand. She turns to Filsan. 'You can't let her die. You owe me.'

Ashamed, Filsan approaches the bed and Kawsar flinches. 'You cannot walk at all?' she asks.

'Not even one step.'

'I always repay a debt. I will do whatever this child asks.'

Kawsar looks around her room, her tomb, and through the window to the red sky hanging over the skeletons of a familiar world. If she goes with them she will see exactly what has happened to her town, she will smell the destruction, taste it. If she stays she will only know her own end. 'I'll go with you.'

A wide smile brightens Deqo's face.

Kawsar's heart begins to pound; she wants escape, but now there is guilt at risking the little girl's life, fear of the soldier and of what she will find outside, and a strange, strange thrill in declaring what she wants rather than what she thinks others need.

They rest in awkward silence until nightfall, and then by the light of a full moon open and share three cans of tuna from the kitchen. Their padding around in the darkness reminds Kawsar of stray cats sniffing through a larder. Her hearing is so acute that their shallow breaths, their mastication, and even the steady beat of their hearts seem deafening. It is easier to not see them; her fate rests in the hands of a scruffy urchin and a brutal, bloodstained deserter. Deqo fills all the flasks she can find with water, while Filsan stands in the middle of the room, almost catatonic. After gathering her thoughts she peers through the window and then opens the front door slightly and creeps out into the courtyard. Deqo watches through the lock and ushers Filsan in when she returns with a wheelbarrow. Stripping the bed of blankets they line the small carriage that Raage used to deliver metre-long baguettes to the local housewives. Kawsar feels soft patches of her skin ooze fluid onto the sheets as she moves closer to the edge of the mattress. 'That's enough blankets, I am not an egg. Come and take my arms.'

Filsan guides the wheelbarrow to the bed and then tentatively places an arm around Kawsar's back. Her touch doesn't feel as distasteful as Kawsar thought it would; it is just a hand, neither evil nor good in itself, but strong as she steers her into the wheelbarrow.

Deqo covers her with the last of the blankets and puts the flasks in the small spaces left beside her.

'Lift the mattress and take out the box underneath.'

Filsan puts the wooden chest on the floor and then lets the mattress drop down. It contains the money Kawsar has saved since Hodan died – the rents she collected from the houses Farah had built and the small police pension she had inherited should have been a sizeable amount, but their value has plummeted along with that of the Somali shilling.

'Give it to me.' Kawsar clutches the box to her breasts and remembers that the key is hidden inside the frame of the tapestry on the wall. She points to it and Deqo unhooks it from the nail, the key falling to the floor.

'Have you got it?'

'Yes!' Deqo leaps up triumphantly and drops it into Kawsar's palm.

'Take warm clothes from the wardrobe.' Kawsar feels awkward and foolish ordering them around from this idiotic throne, but tries to keep her voice authoritative.

'No, we don't want to be overburdened.' Filsan speaks softly but there is an edge to her voice.

'Just take a jumper, then,' insists Kawsar, jabbing a finger at the wardrobe.

Deqo obeys Kawsar's instruction and piles on warm clothes, knowing just how cold a night in the desert can be.

Filsan grasps the handles and tilts the wheelbarrow up. 'How is that?'

Kawsar grips the sides, afraid that she is about to be tipped out, but holds her nerve. 'It's fine, let's take our chance.'

With Deqo guiding the front and Filsan shoving from behind, Kawsar finally leaves the bungalow. She resembles a lizard that has crawled out of its burrow: scale-skinned, slit-eyed, ignorant of what it might find. After the concrete yard they sink into the deep sand of October Road, into a pale white moonscape that seems surreal yet familiar. Kawsar turns to her bungalow and bids a bittersweet farewell to the grief-blue walls.

They move slowly, as if through water, Filsan pushing with her whole body and stumbling repeatedly. Kawsar huddles under the blanket and tries to piece together the broken shards of the shattered neighbourhood into something she recognises. Raage's exceptionally tidy little shop has been ransacked; Maryam's goat pants half-dead on its side; Umar Farey's hotel has received an intense barrage of mortars, its green windows mostly splintered and blackened; the cassettes from the video hall have been smashed and tape flutters in the trees like mourning banners; a fire smoulders on Fadumo's roof. Deqo pulls the wheelbarrow to the left, away from the three bodies lying on their stomachs. Kawsar puts her hand to her eyes to avoid the sight but feels drawn to look, recognising Maryam and two of her children from the gaps between her fingers. Neither Deqo nor Filsan look in their direction. Kawsar says a prayer for the family, ashamed that she cannot even stop to bury them. Maryam with her alligator bag full of medicines deserved more than this country had given her and her children. It has now reduced them to hide and meat for the vultures to pick over. Kawsar is humiliated by the sight of them. Nothing she believed in matters anymore: religion, tradition, civilisation has been swept away. Hodan was right to have gone when she did.

Apart from desultory gunfire and the far-away rattle of trucks crossing Hargeisa Bridge, it appears as if the soldiers and rebels have exhausted each other. The first orgy of violence has been enacted; now it is time for bodies to be buried, wounds to be attended to, sleep to be caught up on. The moonlight is so bright that Kawsar can see to the end of the street where short, velvety shadows huddle beneath the bushes like *jinns*. The tanks, the planes, helicopters, armoured vehicles and cannons have been put to bed and the few songbirds that haven't fled begin to trill, calling out disoriented, despondent songs to one another for comfort. They will have to be the poets recording what happened here, indignation puffing their chests and opening their throats wide, the sorrowful notes catching in the trees and falling, if life returns, like dust over heads that would rather forget.

Filsan pushes deeper into the wheelbarrow to keep it moving; the frail old woman seems to weigh a ton, and the force it takes to move her over the rough ground makes her arms twitch uncontrollably. Bolts of pain shoot up and down her spine and she endures it silently, seeing them as part of the restitution she has to make, a physical purification if not a spiritual one. The pain worsens, beginning at the soles of her feet and slicing up to the top of her skull. Panting, sweating, she drives Kawsar out of Guryo Samo and into the scrubby patch of land behind, an oasis of sand, acacias and discarded mechanical parts. The entire wheel slides into the deep, fine sand and it falls to Deqo to dig it out while Filsan catches her breath. It is another three or four miles before they reach any of the roads leading out from Hargeisa. If they are lucky they will make it before dawn. If not, they will certainly be discovered by the army. Deqo passes around a flask of water and then slings the empty vessel into the aloes.

Filsan's thoughts return to her father, asleep in his empty house in Mogadishu; this is the longest break in communication they have ever had. She has ignored his calls for two weeks but constantly hears his voice in her head anyway, the restrained but contemptuous tone: 'What do you know?' and 'Don't be such an imbecile' run around and around in her mind. She knows in her bones that she has turned irrevocably against him; hating how she curled and shrank in his presence. There is no way to wipe the blood from her now, but she can turn her back on that old life.

Filsan strains against the wheelbarrow, biting her lower lip, gathering the last of her strength like a whipped mule. Careering left and right, they make slow progress to the poor neighbourhood the other side of the oasis. Here the stick and cloth houses have burnt to ash – finding nothing to loot, the advance party of soldiers have smashed, torn and incinerated every last thing the blacksmiths, latrine cleaners and shoemakers left behind. Five-shilling *whodead* flip-flops smoulder in the ruins.

Filsan trips over the debris and puts a hand on Kawsar's shoulder to steady her feet. Kawsar responds with an accusatory look as if she holds Filsan personally responsible for what she sees.

Deqo walks a few feet ahead, scouting the horizon, looking back every few seconds to check they are still with her.

'Don't go that way, there are only wild animals that

way. We need to go uphill to get to the main road,' Kawsar
calls out.

Filsan pushes the wheelbarrow to the crest of the hill and,
when Kawsar is safely level, collapses onto her back.
They have walked all night and now the diaphanous blue
sky spins in dizzying circles over her. Deqo pours water
into her mouth but it chokes her. She pushes the flask
away and closes her eyes.

'Come on, the road is in sight,' Kawsar orders.

'I can't . . .'

'It's already light, we can't just sit here.'

Filsan doesn't reply but covers her eyes, trying to
imagine her companions and the situation away.

Deqo, tireless, jumps impatiently on the spot. 'I am
going to check the road,' she shouts.

'Keep your voice down,' Kawsar hisses after her.

In the ten minutes that Deqo is away, Filsan falls asleep.
The girl returns and shakes her roughly awake. Stretching
her weeping, blistered hands over the wheelbarrow
handles, she follows groggily as Deqo jogs and points to
something ahead.

Fifty feet away a white lorry comes into sight, the open bed
of it crammed with refugees and crates of *qat*. It pulls over
with the engine running as a man chewing a matchstick
approaches them. The *qat* smuggler is around thirty years old
with a deep scar on his cheek and uncombed, clumpy hair.

'Half a million shillings to take you all to the Ethiopian
border.'

Kawsar unlocks the chest in her arms and rifles through it. Add to it the gold earrings she is wearing, and it might be enough.

Filsan stands impotently behind as Kawsar removes her earrings and passes everything to the smuggler.

He puts the matchstick behind his ear and re-counts the haul, showing off his green and gold teeth, then he grunts assent and takes the wheelbarrow from Filsan, running with Kawsar as if she is weightless before lifting her onto the flatbed. The morose passengers shift a little but offer no help as she yells in pain. Deqo jumps on beside her and then Filsan crawls aboard just as the lorry speeds away.

The smugglers drive as fast as their forty-year-old vehicle can take them, dodging all of the checkpoints by driving off-road, the *qat* dealers comfortable in their cab while the refugees are thrown about, cracking teeth on the metal railings, hitting noses against skulls, bruising ribs on the *qat* crates. A pregnant woman opposite Deqo sits weeping as blood pours from between her legs. They cross the Haud desert and enter a slice of the Ethiopian wilderness within two hours; the refugees are ordered to disembark at this barren place, Harta Sheikh, while the truck continues to Dire Dawa. The smugglers deposit Kawsar under a tree.

'Just over there, the camp is just over there,' the gold-toothed man bawls, pointing into the distance.

Filsan stays with Kawsar. Following the other refugees,

Deqo walks for half an hour before stopping dead. One side of the horizon to the other is covered in *buuls*, clutched so low to the ground that they seem to be sand dunes rippling in the desert heat. Saba'ad could be dropped five times into the expanse. It takes her an hour to reach the camp. It is full of men in suits, women in dusty floral *dirics* and children wailing and scratching at the lice in their hair. Some of the men carry blue UN tarpaulin in their hands, but most of the structures are cobbled together from cloth and sticks, some expertly built by people who had once been nomads, others barely holding together. The camp is too new to have any water standpipes, clinics or latrines, and there is still vegetation – aloes, euphorbias, acacias – for people to raid for firewood and construction. A queue forms beside the only official tent, a massive structure with the UN crest on it, and Deqo joins the line, falling quickly back into the inquisitive, impatient stance she had in Saba'ad.

Eventually she is inside and beckoned forward by an Ethiopian woman with a tattooed cross on her forehead. A white ledger covers the wooden desk and her eyebrows furrow behind her glasses, 'Name?' She speaks Somali with a lisp.

'Deqo.'

'Age?'

'Around ten?'

'Are you alone?'

'No.'

'Who did you come with?'

Deqo pauses for a second to explain the situation, but then tells the lie her heart wants to tell. 'My mother and grandmother.'

'Where are they?'

'Outside the camp, they need help, my grandmother can't walk.'

'We'll get someone to assist you.' She waves Deqo to the side and then a young Somali man with a wide smile and a red T-shirt with English writing on it approaches.

He places a hand gently on her shoulder and leads her out of the tent. He collects a wheelchair and she guides him to where Filsan and Kawsar wait. She is back in her familiar world; the war and all that time in Hargeisa just a complicated trial to achieve what she has always wanted: a family, however makeshift.

ACKNOWLEDGEMENTS

First, I would like to thank my mother, Zahra Farah Kahin, from whose stories this book emanated, and my father, Jama Guure Mohamed, for his unwavering support. Dahabo Mire, Nadifo Cilmi Qassim, Fadumo Mohamed, Ayan Mahamoud, Jama Muuse Jama, Dr. Adan Abokor, Dr. Aden Ismail, Edna Adan, Fadumo Warsame, Assey Hassan, Ahmed Ibrahim Awale, Siciid Jamac, Hodan Mohamed, Amran Ali and Ikraam Jama have inspired and encouraged me to carry on with this book even when it was proving too difficult. Thank you to the Authors' Foundation and to Robert Elliott, Scott Brown and all my colleagues, friends and family for their patience. Clare Hey, Courtney Hodell, Ben Mason – *mahadsanid*.

These works proved invaluable to this novel:

Somalia – the Untold Story: The War Through the Eyes of Somali Women, edited by Judith Gardner and Judy El Bushra

Somalia: A Government at War with Its Own People, by Africa Watch Committee

Environment in Crisis, by Ahmed Ibrahim Awale

Sharks and Soldiers, by Ahmed Omar Askar

ACKNOWLEDGEMENTS

The Mourning Tree, by Mohamed Barud Ali

A Note on My Teacher's Group, by Jama Musse Jama

Daughters of Africa, edited by Margaret Busby

Lyrics from 'Shimbiryahow' are from the song by Hussein Aw Farah.

Nadifa Mohamed was born in Hargeisa in 1981. In 1986 her family temporarily relocated to London; this move became permanent with the eruption of the Somali Civil War. She was educated in London and went to Oxford to study history and politics. She finally returned to Hargeisa, now in the new Republic of Somaliland, in 2008.

Her first novel, *Black Mamba Boy*, won the Betty Trask Prize, was long-listed for the Orange Prize, and was short-listed for the Guardian First Book Award, the John Llewellyn Rhys Prize, the Dylan Thomas Prize, and the PEN Open Book Award. In 2013 she was selected as one of *Granta*'s Best of Young British Novelists.